Sharon Ward is a professional astrologer and writer with over twenty years' experience in her field. She lives on the beautiful island of Guernsey with her husband Rob, daughter Yvie and son Finlay. She loves her family, astrology, animals, travelling the world and watching the wonderful collage of life unfold. She's also fairly adept at getting herself into trouble with cynics and non–believers.

In the words of Albotain…

"...to be open to new ideas or concepts is indicative of genuine intelligence. To choose to abandon something that you have studied carefully is a sign of discernment. However, to reject something that you have not even considered is outright ignorance."

www.sharonward.co.uk

With love and thanks to the following people,
without whom I would not have been
able to bring this dream to fruition.

Rob, Yvie and Fin

Gill, my mother

Alex, my mother–in–law

& last but not least, my friends,

Catherine Plevin of Kyphi Design

& Jo Henton

ALBOTAIN'S TREASURE

By

Sharon Ward

Saturnus ❦ Limited

ALBOTAIN'S TREASURE

Published in Great Britain in 2012 by Saturnus Limited

ISBN 978–0–9572751–0–2

Set in Times New Roman 9/11/14pt

Printed in the UK by Print Resources, 58 Brockswood Lane,

Welwyn Garden City, Hertfordshire AL8 7BG

All materials or goods used in connection
with promoting this book have been ethically sourced.

£1 will be donated to the Born Free Foundation for every sale of 'Albotain's Treasure', Registered Charity 1070906 www.bornfree.org.uk

Saturnus ✂ Limited

www.saturnus.co.uk enquiries: info@saturnus.co.uk

ALBOTAIN'S TREASURE

Chapter I

Ed stared at the house, large and imposing, its outline dull, grey and jagged against the moonlit sky. He frowned as he tried to spot any signs of life. Nothing, nothing at all. He put down his holdall, zipped up his leather jacket and sat down on an old wooden bench just inside the large wrought iron gates. It was icy cold in the exposed driveway and the wind cut into him through his clothing. Mind you, he thought, it wasn't as cold as it had been on the ferry over to Guernsey. The Channel crossing to the small island had been more than a bit bumpy as well, the ship swaying steadily from side to side as it lurched through the moonlit waters.

He huddled into his jacket and yawned, it had been a long day and he had a little while to wait yet. Frank had promised that someone would meet him here at 10.30pm. Ed hoped that Frank was more organised than he'd seemed. He'd met Frank Arvil, the solicitor, for the first and last time only yesterday. It felt like ages ago, but Ed could still recall the smell of stale sandalwood that hung in the air in the man's scruffy London office. He glanced at his watch, it was an hour at least before whoever was meeting him was due to turn up. An owl hooted in the distance, the eerie sound gliding through the icy air. The young man glanced over to the dark woodland behind him and shivered. He was chilled to the bone, but he was also a little nervous – more than he liked to admit. The cobbled road and old streetlights were all very quaint; it was just a bit too dark and isolated here for a city lad to feel safe.

He felt in his jacket pocket and found the piece of paper, which crackled comfortingly between his fingers. Ed was glad that he had Martin's phone number. He'd met Martin on the boat to Guernsey and they had gotten on like a house on fire. Martin was a funny, energetic lad with a dry sense of humour and a cutting tongue. Ed liked him. After they'd arrived in Guernsey, Martin's skinny mate, Sparrow, had given Ed a lift from the boat. The three of them had travelled up the steep, winding country roads in Sparrow's very old and dirty Ford Fiesta, leaving the brightly lit harbour behind them. The car had smelled terrible and Ed had had to hold his breath for most of the way. Martin and Sparrow dropped Ed off, shoving the crumpled paper into his hand with the words, 'ok mate, call us if you ever want a pint.' Ed had wistfully watched the one red tail light of the old car disappear around the corner, wishing he didn't feel quite so alone.

His mind drifted back to his flat in London. The grimy bedsit was one place he was never going to miss. Life hadn't exactly been a bed of roses so far for Ed. The first twenty-three years had definitely been sorely lacking as far as luck and love went. Up until the day before yesterday he'd been working in a restaurant in Shepherd's Bush, washing dishes. After an unfortunate incident with a large freezer and a bad-tempered chef, he'd been sacked. He still wasn't sure how he'd managed to lock the man in the cold room. Still, he thought, no harm done. At least, he was fairly sure that hypothermia didn't cause any long-term effects.

Ed looked into the darkness, peering through the tall granite gateway at the house that was to become his home for the foreseeable future. Despite his nervousness, he knew that he was never going back to his old life. He'd been offered something new and he was not going to run away this time.

Oh no, Ed had had enough of his dismal existence – it was time for a new start. Leaning forward, arms wrapped around his shivering body, he stamped his frozen feet up and down trying to thaw them out. A shadow moved in the darkness, just out of the corner of his eye. He turned slightly, the freezing wind making his eyes water. He couldn't see anything, but he knew who it was. He decided to ignore him and turned away.

The shadow was an old friend of Eds, partly imagination and partly real, an emanation from the Dark Planes of Being, a place never seen by the living. Harsh Reality had been following Ed for many years. HR, as Ed preferred to call him, made very sure that nothing really special or good happened to him. Ed knew precisely who this ghoul was because when he was very young he'd asked his mum why nothing nice or fun ever happened to him. His mother, Marlene, blew on her newly varnished fingernails and replied tartly, 'that my boy, is Harsh Reality…one thing you'll never escape from,' and she'd floated out of the room in a haze of cheap perfume, no doubt off to the next romantic liaison with her latest prey. So, thought the young Ed, at least I know what his name is.

From that point onwards in Ed's mind Harsh Reality became a distinct figure, a being who wore a black tattered cloak, part skeleton and part cracked, yellow parchment skin. HR followed Ed everywhere, making sure things went as wrong as possible, gloating happily at Ed's misfortune. However, HR was by now more than just a by–product of a sensitive boy's imagination, he was a creature in his own right. Ed's constant belief in him had allowed HR to exist. He was manifest and, boy, did he love the power. Ed, however, was determined that this new beginning would remove this horrid creature from his life once and for all.

His mind went over the events of the last few days. Following the abrupt end of his career in catering, Ed had returned home to find a letter from Frank Arvil, the solicitor based in Earl's Court, asking that he attend his offices the next day. He had no idea what the solicitor wanted, but he'd been persuaded to attend the appointment by his definite lack of future employment or, to be honest, any kind of future at all. At the solicitor's office, he met with Frank, a large untidy man with a nervous habit of saying everything twice. He didn't seem very efficient at all. In fact, he had even misspelled Ed's surname. Instead of Ed *Blyte*, Frank had him recorded as Ed *Bryte*.

Frank had explained that Ed's father, Ivan, had a brother called Lance, who had recently passed away. Not being able to trace Ivan, Frank had found Ed through his maternal grandmother. Ed's father had escaped the clutches of Marlene, Ed's mother, years ago. According to family rumour he had run away to live on a traveller's site in the Welsh hills. Ed secretly thought that the man had had a lucky escape. For years he had wanted to see his father, but Marlene would turn a nasty shade of puce every time Ed mentioned his name. The young boy soon relegated Ivan to a land of fantasy, one where mums cared and dads were at least contactable.

He jumped, startled as a car came round the corner, its headlights temporarily lighting up the road. Ghostly shadows moved and danced, synchronised with the passage of the vehicle. Trees seemed to loom out of nowhere and the chimneys of the large house looked enormous in the distorted

glare. Ed shrank back as far as he could away from the light,
turning up the collar of his jacket. He wasn't sure why he
wanted to hide; it was just a natural response after living in
London for so long.

The car disappeared and Ed returned to his previous train
of thought. The solicitor was obviously desperate to get the
house sold and the matter cleared up. He'd explained, in his
very well executed sales pitch, that Guernsey was a beautiful
and safe place, one that he would have loved to have the
opportunity to visit. At first Ed had been under the mistaken
impression that there might have been an inheritance, some
financial gain to be had from his uncle's demise. Frank soon
put the dampers on that, explaining that his uncle had no
money and had, in fact, left behind some very large debts.
So, he continued, Ed was simply being offered a caretaker's
job until the house was sold. All of this was a source of much
glee for HR who had been skulking in the corner of the office;
just to make sure things went as badly as possible for Ed.

The solicitor explained that Lance had collected a large
number of antiques and collectable items that also needed to
be sold to pay off his debts. Ed suspected, considering
Frank's obviously manufactured enthusiasm, that the man
was more than a little keen to collect his own fee. Lance had
specified in his last will and testament that a member of the
family must be given this job. The offer of a free boat ticket
and some cash was too much for Ed to turn down in his
current position. Before he'd had time to think about what he
was actually doing, he was on the train to Portsmouth, on his
way to the cross channel ferry.

He blew lukewarm air into his hands and resigned himself
to the possibility of frostbite. From what little he knew of

Guernsey, Ed was sure that it was supposed to be warmer than the mainland, even in March. Right now though, exposed to the elements in the dead of night, he felt like he was in the North Pole. The sound of a door slamming made him jump once again. He looked over and saw a tiny figure moving at a rapid pace toward him. At first, in the gloomy light he couldn't tell if they were male or female. As they drew closer, he could just make out that it was a small, slim woman of indiscernible age. She was wearing a long coat and her face was hidden beneath a large fur–trimmed hood.

'Hello love,' she called out, her thin, reedy voice echoing slightly in the courtyard as she moved towards him.

'Here's the key…Ed isn't it?' without giving him chance to reply, she continued on, 'I didn't realise you'd been waiting here. I'm sorry. I only live next door, I should have checked to see if you'd arrived early.' She thrust the key at him, 'you'd better get yourself inside in the warm my boy. I'll pop in and see you in the morning, just to make sure you're ok.'

Ed took the key, nodded and before he had chance to answer, she was gone, a fleeting figure melting back into the darkness. He was slightly stunned by this whirlwind visit, but decided that he was definitely ready for some food and sleep. He picked up his bag and made his way down the driveway.

He walked down the cobbled driveway towards the dark shape of the house. The wind was still chilly, though not as ferocious as it had been along the sea front earlier. The air smelt wonderful though, of freshly dug earth and the saltiness of the sea. The house loomed in front of him and he stopped at the large door before him. A small outside light shone dimly onto the front porch. The dark wooden door was ornately carved, some kind of animal he thought, maybe a lion. However, despite the light it was still too dark to see properly. He put the key into the lock and it turned.

The door opened easily considering its size, almost hitting the inside wall. Ed stood at the threshold. Hesitantly, he groped around for a light switch inside the doorway. Pale yellow light flooded the hall, illuminating a large foyer with a large curved staircase in front of him. Picking up his bag, he stepped inside. The air inside smelled musty, like old carpet and the place was thick with dust and time. He immediately felt as though he had travelled back a few hundred years, back to a place forgotten by the present. Strangely enough, he didn't feel nervous any more. The house, so far at least, was a comforting place, a sanctuary, still and silent. It was somehow separate from the outside world, protected from the harshness of life and the sharpness of reality.

He closed the door behind him and took a closer look at his surroundings. He leaned his bag against the wall just inside the doorway. The stairway was graced with beautiful banisters, trailing flowers and ivy were carved into the rich dark wood, fading slowly upwards into the darkness above. The bottom of the staircase was flanked by two pale stone archways. The stairs themselves and the floor were also made from stone and both were partially covered with faded, red carpet. Although the hall was regal, it was still friendly, like a scruffy old lady wearing her best jewels and a warm, lipstick smile.

Not knowing which direction to go, Ed walked over to the stone archway on his left. He walked through the opening and looked into the darkness. Again, it was pitch black and after some fumbling, he found the light switch. In a large lounge area stood two old cracked brown leather sofas,

13

huddled companionably together, both facing a large stone fireplace. Ashes from the last fire were still piled in the grate, littering the hearth, remnants of some cosy evening past. Ed noticed that the room still smelt of wood smoke, so obviously it hadn't been aired for a while, he thought. There was a layer of dust covering everything.

A loud noise came from behind him, startling him; he very nearly jumped out of his skin. Turning round, he saw behind him a large grandfather clock. It told him quite forcibly, that it was 11pm. He yawned and rubbed his eyes, he would have to get some sleep very soon. Still a little jumpy after the clock incident, combined with tiredness getting the better of him, Ed hadn't the desire, or the energy, to explore any further. He went back through the lounge and into the hallway, moving towards the other archway. Judging by the warmth of the house and the soft clanking of the pipes, the heating was obviously on.

Feeling surprisingly optimistic, Ed decided to look for something to eat. HR watched him from the shadows, his cracked lips pursed together as he tried to work out what was going on. He was out of his comfort zone in this strange house and he was a little worried that he could potentially lose control of the boy. He really didn't want that to happen, he'd had far too much of an easy ride so far.

Ed sensed HR's presence. Feeling surprisingly brave, he muttered quietly, 'just go away will you.' HR was taken aback by Ed's sudden burst of courage and retired to the hallway. There, he worked on a plan to make the boy suffer for his insubordination, his bony fingers tapping on the wooden banister as he pondered his next move.

Crossing the hall and going through the other archway, Ed found himself in a library come dining room. An elegant formal table, coated with dust and surrounded by eight, slightly worn, regency chairs took centre stage. The walls were lined with shelves and there were more books than Ed have ever seen in his life. Ed's spirits soared. He adored books, they were his escape from a life that held little promise and yielded even less.

As a child, on a Sunday afternoon, Ed would sit quietly in the corner of his gran's living room, reading avidly. Curled up into a ball on her brown stained settee, completely lost in his latest fantasy story, the whole of him was alive and vibrant. In this world he was a true hero, valiant, super–strong and, (of course), outrageously good–looking. He would battle villains, save Universes and fight off gorgeous women by the bucket load. In a place far away from the dingy green flock wallpaper and the grubby shag pile carpet, Ed was more than just an undernourished youngster with stick–thin arms and legs – he was superhuman. As the pervading aroma of Benson and Hedges, old cabbage and lager filled his lungs, he would become God of his own Universe, Master of his own Reality.

All of his mother's family would gather at his grans for lunch on Sundays. This feast usually consisted of reconstituted chicken pieces, oven chips, lager and cheap white wine. The family, including his gran, were a raucous, insensitive, ill–mannered lot. They preferred bingo to books and believed that shouting was a far superior form of communication than civilised conversation. Ed never fitted in, he learned from a very young age that he couldn't compete with their kind of verbal and physical brutality and so kept quiet. If they weren't actively taunting him, the only time that he was really aware that they noticed him was when he heard the odd comment, floating across the smoke–filled room. Ed couldn't always catch what they were saying, although the words, 'freak' and 'just like his father,' were often to be heard. On these occasions his mother would glance at him irritably, as if he were a chipped fingernail that she had forgotten to repaint, a part of her that was not quite up to scratch.

Ed looked around the room, drinking in the wonderful sight of hundreds of books. Heaven, he thought, delighted to have found such a treasure trove. He was tempted to have a good look at this magnificent selection of reading material. Common sense and exhaustion prevailed however, and he reluctantly took the archway leading away from the library. He opened the wooden door in front of him, turning the large iron circular handle. The opening took him down a small flight of stone steps into the next room.

Chapter II

Turning on the light, he saw that he was in the kitchen. Cream wooden cupboards lined the walls and the red tiled floor gave the room warmth and depth. It was clean, very clean in fact, not at all dusty like the rest of the house. It smelled of pine and a freshly ironed tea towel hung over the bar of the shiny cream oven door. In the centre of the room was a pale wooden kitchen table, on it was a note that read…

'Food in fridge, help yourself
Bedding at top of stairs, use first bedroom on left
Will see you in the morning
Mrs P.
Ps: Be careful of Gideon.

Ed assumed that the woman in the driveway must have been Mrs P. Then he frowned…Gideon? Shrugging, he went over to the large fridge next to the window. He was absolutely starving. Thinking about it, he couldn't remember the last time he'd eaten. He opened the door and took out a plate of ploughman's covered in cling film, along with an unopened carton of fresh Guernsey milk. There was a bottle of cider in the fridge. Ed picked it up, the label told him that it was called *'Rocquettes'*. The cool, golden hue made it look very tempting. However, Ed wisely decided against drinking on an empty stomach. He'd never been able to drink more than one glass of any kind of alcohol at the best of times and he was too tired to risk it now. He would save it for another time.

Taking off the plastic covering from the ploughman's, he sat down at the table and began to devour the crusty white bread, creamy cheese and sharp pickle, gulping the milk straight from the carton. After a while he slowed down, his hunger subsiding a bit and he surveyed his surroundings more thoroughly.

Harsh Reality slid quietly into the kitchen. He felt more hopeful now. He wasn't about to give up on his favourite protégée just yet.

The kitchen doorway was behind Ed and to his right was a large, arched window. It was too dark to see anything much outside though, just the vague shapes of the trees at the bottom of the driveway. The moon lurked behind them, tossing in the branches. The kitchen itself was L–shaped and turned to the left. Ed couldn't see what was round the corner. He got up, a hunk of bread still in his hand and went to have a look.

Suddenly, an almighty screech filled the air. Something very large flew at Ed's head. He ducked, only to find that whatever it was had removed the piece of bread from his hand. He covered his head with his hands and crouched down, petrified. The screeching continued and the thing came back, dropping the bread directly onto Ed's crouching frame.

'*Go away you stupid mutt,*' it shrieked.

Ed decided that he was going insane, either that or the ploughman's had been drugged. Panicking, his fertile imagination taking the upper hand as usual, he crouched even lower in an attempt to avoid his attacker. *What* was going on? Everything went quiet. He looked upwards, hesitantly, hands still covering his head. Nothing. Silence. He got up slowly, he was feeling decidedly sick and his heart was racing. Trying to breathe slowly to calm himself down, he looked towards the end of the kitchen. There was another window, next to that was a closed door and to the right of it was what looked like a pantry or larder. Ed could just see inside the slightly open door, tins and bags of food were placed neatly in lines on shelves. Sitting on the top of the door was the largest, ugliest, evilest looking parrot that Ed had ever seen. (Admittedly, tropical birds had not been exactly thick on the ground in London, but it still looked like a very unattractive example indeed.)

Ed, despite his soft nature and love of animals, took an intense dislike to this creature. This was a feeling that was quickly endorsed by the fact that the bird looked as though it was going to attack imminently. Its huge wings were flapping manically and it was screeching like some mad ghoul. Its dingy green feathers were tinged with dirty blue and dull yellow. It must be the size of a small dog, Ed thought, still very, very scared. The bird suddenly stopped flapping, held its head on its side and glared menacingly at Ed with one mean, yellow eye. Its sharp beak opened and closed softly, as if already tasting his tender flesh.

Ed stood stock–still, too afraid to move. He had absolutely no idea what to do next. He really had had enough now, he was tired and very, very scared. He took a deep breath, letting it out slowly and decided to try to negotiate with his newfound enemy, this feathered nemesis. Slowly and very carefully, he reached to the floor and picked up the piece of bread.

'Hello boy, do you want this?'

Holding the offering at arms length, he took a very tentative step towards the door.

'*Go away you stupid mutt,*' was the reply.

'Ok, right, I will.'

Ed stepped back quickly, afraid of a second onslaught. The bird eyed the bread, tilting its head a little more. A little encouraged, Ed again stepped forward. The bird didn't move. He took another step.

'*Stop licking my feet, you stupid creature.*'

Despite his fear, Ed wondered what on earth the bird was on about. Sidling closer, his hand only inches away from the vicious looking beak, he gingerly offered the bread. Then, surprisingly gently, the parrot took the proffered food and using one claw began to tear it apart with its beak, swallowing large chunks enthusiastically. Ed sighed with relief that it was just a piece of bread that the bird was enjoying so heartily and not one of his body parts. Still shaking, he decided that he best make the most of the time that the parrot was busy and exit the room. He hastily backed out of the kitchen and firmly closed the heavy door behind him. That was, he supposed, the Gideon that he had to be careful of. Valid point – only if he'd actually known who Gideon was, he may have been able to avoid him more effectively.

Entering the hallway and picking up his bag, he took the stairs to the first floor. He was more than a little hesitant after the parrot experience, who knew what else was in the house? He found a quilt and a pillow at the top of the stairs as promised. He surveyed this new area of the house. There were in total six wooden doors, three on each side. All but one of the doors on the right, which was obviously the bathroom, were closed shut. At the end of the hallway was another stone archway with a narrow flight of wooden stairs leading upwards. Ed tried the first door on his left, it opened and he stepped inside. Turning on the light he found himself in a dusty, but comfortable, bedroom. A large double bed, its mattress bare, with a huge wooden headboard, dominated most of the room. A carved dresser, with an old–fashioned china washbasin and jug, sat next to a big oak wardrobe. This'll do just fine thought Ed, desperate for some sleep.

He put his bag in the corner and took off his jacket. Quickly making up the bed, he fell into it without even washing or undressing. As he fell into a dead sleep, he promised himself that he would shower in the morning. He dreamed that he was in a prehistoric landscape and that he was being chased by large yellow and green dinosaurs. Strangely, they were throwing bits of bread at him.

HR was still quiet, still sulking. The parrot incident had cheered him up a bit, but he still felt unnervingly insecure.

Chapter III

The staccato shriek of seagulls woke Ed up the next morning. The unfamiliar sound startled him and his head was groggy from sleeping too heavily. He disentangled himself from the covers and half–rolled off the bed. Sitting on the edge of the mattress, he rubbed his eyes and yawned. The realisation of where he was slowly came back to him. He got up and went over to the window. The scene that greeted him took his breath away. Rolling green lawns flanked by large trees, still bare from the winter, lead the way steeply down to woodlands below. Through the gaps in the trees, Ed could see luscious green cliffs, dotted with tiny yellow daffodils and purple heather. The craggy hills clambered sharply down to greet the bluest sea he had ever seen. In the distance, the sun shone onto the water which sparkled and breathed with a life of its own.

He opened the stiff metal latch on the window and pushed it open as wide as it would go. The cool breeze swept into the musty room, filling it with the fragrant scent of wood and sea. Ed took a deep breath, taking in the cold morning air. As well as the seagulls, he could hear many different kinds of birds, their enthusiastic chorus filling the air. The winter sun was warm on his face and he felt as though he was dreaming. It was as if he had been brought by magic to a beautiful new world, one far removed from the grey, dismal place from where he had come. The colours were so vivid, the air so clear, that Ed wasn't sure if he was dreaming, or if in fact he'd woken up from a nightmare and this was actually reality.

After drinking in the scene before him, he reluctantly turned away from the window and went over to retrieve his bag. He left the room and made use of the old fashioned, but functional, bathroom. After cleaning himself up, he changed into some fresh clothes and went downstairs.

Venturing very cautiously into the kitchen, he was relieved to find that all seemed to be quiet. He found some cereal in a cupboard above the sink and using the remainder of the milk from the night before made himself breakfast. He was just wondering if there were any teabags, when he heard a knock at the front door. Upon opening it, he was presented with a small, middle–aged woman, neatly packaged in a pink velour tracksuit, complete with blindingly white trainers. She had short, ash blond hair, framing a face that had, he thought not unkindly, seen better days. The tracksuit seemed a little incongruous considering the age of the lady thought Ed, like rap music in a church. Then she smiled and suddenly her lined face seemed younger, a burst of youthful energy shone through her eyes, transforming her worn features.

'Hello my dear, we met briefly last night. I'm afraid I was very rude and didn't even introduce myself. I'm Mrs Perriman, but you can call me Mrs P!' she added as she beamed at him. 'I've got my own key, but I didn't want to disturb you. As I said I live just next door.'

She gestured to her left. Ed peered round the doorway, taking in the cobbled driveway, beautiful flowerbeds and conifers lining the periphery of the garden. All of which, of course, he hadn't been able to see in the darkness of the night before. Just behind the conifers, in the direction that Mrs P had pointed, about a hundred yards away, he could see a grey, granite house. Its tiny square windows glinted in the sunlight and two beautifully ornate chimneys pointed to the blue sky above. It also had a tiny circular turret on the right gable end, making it look like a miniature castle. From what he could see, it looked very old, maybe over three hundred years. He realised that he hadn't even seen the outside of his new home, something he would have to rectify later on, he thought. He introduced himself and asked Mrs P to come in. It felt very strange asking someone to enter a place that he hardly knew himself.

They made their way to the kitchen. Mrs P took the lead, she moved very quickly for an older lady, thought Ed, hurrying to keep up with her. When she opened the door to the kitchen, Ed said quickly, 'be careful, there's a horrible parrot in there. I think you warned me about him in your note. I thought he was going to kill me last night.'

Mrs P turned to Ed and nodded, 'yes, that's the little sod. Gideon. Lance rescued him from a fairground years ago. Now, he can be alright if you've got some food he wants. He takes some careful handling though I can tell you.'

Ed nodded in agreement. Despite the newness of his introduction to the bird, he was already very aware of this fact. He told Mrs P of his encounter with the animal the previous night.

'Oh Gawd, sounds to me like he managed to get into the larder again,' she responded as they made their way down the stone steps to the kitchen.

Mrs P walked across the tiled floor with Ed nervously following her. Fast asleep on the curtain rail was the bird, head partway under its wing, its gnarled old feet clutching onto the rail. Despite the fact that it was sleeping, it was still one ugly, mean–looking creature. It looked no less frightening in the daylight and Ed's stomach felt a little unsettled as they moved slowly towards it.

Mrs P glanced at the open larder door. 'Mmmm...just as I thought. It's alright, he's sleeping it off. He'll be calmer when he wakes up, I don't think you'll have a repeat of last night's escapade.'

'Sleeping what off exactly?' asked Ed, frowning.

'If he gets into the larder, he nicks the coffee beans out of the packet. He only nibbles at them, but they make him very agitated. He's addicted you see. Once the effects go out of his system and he sleeps it off, he's fine. Well, at least he's better behaved than when he's off his head on caffeine.'

At this, Gideon woke up, croaked sleepily, took his head out from under his wing and eyed his two visitors suspiciously.

'Once he ate a whole load of beans and had a seizure. They're toxic for parrots. Nearly killed him.' Ed thought that Mrs P almost sounded sorry that it hadn't done the trick.

The parrot put his head to one side, as if absorbing what the woman was saying about him,

'*Get lost you smelly old rug,*' it squawked venomously. Mrs P was apparently unfazed by this tirade of abuse.

'That,' she said glaring back at the bird, almost matching its own vitriolic stare with her own steely gaze, 'is how Lance spoke to Lionel. He loved him really, but Gideon takes great delight in somehow only being able to repeat the *rudest* bits.'

The parrot cackled and leered at them from across the room. It flapped its wings and took flight to the other side of the kitchen, landing gracefully on a perch which was tucked away in an alcove in the corner opposite the larder. It settled down and started to pull its feathers out one by one, ignoring Ed and Mrs P completely.

'Ha, withdrawal symptoms from the caffeine. Hope you've got a headache! Serves you right you manky old pile of feathers,' Mrs P remarked triumphantly.

26

She shut the larder door firmly and jammed the latch down defiantly. 'That'll stop the daft animal from pinching any more coffee beans.'

'Who's Lionel?' queried Ed, hoping to goodness that there weren't any more creatures like Gideon in the house. His nerves just wouldn't be able to stand it.

'Lionel? Come with me.' Mrs P's voice took on a definitely softer tone and she smiled at Ed, youthful energy bursting through once again like sunshine after a storm.

They went past the larder and Mrs P opened a wooden door and motioned for Ed to go through. Beyond was a small porch leading to another door that went out to the gardens, which Ed could see from his bedroom window. Inside the porch was an old wicker dog basket and lying in it was a large, black, long haired dog. At hearing the door open, the animal lifted his huge head, panting excitedly, his teeth bared in a welcoming smile. He tried to get up, struggling to get out of his bed so that he could greet them. After a while he managed to get upright and walk towards them, but his legs were obviously stiff with age. As the big dog crept slowly closer, Ed could see that his eyes were milky and his muzzle was greying. His heart softened and he bent down to stroke the animal on the top of his head and scratch behind his ears.

'Hello old boy,' he murmured gently.

The dog wagged his tail, the length of tangled black fur moving back and forth happily. He licked Ed's hand and grunted like an old bear.

'He loves fuss,' said Mrs P, beaming at the dog. 'I've been feeding him and letting him out. He can come out of the porch now you're here, as long as you don't mind him.'

Ed smiled, 'no, of course not. He's lovely. Maybe if you have a lead I could take him out for a walk later?' At hearing the word 'walk', Lionel began to wag his tatty tail even faster and grunted enthusiastically.

'That's fine, the lead is there on the door. He's as good as gold. Hope you're not in a hurry though, the old chap can't walk very fast!'

'Not a problem, I'm in no hurry at all,' said Ed as the three of them made their way to the main part of the kitchen. As they passed Gideon, Lionel moved a little closer to Ed. Sensible dog, thought Ed and patted him on his furry back reassuringly.

Ed and Mrs P sat down at the table. Lionel seemed to have adopted Ed already and sat at his feet, leaning heavily on his legs as if to make sure he wasn't about to go away. This wasn't very comfortable for Ed, but he didn't have the heart to move. In the background, HR was very quietly grinding his teeth, his bony jaw moving slowly back and forth as he watched the comfortable scene unfold.

'Right,' said Mrs P, rummaging in her tracksuit pocket and bringing out a small white envelope together with a pile of white paper.

'First of all, in this envelope is a month's money for food and also directions to the local shop. There's a bit to eat in the cupboard and fridge for now. The shop is only down the road, so you'll have no problem finding it.'

She handed the envelope over to Ed, who looked surprised.

She continued, 'I know a month seems like a long time, but believe me, it's all in a bit of a muddle upstairs and there are literally thousands of items that need packing up. I reckon you'll probably be here for a good while, maybe six months or more. I'll keep an eye on you though. I'll pop in to clean up the kitchen, but it's up to you to take care of the packing up of the artefacts. You'll need to feed the animals though.'

'Although,' she continued sighing, 'I really don't know what'll happen to Lionel and that revolting bird when it's all done and dusted.'

Ed was silent, trying to take in everything that the woman was saying. Up until now he had been so preoccupied with his new surroundings, he'd forgotten that he was here to do a job and he was finding it hard to concentrate.

However, Mrs P was being very efficient and Ed tried his hardest to focus on what she was saying.

'Now, here's a list of all the items that are to be packed into boxes.' She handed a wad of papers stapled together to Ed. He took it and looked at it vaguely, feeling a bit overwhelmed.

'You'll find all of the articles and objects in the spare bedrooms, ornaments, paintings, books and suchlike. Some of them are in boxes, but most have just been left in piles on the floor, along with a lot of rubbish that needs to be thrown away.'

Ed finally gathered himself together, 'how long was Lance in this house for?'

'Your uncle lived here for,' she thought for a moment, 'must have been thirty years. Over that time he put this list together.'

She pointed at the list, 'you'll find a white sticker on each item with the reference number on it, but nothing's in order. Next to the reference number on the list here, there's a description of each item, where it came from originally and its approximate age. It's up to you to repack the existing boxes and pack up all of the loose items. You'll find new boxes in the last spare room on the left. Wrap everything up individually and put them into the boxes carefully, marking the outside with the relevant reference numbers, so the auctioneers know what's in each box.'

She stopped and put the list down in front of Ed, 'afterwards, make sure that you mark the item off on the list, so they know what they've got.'

'Why did he catalogue everything?' asked Ed, trying to make sense of the list. It was written in various coloured inks, with splodges and marks all over it and teacup stains obliterated much of the writing. It was hard to make out what it said – it was so untidy.

'Auctioning off the collection of antiques wasn't your uncle's original plan,' replied Mrs P, 'he thought that when he died, it would all be donated to a museum for display. That's why he kept the list. He thought he could give something back to the world through his collection, information about the past I suppose.'

'Give something back, how d'you mean?' Ed queried.

'He'd profited from his travels and at one point was making quite a bit of money from antiques. He wasn't the most practical of people though and in the past ten years or so, his mind began to go a bit. I think he suffered some kind of breakdown. He was always one for the good life, he didn't take care of his finances and over the years he'd built up far too many debts to be covered just by the sale of this house. A few years ago, he realised that when he died it would all have to be sold off to cover his debts. So, he stipulated in his will that your father was to clear up the house once he passed away.'

'My dad's only about 45, I think, so how old was my uncle when he died?'

'There was quite an age gap between them then. Lance was only in his sixties though when he died. It was a heart attack – a terrible shame. He was such a nice man, even if he was a bit irresponsible. He didn't know how to take care of himself though. I always said that he should have got married. There were always plenty of young ladies around when he was young, never any shortage of callers. He seemed happier to play the field though. He just enjoyed life and lived for the moment.'

She sighed and stared out of the kitchen window, visiting another time in her mind. Ed thought that she looked really sad. She must have been very fond of Lance, he decided.

Ed suspected that his dad and uncle were very different. He always got the impression that his father was a quiet man, not an extrovert at all. His mum and her family always said his dad was useless, a spineless good for nothing. But then, mused Ed, their assessment of people was not always very astute.

'What happened with my dad's family?' asked Ed, 'my mum never talked about them.'

Mrs P ran her hand across her face, as if brushing away her thoughts. She turned back to Ed, 'from what I know, your dad and uncle had a falling out, a long time ago when they were just youngsters. Their parents, your grandparents, Ariadne and Hector were killed in a car crash and there was some dispute about the division of the estate. I think your dad decided that he wanted none of it in the end and Lance got the lot.'

'Did they ever see one another again?'

'Your dad did get back in touch with Lance when he and your mum got married. That was about twenty–five years ago, I suppose. Your dad invited him to the wedding. Lance went and that's where he met your mum and gran.'

'So, what happened then?'

'Well, at the wedding I think that old wounds were reopened, things were said that couldn't be taken back and so they went their separate ways again. It's a shame really, Lance missed his family terribly.'

However, something that had been bothering Ed since he left London came back to him, something that in his rather confused state of mind he had forgotten to ask the solicitor, Frank Arvil.

'How did Frank Arvil know I existed and why me?'

'Well, it was supposed to be your dad that came here, but Mr Arvil couldn't trace him.'

'So how did I come up? I mean how did anyone know about me?' asked Ed, perplexed.

'Your mum and Lance had met at the wedding as I said. Some years later she wrote to Lance asking for money, said it was for you. So that's how he knew you existed. Lance knew what your dad was like, never in one place for very long. Once he found out about you, he instructed the solicitor to locate you if, when the time came, your dad couldn't be found.'

Somewhere in the back of his mind, Ed remembered something about his mother writing begging letters to distant relatives. He'd been about eight years old. Marlene was in–between men, penniless once more and they were living with her mother. This was a grim memory that Ed had tried to forget. His grandmother and mother were a dreadful combination, ignorance combined with viciousness was a toxic cocktail and he had suffered dreadfully as a result of their constant jibes and criticisms.

'But why did he want dad to sort out his stuff? They hadn't spoken for years and I don't mean to be rude, but he was hardly going to meet him again was he? It was a will after all, and he was going to be, well…dead,' Ed felt a bit embarrassed at having to address such a sensitive point.

The woman frowned, 'Lance was a funny old one. I knew him for a long time. We were good friends and he used to confide in me quite a bit, both of us being alone. He told me that when he was young, he was very thoughtless. He regretted many of his actions and he felt he'd made a lot of mistakes. He'd softened as the years went by though, mellowed a bit. He missed his brother, he felt bad at how things had ended. In a strange way, I think he felt that if your dad cleared up his estate he would have a connection with his brother. His collection would be a reminder to your dad of his existence, as if he hadn't been completely forgotten by his family.'

Mrs P got up and made her and Ed a cup of tea. She sat back down and continued on, nursing the hot drink between her cupped hands, obviously enjoying telling the tale. 'When your dad couldn't be found Frank, the solicitor, contacted your mother's mother looking for you and she gave him your address. You're second best, but a good one anyway!' she said smiling broadly.

Ed thought about what Mrs P was telling him, there was something he didn't understand though, 'why, if my uncle cared so much about my dad didn't he leave him any money? I know there are a lot of debts, but he hasn't left him anything at all, not even anything from the collection.'

'Well, I believe that your dad made it very clear when they last met that he wanted nothing of his brother's. Lance said that your dad might be permanently penniless, but he knew that he was a proud, independent man underneath all that quietness. I think he respected that in a funny sort of way.'

Ed let all of this new information sink in. His uncle sounded like an interesting character. He felt terribly sorry for his dad though; his parents dead and him left without anything at all, not even his brother. Although he actually felt sorrier that the poor man had ended up with Marlene. That must have been the straw that broke the camel's back, no wonder he had scarpered to the hills – literally.

Mrs P seemed to have imparted as much information as she was going to for the time being.

'Right young man, keep me posted and let me know when you've run out of cash and I'll get some more to you. Once you've got the boxes packed up, call the telephone number at the top of the first page of the list and call Mr Huntington, the auctioneer. The 'phone's in the hall out there. He'll take the boxes away and sell off the items. All the proceeds will go into a fund which Frank Arvil will use to repay your uncle's debts. Only after he's taken his own hefty fee though, I should imagine.'

'Thanks,' mumbled Ed, not sure what else to say.

'Ok, I'll be off then,' Mrs P got up from the table and then turned to Ed, 'you'll be alright, love. Pop round for a cup of tea if you get lonely,' she said kindly and added, 'although I've got lots of friends, I am on my own quite a bit in the house.' She patted Ed's shoulder with her tiny, birdlike hand.

It was only when he heard the front door close that Ed realised that he had entered a whole new world. It all felt a bit strange, but at the same time, he was actually quite comforted by the fact that he knew a little more about his dad's life. Even though his dad had never been to the house, he felt a bit closer to him somehow. He wondered what Ariadne and Hector had been like. They sounded quite posh, about as similar to his mother's family as pork scratchings to sushi. He wondered what they would have thought of him.

Lionel nudged Ed with his large black nose, looking up at him intently through opaque eyes, as if willing his new friend to understand what he was trying to tell him. This attempt at canine telepathy worked and Ed remembered his earlier promise to take the dog for a walk. He grabbed his jacket and the dog's lead, clipping it to the dog's old brown collar.

'Right boy, let's go and see what's out there shall we?' Lionel gave a short, gruff bark in response and immediately began dragging Ed across the kitchen floor. Ed, hanging on to the lead, struggled to slow him down. He was large dog and despite his advanced age, he was surprisingly strong. Mrs P had vastly underestimated the animal thought Ed, he didn't seem to be slow at all. After a bit of a tussle, they came to a kind of arrangement, Lionel continued onwards at the same pace and Ed hurried to keep up with him. Although this wasn't much of a compromise on Lionel's part, it was actually preferable to Ed having his arm pulled out of its socket.

Chapter IV

As they left the house by the front door, Ed, still moving at a rapid pace turned to look at his new home. Luckily, at that point Lionel decided to slow down for a few seconds, giving him the chance to look at the large house properly. The dark granite building was more than a touch impressive. It wasn't traditional in any way at all, but it was still stunningly beautiful. Ornately carved chimneys cut regally into the skyline, claiming the space above without deference. The leaded windowpanes set in stone arches glinted in the sunlight. It was old, very old, Ed guessed that it was from the gothic period and was at least four hundred years old.

As he passed through the gateway, he spotted a large brass plate announcing that the house was called 'Le Chateau de la Demiange'. Ed was already aware of the house's rather austere title, as Frank Arvil had given him the address when they met in London. The French sounding name had initially filled him with trepidation – the furthest south he'd ever been up until this point was Crawley. However, seeing the nameplate there in front of him now filled him with excitement. He had never seen anything like this wonderful house. He felt strangely proud that he had ended up here, as if the house were a kind of message to him that life held other treasures yet to be discovered.

He and Lionel walked on together down the driveway to the road. It was sunny, but the wind was cold in the open road and Ed was glad he'd remembered his jacket. They left the driveway and turned left following the narrow lane, each side flanked by high grass verges and crumbling granite walls. Apart from Mrs P's house, there were no other houses to be seen and Ed felt strangely free in this remote area of the island. He had no idea where he was going. However, this didn't matter too much, as Lionel seemed to have a particular route in mind. Ed hung onto the dog's lead in the hope that they would be able to find their way home again.

They took a left turn again and Ed found himself walking through another woodland, larger than the one opposite the house. The trees looked very different from last night in the bright sunshine. Shadows had been replaced by dappled sunlight and a carpet of flowers covered the ground. Through the forest, Ed could see the grassy cliffs and the bright blue sea that lay just below them. The white waves were breaking through the turquoise water and he could smell the salt in the air. He and Lionel walked along a broad path of sodden leaves and wet soil. It was soft and yielding underfoot. Lionel splashed copious amounts of mud onto Ed's trousers as his large paws ploughed into the squelchy earth. A sudden flurry in a nearby tree startled both of them. Ed ducked down quickly; he'd had his fair share of unexpected attacks recently. He looked up and relaxed as he saw that it was just a large hen pheasant leaving the tree. She fluttered ungainly to the ground, landing in a heap. She eventually gathered herself together and ran as quickly as her short legs would allow her, into the safety of the undergrowth. Ed and Lionel carried on, the surroundings were beautiful, but more than anything, it was just so peaceful. The sea breeze gently ruffled Ed's hair and the sun glistened through the bare branches of the trees. The sound of birdsong resonated through the woods, breaking the silence delicately. It was as if only the purest sounds had been given permission to intrude upon this small slice of paradise.

At this moment, Ed was totally at peace. He felt as if he had found a part of himself, that he had reclaimed something that should have always been his, something good and bright that his previous life had taken from him. He felt warm and golden inside, like a child feels when it knows it's really safe and loved. This new feeling enveloped him and with it came a sense of contentment, safety and strongest of all, of not being afraid. He realised that this unfamiliar emotion was happiness, something he had not felt for a long, long time. Ed was soft, a hopeless romantic and a sucker for a sad story. However, he was not, up until this point, inclined towards positive thinking, optimism or even half–hearted high spiritedness. Ed and happiness were not familiar with one another. Like a Franciscan monk doesn't need a laptop, the combination of the two just hadn't ever been called for. Ed's spirits soared. He wondered how, in London, surrounded by thousands of people, he had felt so empty, so lonely and yet here, with not a soul in sight, he felt surrounded by positive energy, by life and light.

Harsh Reality was, as per usual, not far behind Ed. However, upon witnessing the transformation that Ed was obviously undergoing, he took a long hard look at him. He was definitely worried. This new energy Ed was giving out was not at all good for HR's well–being. He would starve without any abject misery or fear to feed upon. Realising that he had lost his grip, (for the time being anyway), he decided to take a long holiday in Grimsby, somewhere he felt he would be much more comfortable. Guernsey was much too beautiful anyway; just looking around gave him a nasty headache. He shrugged his bony shoulders and turned away, his ragged black cloak flapping behind him. He was hoping that when he got back that Ed would be back to normal.

Ed wandered on, talking softly to Lionel, who by now had slowed down a little and plodded along by his side. As they rounded a corner, Ed could see that they were at the back of the house, the garden sloped up towards the house and he could see his bedroom window. There was an old black iron gate in the surrounding granite wall and Ed tried it to see if it would budge. After a bit of struggle it swung open. Lionel and he entered. They passed a wooden garden shed and a small ornate goldfish pond, complete with a spouting cherub as a central feature. The cherub's spouting was a bit feeble, and the surrounds of the pond were rather neglected, but the fish looked as happy as goldfish usually look. The two of them made their way up through the main part of the garden, back up to the house.

They arrived at the back door and Ed noticed a large quantity of logs neatly piled up against the outside wall underneath a makeshift shelter. He picked up a few and carried them inside, letting Lionel's lead go. He decided that he was going to make a fire. He was still tired from the journey and he needed to rest a bit before he got on with sorting out the collection of objects. He was a bit hungry as well. He knew that he was kidding himself a bit though. He wasn't actually that tired at all and the hunger in his belly would not be satiated by food. He wanted to look through some of the books in the library and couldn't wait to see what he would find.

Even as a child, Ed had been compelled to read incessantly, he would beg his mother for new books all the time. She would get very irritated with him and make him read the same ones over and over again. Marlene thought that books were a complete waste of money – she had make–up and toiletries to buy.   Ed's life took on a whole new meaning once he discovered public libraries.

Once inside, he put the small pile of wood by the pantry door and took off his muddy trainers. He let Lionel off the lead, making sure that he had enough water and biscuits. Gideon, thankfully, had dozed off again. Ed wondered when he would wake up properly. Bravely, he ventured over to the perch to check if the bird had food and water. He might not like the animal, but he wouldn't like to see it suffer, (well, not *too* much).

He retrieved the wood and went through to the lounge. Lionel dutifully followed him, his nose almost touching the back of Ed's leg he was so close. After a bit of searching, Ed found some matches in a wooden box on the mantelpiece and some old newspapers under the sofa cushion. Despite his lack of experience, he managed after a few attempts to build a roaring fire. He went back through to the library, grabbed half a dozen assorted books and went back to the lounge. The sofas were old, but very comfortable. He and Lionel spent a wonderful afternoon lazing by the fire, Ed reading and the old dog sleeping soundly on the rug in front of the hearth. Ed realised after a while that whilst log fires were wonderful, he did have to watch that Lionel didn't singe when the wood spat out the odd glowing ember. The only sounds to be heard in the room were the occasional chiming of the grandfather clock, Lionel's gentle snoring, and Ed occasionally patting out a bit of smoulder on the dog's fur.

When the big clock struck six, he realised that he'd had nothing to eat since breakfast. He and Lionel went into the

41

kitchen and he found some ready–made pasta and sauce in the cupboard, which he quickly heated up. It looked surprisingly edible for one of Ed's culinary creations, which usually resembled something already partially digested. He grabbed the bottle of cider from the fridge, (he was feeling brave). He ate at the table, sipping at the delicious cider and passing Lionel bits of juicy pasta, which the big dog wolfed down.

When he had finished his supper, he thought about what he was going to do next. He decided that he would have a look around the house and find out where the collection was stored. First, he checked on Gideon, who was awake, sitting on his perch. He spotted Ed and Lionel and glared at them malevolently, his yellow eyes cold and calculating. If he hadn't just been a brainless old bird, Ed would've sworn he was plotting something horrible. He felt that it was probably wise to give the parrot some space and so left him alone, closing the kitchen door as he left with Lionel still close behind him.

They went upstairs and Ed stood on the landing, wondering where to try first. He considered the second staircase at the end of the hallway and then decided to explore this floor first. The house was large, but not huge. He went past his bedroom and tried the next door. Nothing, it seemed to be stuck, he pushed it a little more forcefully. Lionel looked at him quizzically, head slightly on one side, ears pricked.

'Don't worry boy, I'll get it open,' said Ed, as he pushed the door hard with his shoulder. It flew open and he hurtled into the room, landing on a pile of cardboard boxes. Dust flew everywhere and he immediately began to cough and sneeze violently. Lionel stood patiently in the doorway, looking at Ed blankly like he'd never seen him before.

Ed struggled up, walked over to the door and turned on the light. He was so covered in dust, he could hardly see his clothes. He tried to brush himself down, the result of which was clouds coming off him and choking him even more. The air was thick and tasted bitter in the back of Ed's throat, but as the dust settled a little, he could see that the large room was full of boxes and bags. At the back of the room were small wooden chests stacked four or five high. He could just make out the top of the window on the other side of them. He realised that there were another three rooms like this. If they were all as packed as this, he was going to be here for years. Not such a terrible prospect, he thought.

Littered around the floor were piles of carelessly discarded objects. Obviously, Lance had just put them in the room anyhow. Perhaps, Ed mused, as his faculties diminished, he just couldn't be bothered to pack them up properly in the boxes. He made his way to the centre of the room, which was comparatively clear. He felt like an intrepid explorer, an adventurer who had discovered a cave full of treasures.

'Christopher Columbus, eat your heart out,' he muttered, feeling suddenly very brave. This surge of bravado was severely curtailed as he stubbed his toe on something, lost his balance and fell in a heap once more. He grabbed his foot, nursing his bruised toe. Lionel, realising that his new best friend was not altogether coping and in need of some help, came over and began licking Ed's face.

'Blurgh, gerrof,' was Ed's unappreciative response as he tried to keep his mouth closed to avoid swallowing dog spittle. Lionel retreated good–naturedly and watched him, panting heavily, pink tongue lolling out.

Still sitting on the floor, Ed looked around him, noticing that amongst the small statues, paintings, china and carved objects that lay around, was quite a lot of what was obviously rubbish. Old pieces of cardboard, crumpled paper cups, empty drink cans and bulging plastic carrier bags lay strewn all over the floor. He reached over and picked up a delicate figurine. It was covered in dust which he wiped off with his sleeve. It was of a young woman, dressed in a white gown, a faded pink cupid's bow for a mouth. He checked the bottom of it. Sure enough, there was a tiny, very grubby, white sticker on the bottom. Ed could just make out a number on it. He realised though that he had left the list downstairs and so would have to start properly tomorrow. Anyway, it was getting late, he guessed it must be at least seven o'clock. Considering the state of him, he could really do with a bath; an early night was probably a good idea as well. He carefully placed the china lady on the floor, making sure she didn't topple over. He yawned and scratched his head, dust once again flying everywhere.

He got up and made his way to the curtainless window. He peered around the edge of the boxes, through the windowpanes, but couldn't see a thing in the darkness. As he turned away from the window, he spotted a carrier bag leant against the radiator. The room was full of overstuffed old plastic bags, but this one looked interesting. He could just see the corner of what looked like an old book. Curiosity got the better of him; he bent down, picked the bag up and took the book out for a better look.

Crouching on his haunches with Lionel's wet nose snuffling enthusiastically in his left ear, he opened it up. The writing was in old English, the 'S's looked like 'F's' and he could only just make out the print, it was so blurred. He was right, this book was *very* old. He was very excited by his find and desperately wanted to read it. He had no idea what it was

44

about, but he'd never had access to genuine antique books, so he wasn't going to be fussy about the content. This was history, right in front of him – in his hands! Ed had always loved reading about the past. The past was contained, familiar and had a pattern to it that put everything into order and perspective. Although history was a factual narrative of human life, with its dramas and disasters, it was about other people, people who were no longer suffering and who could be safely watched from a distance. The past contained no unpleasant surprises, no chance that something nasty would leap out of the darkness and hurt him.

Closing the book, he got up and started towards the door. A sudden thought made him stop in his tracks. He didn't know if everything in the bag should be kept together. He had no idea if its contents were part of the collection and as there were so many bags in the room, he could easily end up putting it back in the wrong one. Better to be safe than sorry, he thought and turned back. He picked up the plastic carrier bag and went downstairs, Lionel following.

He went into the kitchen and putting the book down, decided to tip the bag out onto the table. He wanted to see if there was anything else of interest in there. A few dusty bits of paper and a couple of dead moths presented themselves to him. He picked up a small piece of paper; it didn't look very exciting at all. In fact, when he took a closer look, he saw that it was a handwritten receipt for two pounds of sausages and mincemeat. It wasn't even very old, the date on it was the 17th of March 1999. He put it aside, a touch disappointed. He went to pick up another piece from the top of the pile when he heard a faint clink from underneath it. Shuffling the papers aside, he quickly located the source of the noise. It was a silver coloured metal disk. Not very big, but it was fairly thick and definitely looked quite old. Ed peered at it, frowning; it had deep, but nevertheless incomprehensible markings on one side of it. He couldn't make them out, nothing recognisable, just a bunch of squiggly lines.

He picked it up. An intense burning heat shot through his hand. Startled, he dropped it, gasping out loud as he did so. He stared at the disc, his heart in his mouth. Then slowly, realisation dawned. Thinking back, he remembered that the bag had been leant against the radiator in the storeroom and that the heating had been on since before he'd arrived. Of course, being metal the disc had retained the heat! Recovering from the shock, he put his hand up to his forehead, half covering his face and laughed quietly to himself. He was such a jumpy coward. Thank goodness no one had witnessed that amazing display of courage, he thought ruefully.

He sat down at the table. His heart was still pounding a little as he took a proper look at the old book. After some time, he realised that it was a book of medieval poetry, although even when he'd got used to the 'S's being 'F's, he still couldn't understand very much of it at all. The language was very strange and the ink frustratingly faint. But actually, none of that mattered to Ed. Just to gaze upon words that were the fruit of someone else's mind, someone who lived in a different world was an experience in itself. To have access to words that had been written so long ago allowed you to enter a secret place, to be privy to something special and hallowed. It was like being invited into a secluded garden full of rare blooms and undiscovered species. Ed knew that beauty doesn't have to be understood rationally to appreciate its specialness, its unique contribution to an otherwise dull world.

After a while however, his eyes began to sting and water with the effort of reading the book. He really was tired now. He put Lionel in the porch and went upstairs. He bathed and went to bed. He dreamed that he was flying over cliffs and beaches, through blue skies, skirting fluffy white clouds.

Chapter V

When Ed awoke in the morning, he remembered the dream. Strangely, he'd felt as though he hadn't been completely alone when flying above the wonderful scenery. He racked his brains, but couldn't recall any other details. In fact the more he thought about it, the less sure he was that there had been anybody else with him at all. He decided that he was just being over–imaginative, as per usual. He pushed the thoughts aside. He actually felt very refreshed and was looking forward to his day.

He did wonder briefly where HR was, then dismissed the thought. Best not dwell on it, he said to himself. He decided to just enjoy the break and make the most of the day. Mrs P had given him directions to the shop, so he and Lionel walked up the hill to buy some supplies. There, they bought a few provisions, (including some rather foul smelling treats for Lionel), and then returned straight home. Ed decided to skip breakfast. He stopped on his way upstairs to put the bag of shopping away and also to shut Lionel in the kitchen. The old dog looked singularly unimpressed at being left alone by his new friend. However, Ed was keen to start work on the collection and thought it better if the animal stayed out of the way whilst he heaved the heavy boxes around. After having found the old book, he was very curious about what other exciting things he might find in the room. He spent the morning packing up all manner of objects, ticking them off the list as he did so. Although by lunchtime he was filthy dirty once again and incredibly hungry, he had really enjoyed himself. A lot of the collection was actually rubbish and some of the objects he pulled out of the boxes looked very ordinary, pieces of china or old pots. Occasionally, however, he would find a truly interesting piece, an African mask or Egyptian relic. Some exotic object from a far away land would suddenly appear from a box, stirring his imagination and his soul, filling him with enthusiasm and spurring him on in his work.

A while later he made his way downstairs. He'd pulled his back lifting the boxes and was now rubbing it, wincing slightly. He went into the kitchen and an overly enthusiastic Lionel greeted him. Ed made himself a ham and tomato sandwich and sat at the table to have another look at his precious find. He opened the book and began to read.

As he was pouring over the words, trying to make them out, he spotted the silver disc out of the corner of his eye. Remembering his stupidity last night, he smiled to himself and continued reading. He finished his sandwich and pushed the plate aside. A few moments later, eyes still on the page in front of him, lost in the aged prose, his hand absently–mindedly wandered towards the metal disc and touched it. It was very, very warm.

He moved his hand away and looked at the circle disbelievingly. His heart began to pound once again, but he was determined to find a logical explanation. He took a deep breath and looked around to find the source of heat. Nothing obvious admittedly, but that didn't mean that there wasn't a simple, logical answer. He got up and walked around the kitchen. As he realised that the answer was not going to be easily found, his head began to spin a little.

'Stop it,' he told himself sternly, 'just get a grip, you idiot. You've just spent too long alone in the house.' He took a deep breath and went back over to the table. He picked up the disc. It was cold.

'See. Ha. It's fine!' and he put it carefully back on the table. He went upstairs to sort out more boxes, grateful for the distraction. However, he felt more than a touch unnerved by these most recent events.

That evening he came downstairs, whistling tunelessly to himself as he entered the kitchen. He made himself some food, humming in a blasé and extremely carefree manner. Anyone watching him would think that he had not a care in the world. However, he studiously avoided the kitchen table, (on which sat the old book and the metal disc), in a manner which suggested strongly that he was trying to hide the fact that he had a problem with it. Like someone pretending to be unafraid of a vicious dog, Ed avoided even looking at the table and carefully kept a good few feet between himself and this innocuous piece of furniture. Strangely enough, he didn't feel so eager to read the old book tonight. In fact, he thought, he wouldn't sit in the kitchen at all. He told himself that he wanted to eat his supper in the lounge and that he had other books he really must look at. He left the kitchen hastily. Lionel, tactfully, didn't blow any holes in this charade and dutifully followed him to the living room.

Ed spent the evening in the lounge. He tried to concentrate on the books he'd left on the sofa the afternoon before, but for some reason he was finding this difficult. Even though the disc had been cool when he'd touched it the last time, the fact that it had been warm a few moments before that was still bothering him immensely. He'd spent the whole afternoon trying to rationalise what had happened. But it was no good, it was weird. He had to admit it, he was petrified and it took all his strength not to run out of the kitchen earlier, the house even. What stopped him wasn't courage, so much as the bare fact that he had nowhere else to go. He could hardly turn up at Mrs P's saying that he had run away from something that looked about as dangerous as a 10p piece!

He looked at his empty plate. He couldn't avoid the kitchen forever. His imagination began to feed his fear. In Ed's fertile mind, the coin or whatever it was began to take on a new, sinister energy. In his mind it grew strong and frightening and the air in the house took on a thick, heavy energy. His breath began to quicken. He had to get a grip, he'd always been easily frightened by the 'unseen.' His family had homed in on this and had always, for a long as he could remember, taken great delight in scaring him. As a small child, they'd hidden in wait for him in the darkness of his bedroom, only to jump out and frighten him when he entered. They thought it was hilarious and when he got upset would tell him he was just a 'spineless wuss' and that he needed to get a sense of humour.

Halloween was Ed's worst nightmare. When he was about five, his mother had had to take him to the doctors. He was so frightened of what his uncle and cousins might do to him on that dreaded night that he'd developed terrible eczema and asthma. The doctor said that he was just over–sensitive and prescribed him some mild sedatives. Even at such a young age, Ed knew that all he needed was someone to listen to him. He carried the nicknames 'Scabby' and 'Wheezy' with him for years afterwards and he never really recovered from all of this, the abject humiliation. It was at about this time in his life that Harsh Reality had started hanging around a fair bit. In a strange sort of way, he missed the old ghoul. Better the devil you know I suppose, he thought, the image of the metal disc swirling around in his head.

He got up and took his plate into the kitchen. He took a deep breath as he entered the room. He put the plate down slowly on the table and deliberately picked up the disc. It was warm, much too warm for comfort. However, he bit onto his lower lip and kept it firmly in the palm of his hand, willing himself not to drop it. He let a sharp breath out, blowing rapidly, as if to expel his fear.

'See, its fine... just a bit warm. Can't hurt me, it's just a coin,' he reassured himself out loud. He felt a bit braver, nothing terrible had happened and the disc actually felt a bit cooler now. Perhaps it was made of a special kind of metal, one that holds the heat, he wondered. He wasn't convinced by this idea by any means, but he desperately needed to be able to put a rational explanation onto these very odd events. Feeling a little better, he put it back down on the table and busied himself washing up the dirty plates. He actually stayed in the kitchen a few minutes more than was necessary. It was not so much that he had conquered his fears; just that he was trying to prove a point to himself – that he wasn't afraid of the disc. He was tired of always feeling that he was a weakling and a coward.

After a while Ed said goodnight to Lionel and went up to bed. It took him a long time to get to sleep. Although he felt a little better since he made himself keep hold of the metal circle, he still felt unsettled. It was as if someone had stuck a wooden spoon in his stomach and swirled it around. The resulting sense was one of weakness and disorientation. It wasn't so much a physical sensation; it was deeper than that somehow. It was a swimming, swishing feeling that made him feel weird and quite nauseous. Ed couldn't really explain it to himself. He remembered that as a child, lying in bed alone at night, this strange sensation would often come over him. It was accompanied by the odd feeling that he wasn't quite alone, that there was some invisible force watching him. He didn't like it at all, not one little bit, but later had decided that it was probably just HR and he kind of got used to it. He wondered where the ghoul had gone – he would certainly have enjoyed this present state of affairs!

Ed didn't know that HR was spending some time in Grimsby. However, with all the improvements going on the town wasn't quite as dismal as the creature had hoped. After a while and seeking a better, more satisfying, holiday atmosphere he had popped over to Whitby. There he paid a visit to the site where Dracula was supposed to have been washed up. He was hoping to meet this august person, maybe get a few tips on how to make life really miserable for this pathetic race. Human beings really were so tedious. Like tenderising steak, it took a fair bit of bashing about just to make them bearable. But HR's efforts were all in vain, there was nothing in Whitby apart from a few seagulls and an ice–cream van. He was devastated. Back to Ed, he thought. Maybe things have gone downhill for him and he's back to his normal, miserable self, he thought hopefully.

Ed turned over in bed and buried himself underneath the covers, as if trying to hide. Eventually he fell asleep. This time he dreamed that he was in a series of dimly lit caves. He was lost and scared. He ran and ran, but found only more caves, dark and dank, the cold air cloying in his nostrils. As he moved quickly through narrow stone passages and gloomy chambers, he could hear a low, roaring, whooshing noise coming from behind him. It echoed as it bounced off the rocky walls and seemed to fill his head with a leaden heaviness and he felt weak, unable to run. He felt as though he were being pursued by something. But by what, he had no idea. He only knew that he was petrified.

He awoke with a start, the morning sun streaming in through the unclosed curtains. He sat up and rubbed his face with his hands. His heart was still pounding and he felt ridiculously scared. It was just a dream, he told himself. He was getting very irritated with his silliness. No wonder his family had loved frightening him, it couldn't have required very much effort at all to reduce him to a nervous wreck! One coin and a bad dream and he was done for.

He got dressed and went downstairs into the kitchen, almost expecting something to leap out from the shadows. He felt tense, jumpy and couldn't relax. He lectured himself sternly as he walked through the house, he had to focus on what he was here for and get on with the job in hand. Although he felt different, he had to admit that the kitchen looked exactly the same, which was a little comforting. The papers and book were where he left them. Through the kitchen window, he could see that the trees were blowing raggedly in the wind. The branches were grabbing at the gales and the strong winds were battering them to and fro. The sky was bright blue though, little fluffy white clouds scooting quickly across it like cotton wool dodgems.

Ed made himself a cup of tea. Again, he didn't sit at the table. Instead, he wandered around, mug in hand, to the other end of the kitchen. Gideon squawked once and cackled like a mad old woman, but mercifully he stayed on his perch. Lionel was still asleep in the porch. Ed had left the door open into the kitchen for him. At hearing Ed's footsteps, Lionel awoke. He padded over to Ed and they exchanged affections. Ed felt a little safer with Lionel and wondered if the dog could sleep in his room. Although, how an old dog could help him with an over–active imagination combined with a serious case of spinelessness, he had no idea.

He fed the animals then let the dog out. The two of them wandered into the garden, Ed sipping the hot tea. Looking down towards the woodlands at the bottom, he could see a small figure moving back and forth. Whoever it was seemed to be sweeping up leaves. However, it was so far away that it was hard to make out exactly what they were doing. Maybe a gardener, Ed mused idly. They had a big job on their hands though, it must take a fair bit of work to keep a huge area like this tidy. Lionel, having done his business, wandered slowly back towards Ed and the two returned to the house.

Back in the kitchen, Ed had to admit that the effects of the bad dream were wearing off and he felt a bit lighter. Little pieces of fear still clung into him though, like sticky cobwebs. He tried to shake them off, splashing his face with cold water from the kitchen sink. He turned back towards the table. As he did so, someone passed the window. He only saw them out of the corner of his eye, but he was sure they had been there. Must be Mrs P come for a cup of tea and a chat, he thought hopefully. He could really do with some company. His optimism faded gradually as he waited, the expected knock at the front door never transpiring. Well, whoever it had been would be long gone by now, he realised. His spirits sank a little and he decided that the best therapy for his anxiety was work. He patted Lionel, gave him a treat and went upstairs to continue packing up the collection.

Ed worked all day, only coming downstairs briefly for food. He ate in the lounge again that night and took Lionel upstairs with him at bedtime. That night, despite Lionel's company, Ed dreamed of the caves again. This time there was someone in front of him. He couldn't see them, but he knew they were there because every now and then he would see a flicker of light coming from ahead. He desperately tried to reach whoever it was, but the noise was still there. It was behind him and in his head, weakening and disorientating him. He woke up feeling sick and shivery and he felt as though he had a temperature. He found some painkillers in the bathroom cabinet, swallowed them down and decided to take an hour or so out before starting work.

Chapter VI

Despite still feeling a little unwell, Ed needed some supplies and so he and Lionel set off for a walk. He was getting his bearings a little by now and so they took a different route to the shop. They took a different lane further down the main road, one that eventually joined the woodland footpath that Ed had discovered a few days earlier. Eventually this took them around the back of the house before joining the road that lead up to the shop. As they passed the end of the gardens, Ed looked up towards the house. There he was again, the gardener chap. Obviously on a break, the man was sitting on a bench halfway up the garden, looking towards the cliffs behind Ed. The figure waved towards him, his tiny arm stretched above a pin–sized head. Ed stopped, responded likewise and then continued onwards. He wondered if he would get the chance to meet the man properly. He had to admit he could really do with a bit of company. He hadn't seen anyone for a couple of days and Mrs P was proving to be hard to track down. A couple of times when he came downstairs after packing up, he would find that the kitchen was spotless, so she'd obviously popped in quickly.

Having gathered supplies for the next day or so, Ed and Lionel returned to the house. He spent the morning in the lounge. He still felt a bit under the weather and dozed on and off on the sofa, Lionel at his feet. Lunchtime came and Ed woke up, feeling quite a bit better. He ambled into the kitchen wondering if he should eat something. He still felt a little nervous generally, but he was getting fed up of worrying about a silly piece of metal and a couple of bad dreams. Really, what was he getting so worked up about? Then he heard a scuffling noise coming from outside near the front door. Not wanting to miss whoever was there this time, he quickly went out of the kitchen to the front door and opened it. It was the gardener chap. He was clipping away at an overgrown rose bush, just at the side of the doorway.

The man looked up, 'hello there, sorry to disturb you.'

'No, no, not at all,' Ed replied, 'I just wondered who it was, that's all.'

'Oh, right. Just tidying up this plant a bit, this one grows too fast.' He carried on with his work, snipping and pulling at the errant bush.

The man was pretty old, seventy at least, Ed guessed. Tufts of sparse, grey hair jutted out haphazardly from underneath an old blue knitted hat. His occasional teeth were a bit brown and worn. He was small and slightly built, Ed guessed that the man only came up to his shoulder. His grey overalls, which hung off his scant frame, were grass–stained and torn in places. The front zipper was broken and held together with safety pins. The trousers were far too long and even though the ends were folded up, they still completely covered his feet. The trouser legs were covered in mud and only the tip of his battered boots could be seen. The old man stopped what he was doing and turned to look at Ed. He had a kind, friendly face, a myriad of lines decorating every millimetre. Ed looked back at him and the lines moved swiftly aside, making room for a wide smile, in spite of the missing teeth. As the old man gazed at Ed unblinkingly, Ed could see that despite his obvious age, the man's eyes were bright blue, completely clear and almost childlike in the directness of their gaze. Perhaps he's a bit slow wondered Ed, feeling sorry for the old chap.

It was pretty cold outside and so Ed, taking pity on the old man, asked him if he would like a cup of tea. The chap seemed a little taken aback by this question

'Oh! errrr, Well, Uhhh, you see.' came the incoherent reply.

This left Ed wondering if it was the wrong thing to do. After all, he'd never exactly had a gardener before and had no idea of the etiquette involved regarding 'staff'.

'Don't worry, I can see you're busy,' he responded, 'sorry, I didn't mean to interrupt you. You carry on, I mean, if that's what you want to do. After all, it's not for me to tell you what to do. Anyway, bye for now.'

Ed gave up; he was starting to sound like a complete idiot. Well, he thought as he closed the front door, perhaps he *was* losing his marbles. Too much time spent alone, that's what it does to you, he decided glumly.

He returned to the kitchen and made himself a sandwich and a cup of tea. He decided bravely that he would sit at the table. He didn't want to admit it, but even knowing someone was outside the front door was better than feeling completely alone. He shoved the papers and the book aside, taking care not to actually touch the disc. He ate in silence, feeding Lionel bits of the crust. Every now and then he would hear the odd noise from Gideon, a manic cackle or high-pitched squawk.

Suddenly there was a knock at the front door. Startled, Ed jumped up and nearly fell over Lionel in his rush to answer it. Standing there was the gardener, woollen hat in hand, his bald scalp exposed to the elements. He looked very cold.

'Do you think that I could possibly bother you for that cup of tea now?' he queried. (He didn't *sound* slow, thought Ed).

'Yes, of course, come in, I'll put the kettle on.'

As the old man followed him into the kitchen, Ed couldn't believe that he was so excited to see another person. He decided that he definitely needed to get out more.

Once inside, the man seemed a bit lost. He wandered around the kitchen, looking bewildered and more than slightly confused. Ed resurrected his earlier theory that the chap perhaps wasn't all there. He did look as though he'd been thrown together like a hastily made Guy Fawkes in his tatty overalls and knitted hat.

'Sit down,' Ed said offering him a seat at the table. Obviously relieved at being given firm guidance as what to do next, the chap did so, putting his hat down carefully next to him.

Smiling benignly at Ed, he said, 'thank you so much. This is really very kind of you.'

'No problem at all,' said Ed, pouring the water into the mugs, 'milk and sugar?'

The chap looked blankly at Ed, eyebrows raised, 'I thought we were having tea.'

Oh boy, this is going to be a bit of a slog, thought Ed, 'Yes, we are, but would you like milk and sugar in it?'

'Oh, I see,' he paused, 'I'll have whatever you're having.'

Ed sat down at the table, introduced himself and explained why he was staying at the house.

'How do you do, I'm Bert,' replied the man, 'this is a lovely house isn't it? I particularly love the garden, especially at this time of year. Lots of new plants sprouting up.'

'How long have you been the gardener here?' Ed asked.

Bert gestured vaguely with his hand, 'oh Lance and I knew each other for a long time. I liked to help him out, you know, keep things in order and make it nice for him.'

'He's lucky to have had you,' said Ed kindly.

Bert blushed and smiled broadly, 'do you think so? That's so good of you to say!'

Ed smiled back. He really was a pleasant old chap, not a bad bone in his body he decided.

The strange thing was that Bert seemed to be having trouble with his cup of tea. He kept taking large gulps, swallowing, and then turning a violent shade of red. The tea was scalding hot, but he didn't seem to realise that it would be much less painful to sip it slowly. He also talked a little strangely. His speech was awkward and a bit clumsy. Ed's assessment of him wandered once more back toward the 'slow' theory. Perhaps the poor old guy's unwell, he thought sympathetically.

Bert looked down at the pile of papers on the table next to him.

'You *have* got a lot to sort out haven't you?' he remarked and picked up the disc, turning it in his hand. Ed watched him a little nervously, waiting to see how Bert responded to it.

Bert just looked thoughtful for a moment, 'do you know what this is?' he asked Ed.

'No idea at all' he replied, reluctant to say very much about it. He'd rather the old man just put it down and leave it alone, then he could carry on pretending that it didn't exist.

'I know a little bit about history. It's a Talisman of some kind, supposed to bring good luck or the suchlike. It's very old, medieval. You should keep hold of it, it could be worth something.'

'Where would it have come from' asked Ed, he was surprised at Bert's response and suddenly curious.

'It would have been made by a magi, or astrologer, to protect and bring good fortune to the owner,' Bert pointed to the markings, 'they're astrological symbols.'

He turned the disc over in his hand, seemingly reluctant to put it down. Eventually the old man sighed, put the Talisman on the table, picked up his tea and began gulping it down again. Ed was relieved to see that it had cooled down enough by now not to scald him.

When Bert had finished drinking, he put the mug down and got up from the table, 'if you'll excuse me, I'll be getting along now. Quite a bit to do this time of the year. Nice tea though, thank you very much.'

'No problem at all, come again, I mean if you'd like to. I'd be glad of the company actually,' Ed admitted.

The old man looked down at Ed, smiling broadly, 'I would like that very much. I don't see too many people either,' he said sadly. He looked away, but Ed saw that his bright blue eyes looked empty for a moment, as if someone had turned out the light behind them.

'Tell you what, come over tomorrow lunchtime, we can have a sandwich,' suggested Ed, eager to grab the chance for more time with his new companion.

'Lovely, I'll be here. Is about one o'clock convenient?' Ed confirmed that that would be fine.

Bert stopped on his way out of the kitchen and turned to Ed, 'I'm terribly sorry, I don't actually have access to a clock. Would you mind awfully if you gave me a shout when you're ready. I'll be out the front again, there are some beds that need weeding.' Ed nodded, briefly wondering why the old man didn't have a watch.

He picked up the remains of his sandwich and sat deep in thought at what Bert had told him about the Talisman. It didn't really give him any answers about its strange behaviour, but he felt better knowing a bit about it, especially the fact that it was used to help people. Perhaps he could stop being so paranoid about it now. However, the articulate way that Bert spoke and the fact that he was so knowledgeable made Ed permanently archive the 'slow' theory. The man was obviously intelligent, if a little strange. Ed was really looking forward to seeing him the next day.

Meanwhile, he decided that enough was enough as far as the Talisman was concerned – time to move on. He hadn't actually finished the old poetry book, but as he couldn't understand a great deal of it anyway, he decided that he really wasn't going to get much more out of it. He bundled the papers, the Talisman and the book back into the carrier bag. He took care to use the book to sweep the Talisman from the table into the bag so that he didn't have to touch it. He put the bag down on the floor near the kitchen sink to take upstairs later.

Chapter VII

The next day dawned, the sky was grey and sullen and dark clouds hung sulkily in the sky. It wasn't raining, but far away out to sea Ed could hear the faint rumbling of thunder. However, he had slept slightly better the night before, he couldn't remember any of his dreams and so felt quite happy as he worked his way through the boxes. By midday, he had done a fair amount. He was getting peckish and was already very dusty.

He went downstairs, washed his hands at the kitchen sink and prepared lunch. He decided to make himself and Bert a toasted cheese sandwich. He'd stocked up the day before and was very pleased that he wouldn't be eating alone for once. He chopped some of the fresh tomatoes that he'd bought at the shop to go with the toasties. Lunch prepared, he called Bert and they spent a very pleasant hour talking about all manner of things. Bert was an extremely interesting chap and he seemed to know a little about everything.

However, his knowledge of history was quite astonishing. During their time together, Ed found himself pulled into a world of ocean travels, great discoveries and famous historical figures. He listened intently as Bert told him about medical discoveries, changes in the world's religions and breakthroughs in technology. The old man described the great plague of London so vividly that Ed felt as though he were really there. In fact, as he listened to Bert describe intricately and with great enthusiasm the horrible symptoms that the sufferers experienced, he actually started imagining that he felt a bit fluey and found himself surreptitiously checking for lumps under his arms and on his neck.

However, Bert seemed to be struggling a bit with the sandwich. He was clearly very hungry, but seemed to have trouble with swallowing the food. He was getting himself in such a state that Ed was worried at one point that he was going to choke. In the end he suspected that the poor old chap probably had problems with his teeth. On closer inspection, they did look pretty dire. Some were missing, the others yellow and so worn they were almost transparent in places. Ed partially remedied the situation by getting a knife and fork and cutting the sandwich up into little pieces for him. Bert was very grateful, but still seemed to have a little trouble swallowing. However, he managed to finish most of his lunch and Ed noticed that the old man looked a little less peaky for a bit of food inside him.

After lunch was finished, Ed decided to find out a bit about Bert and so asked him where he lived.

Bert's response was evasive, 'oh, not far from here at all, just down the road actually. You can probably see it from the upstairs windows,' he told him. As there were no other houses nearby, apart from Mrs P's, Ed was puzzled. He was just about to quiz Bert for more specific details, when a large, horrid smelling object threw itself across the room and landed smack, bang in the middle of the table where they were sitting. Gideon glared up at them, his feathers ruffled up aggressively. His cold eyes moved towards Ed's plate and stared fixedly, Ed tensed, not daring to move. He had no food to give the parrot and daren't leave his seat to get him anything.

'I think he's hungry,' said Bert smiling innocently at the bird.

'Yes, I expect he is,' replied Ed, swallowing nervously. Lionel grumbled from under the table and moved closer to Ed.

'Well, let's see what we can do about that,' Ed was just about to warn Bert that Gideon was about as friendly as a feathered komodo dragon, when Bert picked up a crust and gently offered it to the bird. He held his breath, the old chap was so slight Gideon could probably carry him off to his perch to snack on if he wanted. Ok, that was a bit of an exaggeration he admitted to himself, but not much. Gideon took the bread and began to eat it. He finished it in a flash and then sidled over slowly to Bert. The bird tilted his head onto one side and took another proffered piece of the sandwich. This went the same way as the first. All the time Bert was talking gently to the feathered monster. Then, Gideon walked up Bert's arm and *sat on his shoulder!* Ed could hardly believe his eyes by now. The old chap looked like an elderly, balding pirate as he fed the parrot and casually chatted to him. After a few moments Bert's new, feathered friend had obviously had his fill and took off over the kitchen, back to his perch.

Ed was silent, gobsmacked and amazed all in one go, he didn't know what to say. Bert smiled at him cheekily, a definite twinkle in his eyes.

'Blimey,' said Ed eventually, 'How did you do that? He's usually horrible!'

Bert looked abashed and shrugged, 'I've always liked animals, its nothing really. If you're not afraid of them they feel secure. That's all.'

'Well,' countered Ed, 'please do come back again. Apart from the fact that you more than likely saved me from a nasty bird attack, it's been good to talk to somebody.'

Bert smiled and told Ed that he would love to come back.

'Perhaps tomorrow lunchtime?' the old man suggested, adding hastily, 'if that isn't too soon, of course.'

Ed beamed, 'that would be great. Shall I shout you again?' Everything arranged for the next day, Bert went back to work on the front lawn beds and Ed returned to his packing.

The next week or so passed without incident. Ed and Bert settled into a very pleasant routine. They would get on with their respective jobs in the morning and then meet up for lunch and a chat, parting company again in the afternoons. Ed really enjoyed their time together and they spent hours discussing all kinds of things. Bert never seemed to run out of wonderful historical stories or amazing facts.

Ed's favourite subject though was local Guernsey history, which was both diverse and incredibly interesting. Bert told him many stories about Guernsey. Bert's knowledge went back as far back as several thousand years, from the Neolithic passage graves up on L'Ancresse common, to the Roman remains found in the main town of St Peter Port. He also described in colourful detail the Roman galley found in the harbour. From Bert, Ed learned many fascinating facts about the German occupation during the Second World War. He was surprised that many of their fortifications were still standing.

Then one day, Ed and Lionel were taking an early morning walk when they saw something strange. They had made their way around the back of the house, intending to walk up through the garden. They were just going through the granite gateway when Ed saw Bert. That in itself was not strange at all, after all he worked in the garden. However, the old chap was not actually in the garden, he was coming out of the shed. Again, that was to be expected from a gardener, except that he'd obviously only just woken up. He was rubbing his face, yawning and stretching and looking very dishevelled indeed. Ed ducked back behind the granite gateway. It was an instinctive move, he wasn't sure why, but he didn't want Bert to see him. The old chap had told Ed that he lived not far from the house and he wasn't lying. However, he clearly didn't want Ed to know that he was homeless; otherwise he would have said something. It all made sense now. Bert was always in the same old grubby overalls and, despite the fact that he could eat more efficiently and was looking a bit better; he still seemed to be permanently ravenous. Ed's heart went out to him and his mind began to connect the facts. Of course, Lance had died suddenly and Bert said that he had worked for his uncle for a long time. Perhaps he just couldn't bear to leave. Obviously, he wasn't being paid any more and so couldn't afford to live anywhere else but the shed. Whatever had happened, it was obvious that the poor old chap needed some help.

Bert wandered off up the garden. Ed and Lionel turned back, retracing their steps, walking on through the woodland, round to the lane and towards the front of the house. Ed thought hard about how he could help his friend. He'd grown very fond of Bert and couldn't stand the thought that the old man was sleeping in a cold shed. He couldn't let Bert know he'd seen him though, obviously the old man was embarrassed. An idea came to him, perhaps he could tell Bert that he needed some help with the packing. Bert was an expert on history and would be so much quicker and more efficient than Ed at listing the artefacts. He often found it difficult to know what was rubbish and what wasn't. He could ask him to move in with him and say it was because he needed some company, like Bert was doing him a favour. Yes, that's what I'll do, he decided.

That day at lunchtime, over eggs and toast, Ed broached the subject. Bert looked at him for a long time, then a smile broke out on his weathered face.

'Oh, Ed, of course I'll come and stay, I would love to help you with the collection.'

Then something occurred to Ed, 'the only problem I can see is that you are always so busy in the garden. How will you manage both?'

The two fell silent, pondering this problem.

Then Ed said, 'I have an idea, we'll do a deal. I'll help you in the garden, if you give me a hand with the collection.'

He was rewarded by a great big grin from his friend, 'wonderful…fantastic idea!' exclaimed Bert.

Ed made up a bed for Bert in the lounge. This, he thought would be more comfortable than any of the dusty bedrooms which had no furniture to speak of and were full of boxes. He also rifled through the huge wardrobe in the bedroom where he slept. He found quite a few clothes that were suitable for Bert. His uncle must have been a similar height, he supposed, although considerably wider. Bert would need a belt to keep the trousers up he realised, pulling one from the hanger above him. He also found a pair of shoes that might just fit the old man. Not wanting to embarrass his friend, Ed tactfully left the pile of the clean clothes along with the shoes in the lounge whilst Bert was busy in the kitchen. Neither of them had mentioned the fact that Bert hadn't bought even one belonging with him. Unless, of course, you counted the huge overalls and old boots he wore. As soon as Bert had discarded his old clothes, they went straight in the bin, along with the old blue hat.

In the mornings Ed helped Bert in the garden. He had to admit it, he really enjoyed being outside, it was so fresh and invigorating and it was good for the old man to have someone to cart around the heavy branches. Ed filled plant pots with fresh soil, ready for the seedlings which were growing in the old glasshouse. Ed felt that he could at last breathe properly. He grew healthier and stronger from this work; he even developed a bit of colour. Courtesy of the weak spring sunshine, the greyness of London fell from him like dust. He was slowly coming to life. Like a man who had been asleep for years, he was finally waking up to a new, colourful world.

Each day after lunch they would pack up more of the boxes. This job was made all the more interesting by the fact that Bert knew so much about the artefacts and so could tell Ed everything he needed to know. They ate together in the evenings, sometimes talking animatedly. Often, however, they were silent, each of them engrossed in whatever book they happened to be reading. Sometimes they would pick some of the vegetables that grew in the glasshouse. It turned out that Bert was pretty good at stews and soups and so, combined with the supplies Ed fetched from the corner shop, the two ate very well indeed.

This went on for a while and everything was going very smoothly. The garden looked wonderful. It was most definitely spring now and the daffodils and crocuses, primula and jonquil bloomed, bringing dazzling colours to the still winter–worn landscape. Bert called the early jonquil `bacon and egg`, and when Ed bent to inhale their scent, he understood why. Wild fuchsia climbed the trees, bringing vibrant colour to the still bare branches. Ed forgot about London, the greyness, the traffic, the throngs of strangers streaming mindlessly towards their next destination. He even forgot about HR – well almost.

The two were slowly working their way through the collection and had found some fascinating pieces. They were about two thirds of the way through the first of the rooms and so were making something of a dent in the huge collection. Secretly, even though he knew it was a long time away, Ed dreaded finishing the packing up and the house being put on the market. He had no idea what he was going to do afterwards. All he did know was that he was never, ever going back to London. He loved Guernsey and he really didn't want to have to leave. He was also very happy being with Bert. Despite the age difference, the two of them were very comfortable in one another's company. Ed felt as though he had at last made a real friend, someone who understood him. For the first time in his life, he felt as though he fitted in, that he had found a place in the world. The beauty of Guernsey had touched his heart and he would never be the same again. He knew the cathedral peace he had found in the woods that first day had changed him forever.

Chapter VIII

One fine spring day, a few weeks after Bert had moved in, they had come in from the garden for lunch to find that they had run out of lettuce. There were plenty of tomatoes as usual, but no lettuce. Ed shook his head in amusement. It was only a few weeks ago that he probably wouldn't have known a lettuce from a cabbage. He'd been more inclined to live on burgers and chips back then. Bert offered to pop to the glasshouse and went off down the garden whistling. Ed buttered the bread and poured them both some fruit juice.

There was a knock at the front door. Ed opened the door, juice carton still in hand.

'Hello love,' said Mrs P cheerily, 'how are you doing, long time no see! I've bought you some cakes that I made this morning.'

Ed thanked her and invited her in. He was presented with a very interesting assortment of cakes. He'd never seen anything like these vividly coloured concoctions, he wasn't absolutely sure that they were edible. Blue fairy cakes nestled next to bright yellow meringues. Radioactive green iced scones and dark red slices of something that looked like it belonged in an operating theatre sat next to one another, like captured alien species from different planets.

Mrs P beamed with pride as Ed carefully, (whilst trying not to look too appalled), closed the box and put them on the side as he muttered a hopefully sincere sounding 'thank you'. Mrs P informed Ed that she had been very busy looking after a sick friend for the past few weeks or so and had only had time to dash in to give the kitchen a quick once over. She was sorry she hadn't had chance to stop for a cup of tea. She did, however, remark on the calm and contended state of Gideon. She raised a suspicious eyebrow and glared at him as she passed his perch on her way to the pantry to check for supplies of animal food.

This prompted Ed to tell her about Bert. Standing a safe way away from Gideon, he explained that the old man was doing a fantastic job in the garden and remarked at what an interesting soul he was. He was just about to tell her that Bert was staying in the house and that he hoped that that was ok, when she said quizzically, 'but there is no gardener!'

Ed laughed, 'what do you mean, no gardener?'

'I mean that there *was* a gardener, but he was a strapping lad of about twenty-five. Aussie, I think…went off back–packing as soon as Lance passed away.'

It took Ed a few moments to digest this information. Then he went cold. His mind began to race and he was finding it hard to catch his breath. Who had he let into the house then? Bert had lived, eaten and worked with Ed for weeks now. His mind began to twist and turn like a corkscrew, trying to work out what was going on. The collection, perhaps he was after that? Some of the pieces were obviously valuable; he could be some kind of conman or burglar. He could even be violent. Ed stopped himself at that point. Although he realised he knew very little about Bert, he was absolutely sure the old man wasn't, and never could be, violent.

Mrs P was peering at Ed, 'are you alright lad? You look very green. Here, sit down for a minute. She led him back to the table. 'Listen you don't know who this chap is. If you see him again, you must call the police. Guernsey's a pretty safe place, but still, you can't be too careful.'

76

Weak with worry now, Ed feebly explained that Bert had just gone down to the bottom of the garden and would be back in a few moments.

'Right,' Mrs P got up determinedly, 'I'll go and get Reg from the farm down the road, big lad he is, I'll come back with him in a few minutes. Reg'll scare him off, no problem. He won't bother you again Ed.'

With that, she marched out of the kitchen and left the house. Ed blankly watched her go down the driveway. Her gleaming white trainers flashing as she moved like an athlete in training towards the road.

Harsh Reality just happened to arrive back from Whitby at that very opportune moment. He spotted his old friend Ed looking dazed and shocked. Seeing that things were hotting up he decided to stay on for a bit. His yellow teeth clacked with excitement as he saw Ed's defeated expression. He gave himself a nice pat on the back for his impeccable timing.

Ed put his head in his hands and groaned. Why oh why was he always such a sucker? If anyone was going to be taken for a ride it was always him – always. He was sick of it. Then, he felt something in his chest, a strange sensation of something building, a solid and powerful energy. He felt like he was going to burst. He realised that he was, for maybe the first time in his life, actually ANGRY. He was really, really angry. Bert had come into his life, taken complete advantage of him and, worst of all, had lied to him. All of it, the times they had shared, the whole friendship was just one big, fat lie.

He was seething with rage when Bert came back in. The man's face paled when he saw Ed's expression. He put the lettuce down on the table.

'What's wrong Ed?' he asked quietly.

Ed looked up, 'Mrs P from next door came round whilst you were gone,' he paused, 'you're not the gardener are you?' he struggled to keep his voice even, the heat of the rage had subsided now and he felt icy cold inside. It sat, a huge jagged block of ice in his chest. It hurt like mad.

Bert sat down, slowly, 'Ed,' he said gently, 'I'm so sorry, I would never hurt you.'

'Well, you have. You've lied to me,' Ed said. He was, to his shame, feeling quite tearful. The jagged block of ice was slowly melting away, making him feel weak and watery.

'Ed, I never, ever actually lied to you,' Bert paused, 'I did, I admit, allow you to think what you wanted to. But you created your own story, your version of the reality around what you saw to be the facts.'

Ed stared at Bert, he could hardly believe what he was hearing. How could Bert turn this around so that it was his fault? How dare he twist everything like this!

'You were wearing overalls and doing the garden, what was I supposed to think?'

'I had nothing else to wear and, to be honest the garden needed doing. That's why I was taking care of the plants,' was Bert's reply.

'Well, I know you're not what you pretended to be and the neighbour's gone to get help. She'll be back in a minute to make sure that you don't cause any more trouble.'

Ed felt strangely elated at being able to tell Bert this – that he was not alone and had outside support. It made him feel strong and powerful to make the old man hurt as much as he did.

Bert did indeed look hurt, in fact he was clearly devastated. His blue eyes clouded over with shock and he put his hand up to his face, as if to block out what Ed had told him. Then he took his hand away and reached out to Ed, not daring to touch him, but still desperate to connect with him in some small way. His face was grey and he suddenly seemed to look much, much older. The lines on his face were deeply etched, like cracks in stone.

'Please Ed, don't let them see me,' he pleaded, his voice cracking with fear, 'you don't understand, I can't be found.' He seemed almost hysterical now, his voice getting louder, 'it will all be over, everything's finished, finished.'

The normally placid old man was now pacing the kitchen, ranting incoherently. He seemed almost to have forgotten that Ed was there. He looked up to the ceiling, fists clenched to his chest, 'I've messed it all up, what am I going to do? I am such a fool, a fool. It's never going to work now. Never!'

This carried on for a little while and then, seeming to have exhausted himself out, Bert collapsed and sat down once more at the table. Attempting to compose himself, he took a deep breath, 'Ed. Son,' he beseeched, 'just do this one thing, I beg you. Tell them I'm not here. Please?'

Ed reeled, his head was spinning, *he's never called me 'son' before.* He looked back at Bert, the old man looked tearful. He was obviously genuinely frightened, this was no act. He wondered who he was running away from and why. A ripple of pain in Ed's belly reminded him of the fact that Bert had deceived him.

The old man seemed to have read Ed's thoughts, 'if you do this one small thing, then I will explain everything, everything, the whole truth. I truly promise you. After that, if you don't feel that you can forgive me, then I give you my solemn word that I will walk out of this house and you will never, ever see me again.'

Ed felt exhausted, confused and hurt; he didn't know what to think. But Bert had called him 'son' and somewhere deep inside a part of him had reacted to that word. He had never been called that by a man. It felt so strange, like golden sunlight flashing off of the surface of a deep, dark river – bright, unexpected and warm. It wouldn't do any harm to let him explain, he thought. He could hear his mother's voice echoing in his head, telling him that he was too soft and to pull himself together.

There was a noise at the front door. Startled, the two men leapt to their feet. Ed remembered that Mrs P had a key – there was no time to get Bert upstairs.

'Quick, go to the pantry, I'll close the door behind you.' Bert turned to Ed and in that moment something passed between them, a flash of light, an understanding that said more than a thousand words. Ed closed the pantry door and returned to the other end of the kitchen, breathing deeply to calm his nerves. He was about as good at lying as Bert was at telling the truth, he thought miserably to himself.

Harsh Reality held his breath with anticipation. This was so much better than being anywhere else. He'd forgotten just how good it could be when Ed was at his worst.

Mrs P and Reg entered the kitchen, a definite air of the Gestapo about them. Mrs P had very determined look on her face and her skinny arms were folded firmly across her chest. Reg was most definitely big, he must have been six foot four with swarthy skin that looked as dirty as it did tanned. He had a massive beer gut, bulging forearms and very short greasy black hair. He was wearing a dirty white vest and tattered army trousers. Ed gulped, he didn't look very friendly at all. His mean eyes glared ferociously at Ed from underneath heavy black eyebrows. He had a look on his face that told the world that he most certainly meant business. By business he didn't mean buying and selling shares – that was for sure.

'Is this 'im?' he queried, lunging clumsily towards Ed, 'right you. Out. NOW!' he roared, as he leant forward to grab Ed by the scruff of the neck.

Mrs P stepped forward and slapped the big man across the arm with a sharp *thwack* and said crossly, 'no, you idiot, that's Ed.'

Surprisingly, Reg stepped back immediately with a startled look on his face. He rubbed his arm and looked very crestfallen, 'oh, right. Just 'e looked a bit dodgy,' he muttered sheepishly.

Ed looked at Mrs P with a newfound respect. For a small woman, she could certainly handle herself, he thought. Reg was obviously all talk and no trousers. Come to think of it, perhaps all talk and no brains was a more accurate assessment. He wasn't at all impressed that the big lug had thought he was the culprit.

'Where is he then?' asked Mrs P.

'He's gone,' said Ed, fingers crossed behind his back. He hated lying, especially to Mrs P.

'Gone, where?'

'Well, when I told him that I knew he wasn't the gardener, he just scarpered. He..er...ran out of the back door and across the garden.'

Ed hoped to goodness that Reg didn't decide to go after him. The big lump would be bound to come back to the house when he couldn't find Bert and he desperately needed Reg and Mrs P to be gone as soon as possible.

'He's long gone by now,' continued Ed, trying his very best to sound upbeat and relieved all at the same time, 'I'm sure he wouldn't dare come back. I think I scared him off.'

This last statement was pushing it a bit. Mrs P and Reg both looked more than a bit sceptical at the idea that Ed could frighten anyone. Reg scowled, his eyebrows dropping so far down that his eyes disappeared completely. However, Mrs P quickly and politely recomposed her features so that she looked markedly impressed rather than disdainfully disbelieving.

'I'm sure you did dear,' she said patting him lightly on his upper arm. 'Just let me know if you see hide or hair of him again and I'll bring Reg back.' Reg grinned at Ed, looking about as friendly as a gorilla with toothache. Ed smiled back, hoping he didn't look too petrified.

'Thanks, I will,' he promised.

Mrs P turned to Reg, 'come on you, let's go. I'll make you a cup of tea and I've got some lovely fairy cakes I made earlier.' Reg grinned again and lumbered after her like an oversized toddler.

Once out of the larder, Bert was profusely grateful. He clutched Ed's hand and kept saying, 'thank you, thank you, you won't be sorry, I promise you.'

Ed was quiet, he was upset at having to lie to Mrs P and felt as though this made him as bad as Bert. Oh well, he supposed they were both liars now. Deflated, he made his way back to the table with Bert behind him. HR was having a field day, he was so glad he'd decided to return.

Ed sat down and Bert made them a cup of tea, he put two sugars in each and made Ed drink some of it.

'It's for the shock,' he said, 'I know you didn't want to lie to them. Honestly, if there'd been any other way....' he tailed off, knowing it was hopeless.

'I shouldn't have had to do it in the first place,' said Ed sullenly. He felt cheated somehow, not only of his friendship with Bert but also of his own integrity. He had always told himself that he would never be like his mother's family, that he would never lie or cheat. His honesty was the only part of himself that he felt even slightly proud of and now thanks to Bert, even that was gone.

HR grinned and settled himself back in, snuggling up in the corner of the kitchen, bony knees folded and arms crossed. He was ready for the show.

'Let me explain Ed,' said Bert gently, 'please. As I said, once I've finished, you just say the word and I will leave for good. I promise.' Ed didn't reply, so Bert continued on, his voice shaking a little as he spoke.

'I have a story that I would like to tell you. It's not a short story, but,' the old man attempted a watery smile, 'it's a story that encompasses history and so you may enjoy some of it.'

Ed really wasn't in the mood for one of Bert's tales. He also couldn't think how it could relate to what was happening now, but felt too exhausted to argue. He didn't answer. Sipping his tea, he stared at the space just in front of him, his face expressionless.

Bert took a deep breath and began....

Chapter IX

'A long time ago, over eight hundred years ago in fact, there was a man who lived in a castle. His name was Albotain and in those days he would have been called a magician or an astrologer. However, perhaps a more appropriate description might be that he was a 'doctor of the soul'.

Albotain had always lived in the castle, as had his father and his father before him. They had all been part of castle life and were as dependable and solid as the walls themselves. They simply had always been there. Everyone came to Albotain with their illnesses, their aches and pains, just as they had done with his father and his grandfather.

You see, in those days doctors were physician astrologers. They were not just academics; they were also mystics who were familiar with the planet's influences upon Man. They took a special interest in the health of the soul as well as the body. They felt that the body was the living, breathing part of the soul. They spent their lives trying to understand why people became physically ill or psychologically imbalanced. These wise men studied the skies for signs of what was to be. Many spent their entire lives developing their inner powers, their ability to connect with other realms and the beings that resided there so that they could help their fellow man. Albotain was one such scholar.

He was content. Well, as content as any true scholar, any genuine 'seeker of the truth,' can be. His days and most of his nights were taken up by his passion, his desire to learn. He spent hours upon hours buried in manuscripts and books, studying the masters of the time. He read all of the ancient works he could find, trying to fathom out the mysteries of existence. He was determined to seek out every piece of information that could help him. He felt it was his vocation, his path and he would let nothing stand in his way.

He sought out manuscripts created by the Egyptians, the Greeks, the French and the Arabs. He painstakingly taught himself a multitude of languages so as not to limit access to potentially valuable material. He studied the works of Plato, Plotinus, Apollonius, Abelard and Ibn Ezra. He read the Socratic dialogues, the Ennead, Mishpetei Ha'Mazalot and the newly discovered Arabian text, the Picatrix.

However, he did not simply emulate these great Masters. He had no wish to become a carrier of others' beliefs. Instead he took what he felt was wise and good and created his own understanding of the universe. He also researched various methods in order to increase the power of healing, to help others recover from what ailed them. He desperately wanted to understand the root of all illness and the reason why Mankind was such a sickly and discontented breed.

He would stroll about the castle grounds at nighttime with his astrolabe, carefully measuring the positions of the planets. During the day he would be found wandering the castle with his almanacs, or star charts, rolled up under his arm. He was always ready to heal the next sick kitchen worker or feverish child. It was who he was, he knew nothing else.

Albotain believed that to be a good scholar, he had to be alone. He felt that other people and personal relationships were a waste of his precious energies. He needed no one and that was rightly so. In those times, the skilled physicians and astrologers actually believed that in order to progress, to learn the true art of healing and understanding, one had to be what they called a 'melancholic'. Today, we would call them recluses, hermits or even depressives. A melancholic is one who lives alone and finds no joy in the spontaneity of life, in light–heartedness or within human connections. But that was Albotain and he knew so much. Yet ultimately he knew so very little, as you will discover.

You see, this was his downfall. Full of knowledge and facts, he left no room for the part of life that is truly alive, that is the essence of life. He never learned how to love or to how to truly give to another. Consequently, the bridge of knowledge that he had built was missing a vital piece. Despite his studying and commitment to the academic part of life, sooner or later the connection with the other side, the higher realms, had to fail him. It had to break through lack of understanding of the human heart. For what is spirit if it is not love and compassion?

Despite his rather unsettled emotional state, Ed nevertheless found himself listening intently. HR was still curled up in the corner, watching the two men closely through slitted eyes.

Now, the Lord of the castle, Vincent, was a loving and wise man. He treated everyone as equals and loved his subjects without exception. He was always able to see the best in those around him, including his faithful magi, Albotain. Lord Vincent was also particularly close to his head huntsman, Reinaud. Vincent loved Reinaud like the brother he never had. Also, they were both widowers and so sought one *another's company often when they felt lonely or unhappy. One day, one terrible day, Reinaud was killed by a stray arrow whilst out hunting. The castle was silent with grief; no one spoke above a whisper for weeks. Everyone loved Reinaud, but more than that they loved Vincent and knew that their master would be devastated by the loss of his dearest friend.*

Then, weeks later, Lord Vincent, frail and unwashed, emerged from his chambers and went to see Albotain. He told him that Reinaud had a son, a young boy who was now an orphan. Vincent may have been grieving, but he was a strong and wise man and even in this time of pain, he was still able to think of what was best for all concerned. His duties meant that he was often away from the castle for long periods of time and so he was unable to be a constant influence in the boy's life. A boy needed a father figure, someone who could teach him a profession. So he asked Albotain to take care of the boy and train him in medicine and astrology. Albotain had never married and had had no children. There was no one to carry on the legacy of knowledge that he carried so preciously, no heir to pass his wisdom onto.

Albotain agreed. To be honest he had little interest in the boy, but felt it was his duty to consent. He decided that he would help bring to Lord Vincent the sense that he had honoured Reinaud's memory. The boy was only ten years old, a small, lost little creature, pale and thin. His name was Daniel. His dark brown eyes were guarded, unreachable and deadened with the pain of losing his only remaining parent. Albotain took pity on him and gave him one of his many chambers. The boy was also allowed access to Albotain's books, charts and maps of the skies. Having done what he felt was adequate; the astrologer very shortly afterwards became engrossed in his own work once more and left the boy to his own devices.

It was about this time that Albotain's journey of discovery took him to uncharted realms which he explored with a passion that was only exceeded by his determination. It seemed that his years of toil and struggle were beginning to bear fruit. He began to develop greater understanding of the other worlds, connections that gave answers as to the true nature of man. He had spent months meditating and purifying his soul with mantras and spells. He had fasted for weeks, living upon just water. He walked for hundreds of miles across the hills and valleys. In a deep trance he sought true union with a race of advanced beings called the Unseen Masters, or the Brotherhood of the Light. It was believed that this benevolent race were as close to God as could be. As pure as sunlight, they held within their consciousness the knowledge of the universe, the eternal truth and infallible knowledge. In connecting with these great beings, the answers to everything, the remedy to all of man's weaknesses and failings, could potentially be at Albotain's fingertips.

As the months went by, Albotain began to sense an energy around him, a surge of inner strength and illumination that he had never experienced before. He felt clearer, stronger and began to know instinctively what ailed his patients. He saw colours surrounding people and discovered that this aura could tell him much about his subject's state of health.

His dreams also altered. He found that whilst asleep, he could travel to different worlds. These were no ordinary dreams; he was lucid, acutely and consciously aware of that which he encountered. He saw beings of light that were human–like, but held within them absolute perfection, no disease afflicted them, no inner torture corrupted their beauty. He visited the Angels and sat with them whilst he watched from on high the migration of souls, hundreds and hundreds of them. They moved from the earth like clouds of silver grey dust, their business finished. He watched in wonder as the new souls, bright with hope, descended onto earth, ready to take up their new place as part of the human race.

Albotain also saw what happened to those who defied the Laws of Spirit – the villains, the murderers and thieves. He watched as the true consequences of their depraved lives were shown to them by the Guardians of the Realms. He saw how they begged for mercy, wracked with guilt and self–loathing as they realised what they had done to their fellow men, their brothers. He watched in awe as they chose their own punishment, eager to revisit the earth, to re–right wrongs and make amends to those they had tainted with their evilness.'

HR had the sudden unpleasant feeling that he was being observed. He felt the eyes of the old man looking into and through him. Even though Bert was actually gazing at his hands, which were clasped tightly in front of him on the table top, the ghoul had the horrible feeling that he'd been spotted.

'As a result of his newfound connection, this increased knowledge, Albotain's talents increased tenfold. Soon, people were visiting from hundreds of miles away, travelling on horseback or on foot for days, or even weeks. Often they would physically carry their sick and diseased loved ones. They would travel just to see this amazing healer, this man who seemed to be so much more than a mere mortal.

As a result of his studies Albotain learned to create Astrological Talismans, engraved discs that held a powerful magic. It took a great deal of talent to be able create these objects. The magician would carefully study the planets and stars and once they were in the correct positions, only then would the Talisman be created. The discs were usually made of silver or gold and had inscribed upon them magical and astrological symbols. Consequently, these special objects possessed highly potent magical powers.

These objects could help the owner in many ways, depending upon what kind of Talisman it was and which planetary influence was held within it. For example a Talisman of Jupiter could protect whilst travelling, bringing with it good fortune and happiness. A Talisman of Venus would bring love, harmony and balance to the owner's life. A Talisman of Saturn bought stability, good reason and common sense.

Albotain was adored by those who came to him. Before now, he had never received this kind of attention. In the beginning, he shied away from the adoration and praise that was being heaped upon him. But, in the end he was no greater than any other man, not really, not deep inside. Soon he began to accept, encourage even, the affections and flattery that his patients and their families bestowed upon him. It was not long before the nobility and their consorts heard of his great skills and so too came to him. They arrived at his door bearing gifts of luscious cloths, jewels set in silver and gold and exquisite fruits from foreign lands recently conquered.

Albotain felt loved and valued for the first time in his life. This weakness, this lack of understanding of the human heart,

91

led him to believe that those who worshipped him truly loved him. He could not see that it was his power that they bowed to, not his heart or his true self. This need to be noticed, to be elevated above others, became addictive. The more he was told he was wonderful, amazing, a true God, the more he needed reassurance that this was so. He hungered for praise, to be told that he was important and worthy. Nothing was ever enough though. Strangely, it was as if each word of adoration spoken to him took a small piece of him away. The acclaim just left an empty feeling in his belly that he just couldn't seem to satisfy. This drove him on further, desperately seeking reassurance and praise from all he encountered, only to find he felt the void within him even more acutely.

Of course, these experiences and his responses to what was happening changed him, they affected his soul. You see, to connect with the higher Gods you must be pure and desire to be with them for reasons that are not selfish or egotistical. Albotain had initially progressed so well, so quickly, because his motivation had been pure. He deeply and sincerely had wanted to understand the universe, so that he could enlighten Mankind and bring clarity to a distorted and chaotic world.

Now, when a person is pure of motivation and truly desires to advance spiritually, there is a change in their soul energy. Essentially it quickens, speeds up if you like. The higher, more evolved spiritual beings are then able to connect and communicate with this Student of the Light. This is because both are on the same frequency. Like a radio tuner finding the right wavelength, a clear connection is established between them.

So, as Albotain became more and more attached to this new way of life, his motives changed. Instead of working for love, he was afraid – afraid that the adoration would stop. He began to believe that he would be nothing without it. He had forgotten how rich and nourishing his inner world had been before he had become so famous. Consequently, his soul energy dropped, its vibrational rate became lower. The higher beings could no longer reach him to protect and guide him.

However, because his psychic powers had been awoken, this drop in his energy field meant that he was now open to the lower realms of beings. His dreams became much darker and for the first time in his life, he felt afraid when he was alone and knew instinctively that he was no longer safe. He often saw dark shapes out of the corner of his eye when no one was around. Strange noises in the dead of night startled him when he was alone in his chamber. They wanted him, they would whisper in his ear. They told him that they would give him everything if they could just have his soul, if he would just go with them into the Darkness. He refused and they became angry and vicious, frightening him further. He was angry, he felt betrayed. He would cry out, asking why the good, pure spirits had left him. He didn't realise that it was he who had left them.

Of course, because of this shift in his energy, his powers of healing began to diminish and so became less effective. In his panic and his fear, he turned to other forms of magic to compensate for the loss of his powers. He studied mind control, he taught himself how to find weaknesses in others. Once he had access to others' vulnerabilities, he could use them to his own ends. He would drain his subject of their energy, leaving them weak and depleted, so that he could then feign healing them. He was willing to use anything that could save him. He lived off of the back of his previous successes, hoping and praying that no one would find out that he was a failure, a fraud. He was petrified, but it was his fear and his greed, his need for more that made him able to justify his actions to himself.

This went on for a few years and Albotain clung to his new life. Desperate not to fall from his pedestal, his elevated status, he spent all of his time trying to hold onto the web of deceit that he had woven together. Meanwhile, he had not noticed the boy Daniel, this quiet, unassuming lad with the empty eyes. He had given him no attention or affection – in fact he had barely noticed him.

However, Lord Vincent realised that he had made a mistake giving Albotain charge of the boy. He saw that the old man hadn't the time or the inclination to care for his charge. So he kept a close eye on the child and made sure he saw him as much as he possibly could. Vincent had also noticed that Albotain had changed, and although he still loved his old friend, he found himself avoiding the man more and more. Therefore he felt in his heart that he shouldn't encourage the empty relationship between the astrologer and the child any further.

When Vincent was at the castle he would visit the boy, talking with him for hours. The youngster had spent a lot of time alone and over time had studied many of Albotain's manuscripts and notes. He had taught himself to draw up charts of the planets and stars and was eager to share this new, exciting ability with his Lord. Lord Vincent soon realised that the boy had talent. He was only fourteen years old by then, but he seemed to possess a wealth of knowledge that belied his years. Over time Vincent began to consult the boy instead of Albotain and found that he was extremely accurate. He also saw that he was honest and pure in his assessment of situations and was tactful and responsible regarding his predictions. Daniel also seemed able to help heal physical illnesses. He was naturally talented with regards medical or health matters. He could tell from the star charts which of the four humors, or bodily substances, were out of balance and could give advice on what should be done to correct them.

Vincent, who was an intelligent and well–educated man, was so inspired by the boy's talent and enthusiasm, that he asked him if he would teach him the art of astrology. The young man agreed and told the lord that he had been studying magical astrology. He said that as well as teaching him the art, he would create something very special for his master. He would create for him an object that would help him in his pursuit of pure knowledge.

Soon word spread around the castle that Vincent was consulting the boy instead of Albotain. Albotain was livid. If his devoted followers found out that the Lord of the Castle was not consulting him, the great Albotain, choosing to see a mere boy instead, he would be finished. He was getting older, what future did he have if he lost his status and power now? He locked himself away in his chambers. He was infuriated and overtaken with anger. He didn't even notice the dark shapes and the whispering voices desperately trying to draw him even further into the shadows. For hours he paced like a caged wild animal back and forth, his velvet robes flying behind him like wings. He was totally deranged and beside himself with fear and madness. After a while, he began to hatch a plan, a nasty, evil plot. He formed an idea, one that he carefully recreated in his twisted mind so that he understood that he was justified, that he had no choice but to get rid of the boy – for good.

Lord Vincent had three daughters. Two were already married and lived far away from the castle. The youngest, however, was unmarried and still living with her father. She was Vincent's favourite. She was petite and beautiful and everyone knew that Vincent did not want to let her go. She was also the absolute image of his beloved late wife. He could not bear the thought of losing the last part of her, his only true love, as well as his favourite offspring. Albotain, of course, knew this and having become a master of using others' weaknesses against them, he knew that she had to be implicated somehow.

He went to the Lord and told him he had received psychic messages from the spirit world. These communications were warning him that the boy had been studying dark magic and that he was intending to use a mandrake root to create a spell that would force the Lord's daughter to fall in love with him. Once this had been done, Albotain informed Vincent, the boy would be in a position of power and could manipulate the Lord in order to ensure that he inherited the castle and all his master's riches.

Vincent asked the old man what real evidence he had of this. Albotain told him that he had followed the boy to gain proof of his intended actions. It was a full Moon and he had seen the lad with one of the castle dogs underneath the gallows just outside the castle walls, digging up a mandrake root. In those times, it was known to everyone with occult knowledge that when the bodily fluids of criminals dripped onto the soil below the gallows, any mandrake root growing *there would be endowed with magical properties. This was particularly potent when used in love spells.*

The Lord was sceptical at first, demanding more details from Albotain. At first, he told him that his story was pure conjecture and this was not enough for him to believe that the boy was plotting against him. Albotain reminded Vincent that this kind of witchcraft was not practised by the pure and good. It was bad magic and he could prove the boy was up to no good. The Lord thought about this long and hard. He was fond of the boy, but more than that, he could not bear the thought of anyone harming his daughter. He asked how Albotain could prove what he was saying. The astrologer replied that he had secretly followed the boy back to his chambers and had seen him place the root underneath his bed, wrapped in a black cloth.

The boy's room was searched and they found the mandrake under the bed, placed there, of course, by Albotain. The Lord was devastated, he was very fond of the boy, but he had to protect his daughter. He decided that the best thing to do would be to send the boy away, far from the castle and from his beloved daughter. However, he wished the boy no harm and realised that he was alone in the world. He worried that it had perhaps been loneliness that had driven him to behave so badly. So, the Lord arranged for the boy to live with a farmer and his wife who lived many miles from the castle. They had no sons of their own and needed some help with the farm. However, they did have a daughter and were seeking a husband for her, so it was an ideal situation. Vincent felt that the boy would be well looked after and would want for nothing.'

HR smirked a bit, but not quite as enthusiastically as usual. Although he liked an unhappy ending, he wasn't sure if it was all going to go the way he liked.

'However, Vincent realised that the boy had taken the wrong path. He had been caught practising bad magic and so was potentially a danger to himself and others. The Lord told the boy that he was banished from the castle, but also that he was never, ever allowed to practice magic or astrology ever again.

By this time, Albotain had gone to see the boy and warned him that if he denied the charges, Lord Vincent was so angry that he would probably put him to death. The boy, confused and frightened by this unexpected turn of events, agreed to Vincent's demands and left the castle, never to return.

So, Albotain was once again reunited with his master and continued to hold power over those who adored and worshipped him for many years. He died at a good age, surrounded by people who were devoted to him. However, as he drew his last rasping breath, he wondered what was going to happen to him next. He knew in his heart he had done wrong and he had a horrible feeling that whatever was going to happen to him next wasn't going to be good.'

Chapter X

Bert stopped, drew in a deep breath and looked up at Ed, who was silent. Eventually Ed asked, frowning, 'what has this story got to do with you not being the gardener? You haven't explained anything at all.'

He got up, ready to leave.

Bert put his hand on Ed's arm, 'wait, that's only the beginning of the story Ed. There's more to tell.'

'More?' Ed asked, eyebrows raised. 'He's dead Bert. There can't *be* any more.'

'Just give me a little more time and you'll understand. At least I hope you will. I'm going to tell you what happened to Albotain after he died.'

Ed looked at Bert, bewildered. Sighing, he sat down again. He had no idea why he was agreeing to listen to more of this rubbish. He was so confused, he really didn't know what to think. Putting his empty mug down, Bert continued...

'Albotain awoke in a place he didn't recognise. It was a great hall; the walls were made of white marble and the high ceilings were supported by beautiful, carved columns. It was filled with sunlight that streamed in through huge windows. Inset in the windowpanes were bright jewels that cast multi-coloured rainbows across the polished floors. It was quiet and incredibly peaceful. Robed figures moved silently past him, smiling gently and greeting him like a long lost friend, softly squeezing his shoulder or touching his hand. He sat up, realising that he had been lying on a couch of some kind, soft

cushions enveloped him and a fine woollen rug was draped over his legs.

He breathed a sigh of relief. He'd got away with it! He hadn't been punished for his behaviour. Here he was in what was undoubtedly some kind of Heaven, some palace in the higher realms. He got up and began to walk towards what looked like a central hall. He felt happier than he had for years, lighter and younger. His bones no longer ached, his stiff back was supple again. He looked down at his hands and saw that they were smooth and free of age spots. He continued on and reached the main part of the hallway where he stood, a little at a loss as to what to do next.

Walking swiftly and purposely towards him was a tall, distinguished looking man. He wore a gown that looked as if it was made from silk. It was very striking and constantly changed colour as he moved. It flowed from delicate rose pink to lilac and then to a deep blue which slowly faded into magenta. The man held out his hand, placing it firmly on Albotain's shoulder and told him that his name was Micah and that he had been asked by the elders of the Higher Council to take care of him.

They talked for a while, leaving the palace and wandering through a beautiful landscape, an absolute paradise of natural beauty. Crystal clear waterfalls and lakes cut through lush green countryside and there were flowers everywhere. Albotain noticed that their colours were brighter and more vivid than anything he had ever seen. They stopped and sat under a huge, majestic oak tree, watching the birds swooping gracefully over the lake in front of them. Children dressed in white played in a field nearby, holding hands and singing sweetly as they moved round in a circle. Their silvery voices floated through the clear air like the breath of angels. Micah explained gently to Albotain that he was indeed in a part of Heaven and that hopefully, one day, he would be able to return here as a member of the Higher Order.

Albotain was puzzled. What did he mean, return? Surely this was his new, rightful home. Micah told him that he, Albotain, was a Soul of the Higher Order. He agreed that Albotain in his earthly life had mainly been a good and devoted soul, a true Seeker of the Light. However, after he attained the connection with the Great Masters and had become an object of adoration for others, he had misused the power given to him. He had truly lost his way when he began to crave greater influence over others and to covet material riches. His weaknesses had overcome him and this had ultimately led to his downfall. His actions and the consequences of his behaviour would, said Micah gently, have to be put right before he could be allowed to reside in this paradise, this place of peace and love.

Albotain argued that yes, admittedly he had wandered off the path somewhat, there was no denying that, but could he not just be forgiven? After all, that's what spiritual beings did isn't it – forgave unconditionally? Micah laughed kindly and told Albotain that it was not just the fact that he had turned to dark practises in trying to maintain his worldly status that was the problem. It was what he did to Daniel that was the real issue. Albotain didn't understand, Daniel was just a boy and he hadn't hurt him really. He told Micah that he had heard through the castle grapevine that the boy had married the farmer's daughter. Apparently he had inherited the farm and so at this present time he lived fairly well. What was the problem? No real harm had been done.

101

Micah looked at Albotain for a long time. When Albotain looked back into the Angel's emerald eyes they seemed to hold eternity, as if the whole universe lived and breathed within him. Micah explained that the boy was no ordinary boy, but a highly developed spirit, one of a group called the Sapphire Souls. These beings were from the highest spiritual planes and so were pure and untainted. They were also highly courageous and strong enough to incarnate into physical form onto the earth in order to help Mankind. The boy Daniel had been sent to help heal the earth and its inhabitants. The wise and all–seeing elders of the Higher Council, the carers of the earth, knew that over the next five hundred years, that man, through his own selfishness and greed, was going to bring upon himself plague and war.

Despite man's failings, the Council loved all of humanity and wanted to help this fragile race if they could. They had to give permission for a Sapphire Soul to manifest on earth. This happened very rarely and was only allowed in the direst of circumstances. This had been sanctioned once before, but that particular Sapphire Soul had been persecuted and then violently murdered.

The difficulty was that no matter how pure and untarnished these beings were in their true spiritual state, as soon as they incarnated into physical form, they became fallible. They were then prey to all of the weaknesses associated with human beings. They lost the conscious awareness of who they were. Even if they did eventually realise what their mission was on earth, their emotions and human–ness corrupted their judgement. They misjudged people, trusted when they should have been suspicious and allowed unscrupulous others to take them away from their spiritual mission.

The Higher Council decided that this next incarnation of a Sapphire Soul needed guidance on earth. Consequently, they had given the boy to Albotain. They believed that the astrologer could help Daniel in his mission, to train and mould him, enlighten him with regard to astrology and magic. Once the child was acquainted with earthly magical practice, then he would be equipped to fulfil his true destiny, to change the course of man's dire fate. Of course, the Council knew that Albotain in his physically incarnated state was also human and as such was flawed, but they had no other option. In whatever manner they chose to bring this Supreme Being to earth and whomever they chose to mentor him, they did not have the power to control people. Man had to be allowed to exercise his Freedom of Will. This was the first spiritual law and as such could never be broken.

Albotain sat on the grass, absorbing the enormity of what Micah had told him. He was shattered; he had not only failed himself, but the whole of humanity. He alone had single-handedly corrupted fate so that it was distorted and ruined. Like a twisted flute, it could no longer play notes that were clear or untainted. It could express no clarity, no resonance of purity. He had, through his foolish and ignorant actions, taken away the boy's powers and rendered him useless. This highly developed being, this Sapphire Soul, was now nothing more than a farm hand and unless something was done, Mankind was going to suffer dreadfully.

Albotain asked Micah what he could do. The Archangel smiled sadly and told him that he must return to earth. It was too late for this Sapphire Soul to step back upon his path, so Albotain must take care of the boy's descendants. Micah told him that he must try to mitigate the damage that he had done to the chain of destiny by guiding these, his subjects, toward the Light and towards good deeds and actions. No matter how small their contribution, each time one of Daniel's descendants gave something of value to the world, it would help heal the damage. No matter how incidental it was, each positive action would fractionally diminish the harm that Albotain had inflicted upon destiny.

This task was, Micah told him, as much about Albotain's development and his reparation as it was about the boy's lost legacy. The astrologer had much to learn and needed to understand about truly giving to others. He needed to understand the issue of human relationships and the concept of unconditional love. It was hoped that through his work with Daniel's descendants Albotain would purify his soul and cleanse his heart and so become a sound guide and mentor for the third Sapphire Soul.

Albotain was puzzled, they were going to send another one to earth? Why? It obviously hadn't worked the first two times! Micah agreed, most certainly, sending these elevated beings to earth had not been successful so far. It had taken the Council of Elders some time to decide upon an answer. However, Mankind was not going to improve his lot on his own. This race was determined to destroy himself and his planet and they knew for certain that if they did not do something within the next thousand years, it would be too late.

The first Sapphire Soul had been without a guide or teacher and had eventually perished alone. The next time, the Council had hoped that the boy, the second of these Higher Beings, would be protected by Albotain. However, after Albotain had abandoned the child and then betrayed him, they realised that the mentor or guide for this next *incarnation would have to be more than a mere human. They would need to be a Divine Being, one that was charged with caring for the third Sapphire Soul. Divine Beings were incredibly rare, but were able to guide other incarnated souls without being prejudiced or corrupted. Unfortunately, Micah explained, due to their high status, these elevated beings were much in demand throughout the universe and were permanently placed taking care of other planets and their inhabitants. So another Divine Being would have to be created for this particular role.*

Now, Albotain was certainly not in this, his present stage of spiritual evolution, a Divine Being. However, in his spiritual/post–life state he had begun to realise what he had done and so was ready to right his wrongs. The Council knew that Albotain was the only soul even remotely able to help them. He possessed the knowledge and wisdom that the child would need to fulfil his destiny as the Saviour of the world. Their plan was that through guiding and teaching the boy's descendants, the man would ultimately become Divine. He would in time become without imperfection. He would be untainted and highly developed. Ultimately, Albotain would be a suitable guide for the third incarnated Sapphire Soul.

This third Sapphire Soul was Man's last chance. They gave Albotain just over eight hundred years to complete his task, to purify his soul and to become a Divine Being. Once he had attained this level of perfection then he would be appointed Guardian of the third and last Sapphire Soul.

However, until that point, as a spirit he would have to be connected to the earth–plane somehow. He would, Micha explained, appear in spirit form to each student and he would teach and guide them in order to purify his and also their soul energy. However, something tangible would have to be used to hold him fast to the earth. It would have to be something that would attach him first to the boy and then after that, to each chosen descendant. Each descendant was destined to have a male child and a physical object was needed, an heirloom that could be passed down from the father to their son. This object would ensure that Albotain was able to connect with those he was to teach and guide.

There was, Micah informed Albotain, one such object. Unbeknown to Albotain, the boy during his time in the astrologer's chambers had discovered some of the magician's work on Astrological Talismans. Micah told Albotain that Daniel had begun to create his own Talismans. Many of his first attempts failed, the planets were not in the correct alignment, or he misunderstood how to create the Talisman effectively. Eventually though, he mastered the art of making them, judging accurately the right time to create them and how to give them the relevant powers. It was about this time that Vincent asked the boy to teach him astrology. Daniel had promised to make his master a Talisman of his own. Of course, thanks to Albotain, Daniel never got the chance to teach Lord Vincent, or to give him the Talisman that he had made for him.

Albotain had had no idea about all of this and listened intently as Micah explained that this Talisman had been very special indeed. It was a Talisman of Mercury in Aquarius. Mercury used at its highest level, its most positive, rules astrology. The sign of Aquarius brings to the owner a love of humanity and a desire to use knowledge to help others. This boy was a Supreme Being and this fact, combined with his deep love and respect for Vincent, had endowed the Talisman with incredible powers. Most importantly of all, as he could *not bear to lose every connection with his Lord, the boy still had it in his possession. This was to be the object that Albotain's spirit would be attached to. It was this that would hold him to the earth–plane until such a time as he was pure enough to be considered a Divine Being.*

And so Albotain's long journey of teaching and self–discovery began... '

Chapter XI

Bert wiped his face with his hands as if to bring himself back to reality and sat looking at Ed. His hands were now still, clasped in front of him as if in prayer.

Ed looked out of the kitchen window. He was beginning to feel angry again.

'Bert,' he said not looking at the old man, 'this still doesn't explain who you are and why you lied to me.'

'You don't understand do you Ed?'

'No. I don't. I don't understand any of this stuff.'

'I am Albotain.' He said this quietly, as if afraid to hear the words himself.

Ed turned to Bert, now looking at him directly. Enough was enough, he thought. The poor old guy was obviously deluded. He began to feel nervous. It was one thing having a conman in the house, another knowing that there was a complete nutter sitting right opposite him. He must have escaped from somewhere. People could be looking for him, he thought hopefully. Although Ed still didn't think Bert was actually dangerous, he was beginning to feel very concerned. His mind was racing. He needed to get help, but who would he call? The police, an ambulance, a doctor? He had no idea what to do next, but he knew he had to get to the 'phone.

HR was delighted, feeling much more his old self, he jigged and leapt around the kitchen, his black cloak flailing like dark clouds. He was having his very own party, disaster and chaos falling about him like astral confetti.

Meanwhile, thought Ed, until he could get to the hallway without alerting Bert, did he play it safe and humour him, or did he try and make him see sense, help him understand that he wasn't well? He decided on the last one, humouring him might just make it worse.

'Bert, have you ever been to the doctor's? Has anyone ever said that you might be, well, a bit poorly?'

Bert looked back at him perplexed. He scratched his head, 'Ed I *am* a doctor, or rather a physician. I have never been ill in my life, apart from a bit of rheumatism and a weakness in my left knee.' He paused, realising what Ed was getting at, 'I see Ed, you mean you think that I'm feeble–minded, insane?'

Ed replied carefully, 'no, no not insane, just maybe a bit confused.' He was playing for time here, he continued, just filling the air with words off the top of his head, 'I mean, one thing you haven't seemed to notice is that you're *real*. You're not a spirit, are you now?'

'Ahhhhhhh,' Bert's perplexed face cleared and he smiled, 'I can explain that.'

Ed sighed, 'really?.... Ok, let's hear it then.'

This should do it he thought, the poor old chap was going to tie himself up in a knot trying to explain this. He realised that Bert was genuinely unwell and he was beginning to feel sorry for him. Perhaps, just perhaps, he could persuade him then that he needed help and that they should call someone.

But instead of seeming worried, Bert looked quite excited. He insisted on making Ed another cup of tea. He obviously thinks I'm coming around to believing him thought Ed. He was feeling a little guilty that he was being so underhand with the poor chap. Well, it shouldn't be too long before I can get him some help he told himself.

'You see Ed, I returned to earth in spirit form and contacted the boy. Although I was entirely unexpected, he was happy to help me. He knew in his heart that something had gone wrong, but in his conscious, human state, he just wasn't sure what it was. Micah was right though, it was too late for Daniel to manifest his destiny. Paradoxically, his particular strength was also his weakness and he had resolutely refused to practice astrology or magic again. He was loyal, he had integrity and he held firmly to his promise to Lord Vincent. He was married by now, he and his wife had had a child, a boy and he agreed to prepare his son for me. He would make sure that when he, Daniel, passed away that his offspring was in possession of the Talisman and was ready to communicate with me. That was the single, paltry legacy that this Sapphire Soul left the earth,' the old man sighed sadly.

After a moment he continued, 'since then I have looked after every descendant of Daniel's. I have had some successes and a few failures. There are, of course, many benefits to be received from ownership of the Talisman. Each father has diligently passed it down to their heir, glad to be able to give such a gift to their son. Of course, none of them changed the world in any large way, but some bought a little Light to the earth–plane. However, my real problems started when Lance's parents were killed and the chain of heritage was broken. They weren't supposed to die at all. Over the past eight hundred years, every now and then an event would occur that wasn't part of the Grand Plan. Through my stupidity, through what I had done to the boy, I had twisted fate and fractured destiny. Their deaths were a tragedy in more than one sense.

Without the influence of Daniel, Mankind had over the centuries ran riot, carelessly destroying himself and the earth. This race may have progressed technically but man used much of his newfound knowledge to destroy the world. Wars broke out, plagues killed thousands and the Higher Powers could only watch helplessly. The Council of Elders tried their very best to fix the Grand Plan, to reinstate what should have been, but it was far from perfect. Like a damaged oil painting that has been restored, it may have looked flawless, but there were always minute cracks that could not be sealed. It is through these cracks that energy leaked, energy that was stray and not meant to be part of the pattern. Throughout my time as a spiritual guide, accidents or strange turns of events would arise every so often and it was I who had to pick up the pieces and try to lessen the damage. It was all part of the deal that I had agreed to, to make amends for what I had done. The death of Lance's parents was one such unfortunate result of this damage. In fact, I wonder if Lance himself was another anomaly, he was such a strange one. Perhaps he was never meant to be born.'

Bert paused, lost in thought. Ed, despite his understanding that the old man was completely unhinged, was nevertheless curious about what happened next, 'so, when Hector and Ariadne died what happened to the Talisman?'

'It went to the wrong son' Bert said simply. 'Lance was loud and brash in those days. He loved beautiful things and collected anything that he thought was worth money. He literally shoved his younger brother aside to take what he wanted. He took all of the inheritance and so obtained the Talisman.'

Bert sighed, 'he had no idea what the Talisman really was, the power that it carried. I used to visit him in his dreams and appeared to him in spirit form. It took a little while to get him to understand that I had a part to play in his life. Once he got over the initial shock of hearing and seeing something that on a physical level was not there, in a strange way he and I got along fairly well. Whilst he never exactly embraced the spiritual aspects of life, he certainly benefited from the Talisman's powers in other ways. He made money and was comfortable in his life. I understood that he had taken the Talisman not knowing what it was. It was after all my fault that any of this had happened in the first place. We existed alongside in a pleasant, if relatively non–productive, manner.'

Bert stopped, deep in thought for a moment and then continued, 'however, I was just waiting I suppose. The laws that govern the Talisman state that once a person takes possession of it, then it, and I, must stay with that person until they pass away. I was tied to him whilst he had the Talisman and I knew I had to wait for him to die before I could find the next true owner. Despite his lack of spiritual intelligence, Lance knew that he had benefited from me and from the Talisman. We agreed that the rightful heir would inherit the Talisman once he had passed away and he was true to his word, even though ultimately your father couldn't be found. In return, I allowed Lance to use the Talisman for his own ends. There was also the condition that he could never marry. I could not allow him to have a son of his own, as he would, of course, have wanted his own offspring to benefit from the Talisman's magic.'

'But,' said Ed returning to his senses and also to his original plan to make Bert face up to his delusions, '*you are real*....you haven't explained that!'
'When we couldn't trace your father, you were the next in line. If fate had been working as it should, Ivan should have received the Talisman from Hector and you should have still been with your father. He would have then trained you and passed the Talisman onto you at the right time.' The old man sighed once again, 'I suspect that darker forces interfered and

blocked our progress. Perhaps that is why you have not been able to find him and why he couldn't be contacted when Lance died. These fractures in fate not only disrupt the pattern of what should be, but they also allow dark energy to slip through, conscious manifestations of the Ethereal Shadows. This causes even more mayhem as the mission of these dark spirits is to ensure that the plans made by the Council of Elders do not succeed. The age old war between good and evil is still with us.'

'So, you're saying that's why I haven't seen my dad and also why no one could find him?' asked Ed incredulously.

'Yes, it's possible, likely even,' came the reply.

Ed just shook his head disbelievingly, 'anyway, besides that none of this answers my question. How come you're here?'

Bert replied, 'anyway, we did find you and here we are. However, unlike the others, there was no one to prepare you for the Talisman. There was no one to teach you how to connect with me and not to be afraid of what was happening. Lance was no problem; he was made of strong stuff. You see, he had no imagination, no fears and as soon as he realised that I could help him gain wealth and possessions then he was a happy chap. However Ed, you are different, you are highly sensitive. You were so frightened by the Talisman and by my trying to contact you, I had to think of another way to get through to you without scaring you half to death.'

'What did you do?' asked Ed. He was feeling confused now. What really was starting to worry him was that Bert's story was beginning to make sense. It explained the Talisman and its strange behaviour and also how he, Ed, had ended up in Guernsey. He was desperately trying to find the holes in Bert's story, but was struggling. On the other hand, he couldn't accept what he was being told either. He wasn't sure what to think any more, he had a headache and wanted to lie down.

'I went to the Council of Elders and asked for them to grant me a favour. I asked to be temporarily re–incarnated in physical form, to reach you in such a way as not to frighten you. At first they refused, they quite rightly said that I would risk damaging fate again by being in physical form.'

Ed was puzzled, 'why, what harm could you do?'

'I could change the course of destiny with one single action. I am not *supposed* to be here. If I kick a stone on a path, if I pick a flower, then I have altered the world. If I speak to a passer–by, I could make them late for a meeting that could change their life. A soul mate could be missed, a destiny ruined. Just imagine if I disturbed a squirrel about to bury an acorn in the path. That oak tree would not have grown to block the path. Then, years later, a woman may not have walked around it. Instead, she may have slipped on the path and lost the child she was carrying. That child could have been a genius, a dictator, a saviour of this race. Do you see what I mean? So many small acts can lead to so many big ones. Think of the butterfly.'

Ed looked confused.

'The flutter of a butterfly's wing in South America can cause a storm in Alaska. All things are connected,' he continued on. 'They told me that had been done a couple of times before – caused uproar apparently. Colliding two worlds without causing tremendous damage is no mean feat and has all sorts of repercussions. It's always terribly difficult to reverse, so many ends to tie up, a kind of celestial macramé.'

Bert sighed, he looked tired, as if he carried the world on his back. 'When I swore to them that I would do my utmost to avoid others, to not be seen by anyone but you, they eventually agreed. They were still very concerned, they told me that once I incarnated into physical form again all of my weaknesses would revisit me. All of the failings that I had worked so hard to overcome during my time as a spiritual teacher would return and they warned me that I may be of no use to you anyway in this state. I am human now and I am little more than a frail old man. I do have some powers in this form, but I am weakened by this inner struggle that you call Life,' he sighed, 'I had forgotten it was so hard.'

Ed got up and walked over to the kitchen window. He felt numb, distanced from reality, as if Bert was talking to him from a long way off. There was no way any of this could be true. He must be going insane himself to even listen to this rubbish. However, small thoughts were scurrying around his head like mice. Unimportant, incidental little facts that on their own shouldn't matter. All together though, they were making quite a bit of a racket and his head was beginning to throb. The Talisman, the strange dreams, the fact that Bert had had no clothes, no belongings. Ed's mind span, Bert also seemed to have no past, well not one that he, Ed, could relate to. The old man also had a tremendous amount of knowledge regarding history, too much really, when he thought about it. Ed shook his head, as if to shake off the ridiculous thoughts that were running round and round in his head. He felt as though he were losing his mind.

Bert winced, 'I'm not at all keen on having a body again Ed, really, it's awful. I had to come back more or less in the physical state that I was just before I died. I feel tired, achy and have so little strength. I had no clothing that was suitable and so I had to wear the gardener's old overalls and boots, which were very uncomfortable I can tell you. I also get so hungry, I want to eat all the time. All I think about is food, it's such a distraction from my spiritual work.' He smiled, 'don't you remember how I had trouble eating and drinking when we first met? I hadn't eaten or drunk anything for eight hundred years! How that first cup of tea hurt, it took me a while to realise what the terrible burning pain was in my throat.'

Ed turned and looked at the old man. If Bert was making this up, he was very convincing. However, none of what he had told him was enough by any means to make Ed believe that the man was an eight hundred year old magician. 'I need some proof, I need you to show me that you are who, or what, you say you are.' His voice sounded unfamiliar – harsh and unfeeling.

Bert's smile faded and his eyes looked empty of light once again. 'You still don't believe me. Alright Ed,' he said softly. He got up, reached into the carrier bag by the sink and retrieved the Talisman. He offered it to Ed.

'I always know where the Talisman is, it's like a part of me,' he said smiling sadly. 'Take this, go for a walk, go to the beach and sit and wait. I will prove myself to you.'

Ed reluctantly took the disc. He put it in his jeans pocket, at the same time checking if his wallet was in there. He hadn't decided what to do and he needed some time to think. He might not come back to the house at all. He only had a few clothes here, nothing irreplaceable. He could catch the boat back to England and forget all of this happened.

HR was listening very carefully, he leant back in his corner, suddenly feeling much better. His old Ed was back, ready to run away and hide once again. Perhaps they could get onto their old footing, Ed terribly miserable and HR very happy and contented. The creature chuckled evilly as he thought of all the good times ahead.

Chapter XII

Ed put on his jacket and left the house by the back door; he didn't take Lionel with him, just in case he did decide not to come back. He walked along the woodland path and took the worn granite steps down to the rocky cove below. The sun shone on the water, it was warm for the time of year. The waves lapped gently over the rocks, the white lace trimmed eddies showing off the deep blue water. The seagulls glided like lost souls high above him, crying out softly, their cold prehistoric eyes taking in everything below. Ed sat down on a convenient flat rock at the foot of the cliff. He took out the Talisman from his jeans pocket. He examined it as if looking for some clue, some sign that it was genuine. Overcome with exhaustion, he put it back in his pocket, turned his face towards the sun and closed his eyes. His face felt warm and the sunlight on his eyelids turned his inner world pink, a rosy glow enveloped him. He breathed deeply trying to clear his head.

He sat for a while not moving, just soaking up the warmth. He felt drowsy and leaned back against the cliff face behind him. His mind turned slowly, images and thoughts swimming around, merging together and making no sense whatsoever. He opened his eyes and rubbed them. He stared at the sea watching the waves, the heat from the sun made the water shimmer. Then something caught his attention. Standing a little way away was a figure. He couldn't make out much in the way of details; the sun was too low in the sky and was in his eyes, blinding him. Whoever it was started to come towards him and then as he looked, they'd gone. Ed peered

119

through the hazy sunlight. Nothing, he'd imagined it, he was going mad after all.

He closed his eyes again, his hands shoved in his jeans pockets to keep warm. He tried to relax and work out what was happening to him. Then just as he was drifting off, an energy passed through him. He couldn't describe it any other way. It was like a push or a shift deep down inside of him. It wasn't unpleasant, just very disconcerting. He felt as though the ground beneath him, or the air, or both, were gently vibrating or humming. He felt odd, like there was movement inside and outside of him. A silent wind buffered him, swishing around inside of him. He opened his eyes, feeling dizzy – the sea and the sky greeted him innocently. Then, as he closed his eyes again, the 'wind' spoke. He could only describe it as being like a thought, only it felt much stronger, like it was being pushed into his head. If a thought could be described as a gentle puff of air, then this was a gale force wind.

The voice said, 'when you return to the house, there will be four stones placed by the back door in the shape of a diamond.'

Ed looked around, the beach was empty. He felt as though an electric current had passed through him, his whole body tingled and his heart was pounding. He also felt nauseous and his stomach was churning. He got up, feeling panicky. He was scared, really scared. His fear made him walk quickly to the steps and make his way back to the path. He desperately wanted there to be someone, anyone, there – someone to talk to, or even just to say hello. The path was empty. He hurried along it, all the while talking to himself. He tried to reassure himself that he was alright, that he was just overwrought and stressed. It didn't work; somewhere in his heart he knew that what he had heard was real. Well, as real as any whisper in your head could be. There was only one way to find out. He walked quickly towards the gate that led to the garden. He kept up this pace through sheer fear and panic. He was afraid that if he slowed down and thought about the consequences of what he was doing, he would just run away, never to return.

His heart was in his mouth as he approached the back door, but he already knew what he would see. Four stones, diagonally placed, silently greeted him, their mute stillness speaking a thousand words. His hand came up to his mouth, he felt as though he were dreaming. He knew they hadn't been there before. He had left the house this way and they would have been right in his path. He turned away and walked back down the garden, back to the pathway. He had no idea where he was going, but he knew that he couldn't face Bert, or whoever the man was. He had to clear his head, try to work out what was happening. His heart was heavy and his mind was spinning as he walked towards the woodland. HR followed closely behind. He was enjoying the feast and he had a feeling that this was only the entrée.

Albotain watched Ed turn back and head down towards the woodland. His heart ached and he felt tears sting his eyes. These were unfamiliar sensations. Throughout all of his time on earth and the centuries he had spent in spirit form as a teacher, he had never experienced emotion like this. Of course, over the years he had cared about all of the boy's family, his students, but he had related to them in a vague, disconnected way. They had been the pathway to his forgiveness and his ingrained sense of responsibility had driven him on to do his job well, to teach and guide them. In many ways, Lance had been the most difficult. However, it had bought Albotain no pain to know that the man was not developing spiritually, just a mild sense of frustration coupled with the desire to move onto something more fruitful.

But this was different. He realised that he felt this way because he, for the first time ever, truly cared about someone else. During his time in his physical, earthly form, he had grown attached to Ed. His heart and consciousness had expanded beyond facts, figures, knowledge and self–interest. He knew at that point, that although he was human and was frail, weak and tired, he had discovered a great strength within him. There was a sense of something awakening within him. Even though he was desperately unhappy, it still felt right somehow, as if something had fallen into place. He was alive, truly alive and this was because at last he desired to give unconditionally, even at the expense of his own happiness. He, Albotain, the great astrologer, finally felt love for another being.

He sat down once again and waited. He had no idea if Ed would return. One thing he was discovering as time went on was that because he was becoming emotionally attached to Ed it was harder for him to use his intuition. Situations or events connected to Ed were cloudy, blocked by his own feelings. He found it almost impossible to see into the future, or to understand situations on a purely spiritual level. The more his heart became involved, the less he was able to see objectively. Right now all he could feel was Ed's pain and his own deep–seated angst.

He wondered what would happen if Ed did not return. During their time together, the old man had learned that Ed was not one for confrontation. It must have been tremendously hard for him today. Albotain thought back to his time in the castle. The people he had known and the events that had shaped his destiny. It was strange, but now that he was in physical form, he found it easier to remember his earthly life. Over the past few months, his memory had slowly cleared. But because of this he was not at peace within himself, his sleep was disturbed by recollections – visions from the past. He would wake during the night feeling afraid and not knowing why. Shadows seemed to flicker in the gloom, as if he wasn't alone. The darkness unsettled him and he would often keep a lamp on next to the sofa where he slept. He felt alone and vulnerable and now that he had felt the comfort of human companionship, he did not want to be alone anymore. That thought frightened him. He had never needed anyone before now; he'd never been vulnerable in this way.

Of course, Albotain had loved his mother and father, but theirs was a meeting of the intellect and the mind. There was no room for sentimentality or unnecessary attachments in his close family. When his father had died, his mother simply said, 'he has moved on to the Great Halls of Learning.' It was as if he had just taken a short journey and in her mind that was exactly what he had done. She showed no sadness, no grief or self–pity.

So, Albotain learned to also close down the part of his heart that could have ultimately been his saving grace. He did not develop that part that loves, cherishes and needs others, the vulnerable and fragile part of all men. He realised now that it is this weakness that is man's strength. It is what makes them powerful and gives to them the courage of a lion and the strength of a bear when their loved ones are in danger. Until now, Albotain had never experienced deep emotional bonds and misunderstood the nature of genuine affection. He understood why he had been so easily corrupted by the attentions of those who adored him. He had been swayed by riches and by the lure of fame and glory. Possessions and adoration from others had falsely promised to fill the void that existed within him, that part of him that did not know true love for another. He knew differently now.

Albotain returned to the table where he sat and waited. Occasionally he would pray, hands clasped and his eyes tightly shut. He spoke to the Angels in a tongue that was unrecognisable to the modern world – Malachim, the language of the Angels. He asked the Higher Spirits for help and guidance, for the outcome that was best for all. Powerless to help himself, he placed himself in their hands.

He sat at the table watching the sun go down. The brilliant rays flooded in through the kitchen window, its parting kisses turning everything to soft gold. Gideon glided over and sat on Albotain's shoulder, nestling into his neck and clicking softly in his ear. The parrot had undergone something of a transformation since he had moved into the house; he was much calmer and seemed to feel a great deal of affection for the old man. Albotain scratched the bird's neck softly and talked to him, asking him what he should do if Ed didn't come back. Gideon didn't reply, he just tutted a couple of times and nibbled on his ear.

Albotain silently acknowledged HR, who was by now quietly cowering in his corner. The language of the Angels uttered by the old man had been almost too much for him to bear. To the ghoul it had sounded like an ear–splitting whistle, one that threatened to shatter his bony skull. Albotain looked over at the dark shape huddled in the corner of the kitchen. He'd ignored him for too long he thought sadly, the poor soul needed setting free. The man raised his arms towards the being and sent out feelings of love and forgiveness that were so strong that HR reeled. He shrank back, willing the wall to swallow him up. His skeletal arms stretched across his withered face trying to hide from the Light that shone from Albotain. He breathed a sigh of relief as Albotain's attention was diverted by the presence of the parrot who was nipping at his ear. The Light faded and the comforting shadows once again enveloped him. HR was exhausted; he closed his eyes and slept. He had horrible nightmares where fluffy kittens chased their tails and tiny bunny rabbits played together under a moonlit sky.

Eventually Gideon returned to his perch, tucked his head under his wing and fell asleep. Albotain also felt sleepy, the strain of the day was catching up with him. He sighed and watched the sun slip away to visit other parts of the globe. His lids began to droop and he nodded off, chin on chest. He dreamed of Heaven where he walked with the Archangel Micha. They strolled through glorious woodlands under high, green trees dappled with golden sunlight. As they walked, they discussed philosophy, the true meaning of existence and the purification of the soul. His body was young and supple once again, his mind as clear as crystal.

He was woken suddenly by the sound of the back door closing. The beautiful dream faded and reality came crashing down upon him as he realised where he was. Ed entered the kitchen. He looked wild–eyed and scared, as if he was ready to run at the first sign of danger. Albotain sat up straight and looked him straight in the eyes.

'Hello Ed. You've come back then,' he swallowed nervously, afraid of saying the wrong thing and scaring the boy even more, 'I'm glad you're here,' he finished.

Ed looked away from him, his gaze fixed on the floor in front of him. He was deathly pale and dark grey shadows flickered across his face as he spoke.

'I had no where else to go,' he replied tersely.

He stood away from the table, his body tense, fists clenched by his side. He was obviously ready to run. The old man realised that it was probably best if he didn't try to push Ed into talking right now. He had had a huge shock and needed time to absorb everything. Albotain got up and busied himself making supper, chatting to Ed about inconsequential matters, the garden, the weather – anything but what was on both of their minds. The unspoken words screamed silently behind the mundane chatter, filling the atmosphere with their fury.

Ed eventually sat down, fists still clenched by his side, his knuckles white. Albotain put the food down on the table next to the boy and sat down. They ate in silence, Ed pushed his food around his plate, staring at it as if its very existence offended him. The truth was that Ed was heartbroken as well as terribly confused. Strangely enough, although he had been given a glimpse of a reality previously relegated to fairy stories and fantasy computer games, his primary emotion was not one of disbelief or amazement, it was of sadness and regret. He was desperately unhappy that the only person he had truly cared for had become something else. He had never felt happier than when he and Bert, (or Albotain), had been together as friends, talking and working on the house and garden. He had never felt so safe, so sure that he finally belonged somewhere. Now it was all different. Bert was not who he had said he was and that was hard to come to terms with.

At this point Ed had not even begun to address the fact that Albotain was from the distant past, recently reincarnated and in many senses of the word, unalive. He was not even human, not in the way that Ed understood it anyway. All of this was completely and absolutely beyond his comprehension. So, in his usual manner, Ed chose to ignore what made him uncomfortable – this collection of unfathomable details. He decided to focus upon the fact that he was still angry with his friend for his dishonest behaviour and that he had been betrayed. He was not ready to talk about his feelings though, how hurt he was and how lost he felt.

'I came back because I have nowhere to go and because you mentioned my dad the other day. I want to find him and it seems that you're the only person who can help. I think after you've lied to me, it's the least you owe me.'

'Yes Ed, you're right I do owe you something, to repay you for what I have done to you. You must understand though, I have only ever cared for you and tried to do what was best for you. I want to help you. You must recall how you felt before you came here to this beautiful island, your loneliness and lack of direction? Those feelings stemmed from the fact that you had no path. Your destiny had been rubbed out by the events surrounding Ariadne and Hector's deaths and so you have wandered the world without guidance or help. You've had no sense of direction, no vocation or understanding as to why you are here. Your life was empty. Think about it Ed,' he pleaded, 'you've never even had a girlfriend. Haven't you ever wondered why nothing positive ever happened to you? Why do you think that you have always escaped through books? Why do you think that dark entity attached itself to you? Think about it Ed,' he repeated, 'you know I'm right.'

Albotain pursued his lips and looked at Ed intently, waiting for him to respond.

Startled, Ed replied before he really knew what he was saying, 'I didn't know you knew about HR – I mean Harsh Reality.'

'Yes, I know about the entity that is attached to you,' Albotain smiled, as if he had read Ed's thoughts. 'He is to be pitied, not hated. He is from a place that has no Light, no hope. As a vulture takes whatever it can to survive, he is the same – he knows no better. He is still here, although he's not so close to you now because he's wary of the changes within you. If you could love him, forgive him, then you would release him.' Ed was quiet as he considered what Albotain had said.

'Please try to understand, I know this is so hard for you. I am telling you the truth and nothing else, I promise.'

Ed didn't reply, instead he stared at the table in front of him as if the answer was hidden in the grain of the pale wood.

Albotain continued, 'in your heart you have known that something was wrong, that the world you inhabited was empty and meaningless. You have used literature to try to compensate for your feelings of unhappiness and desolation, to escape from this No Mans Land that you have found yourself in. I know you Ed, better that even you know yourself. You have been happier since you came here haven't you?' Ed looked up and shrugged, he felt vulnerable now, like a child, alone and scared.

'I can help you Ed, I can bring you more happiness than you could have ever imagined possible. I promise you that, I swear that I can make your life complete Ed. Trust me ...please.' The old man stopped, his voice cracking, his emotions threatening to overwhelm him.

Ed looked at Albotain, 'How? How can you help me? Can you tell me where I can find my dad? '

'Ed, I can teach you many, many things, knowledge that will broaden your mind, techniques that will enable you to understand humanity and the world of Spirit. I can show you how to heal yourself and others. Once you have learned all I have to give you, then you will be given the opportunity to find your father yourself.'

'So if I let you teach me, then I'll be some kind of superhuman being?' Ed was incredulous, sure now that he was being taken for a fool.

Albotain smiled, 'no not a superhuman being Ed, just the best human you can be. You'll be stronger certainly, but I don't mean the kind of strength that can bend metal bars, or lift buildings. You'll possess an inner strength that comes from a true understanding of life and people. I can't promise that you'll be rich either; the wealth I offer feeds the soul and the heart not the wallet. What I am able to teach you will help you lose your fear, to develop faith in yourself and others. I can show you how to find fulfilment. However, most importantly I can bring you inner peace, something that many pursue but few experience.'

'Exactly how do you intend to do all of these amazing things?' Ed was curious now. He was still trying to come to terms with what was happening. What Albotain was offering sounded wonderful, but how did he know he was telling him the truth?

'Through teaching you the Spiritual Laws of the universe, the Truth that all men seek, I can set you free so that you are able to live without fear. You will be one of the few in this world who live at the highest level, to transcend the mundane energies of human life. You will rise above the shadows of fear and ignorance that inhabit the lower levels of human consciousness. You will be complete.'

Albotain stopped, frowned for a second and then said, 'I can show you something now if you like, something that may help you.' He suggested this tentatively, as if afraid that he was moving too quickly.

Ed stood up from the table and walked to the window. Although it was almost dark outside it still gave him a sense of space and freedom to stare out into the garden. The silhouette of the conifers showed black against the dimming light, the wind moved them back and forth, breathing life into them. He didn't know what to think anymore. Even though his rational mind baulked at the idea of accepting what the old man had told him, the truth was that in his heart he wanted to believe that he was genuine. Also, the idea of happiness and inner balance sounded wonderful.

Most of all though, he wanted his friend Bert back. By accepting, or even appearing to accept what Albotain was saying, he could theoretically re–establish his relationship with him. If the man was genuine, then he, Ed, might finally understand what his life, for what it was worth in its current state, was all about. All in all he actually had nothing much to lose. He'd already been hurt and so it really didn't matter that much if it all turned out to be some kind of trick, or just plain madness on the old man's part. He was used to having nothing and this situation at least held the vague possibility of bearing some fruit. On the plus side, he wouldn't be alone for the foreseeable future, a state of being he was not anxious to return to. If Albotain was telling him the truth, there was also the possibility that he might be able to find his dad. Although he wasn't entirely sure exactly how he was going to do that, a slim chance was better than nothing.

He turned to Albotain and nodded, 'Ok.'

The man smiled, a million candles illuminated his eyes and pure happiness shone from him.

'You won't regret this Ed, you really won't,' he exclaimed excitedly, 'oh what a happy day. I have the chance to repay my debt to the world *and* I have my best friend back!'

The years seemed to have dropped suddenly from Albotain, revealing a joyous and more vital being. His face seemed suddenly younger and his blue eyes blazed with life.

The old man moved quickly. He was agile and nimble once again, energised by joy and the relief that there was hope for both of them and for the future.

Chapter XIII

Albotain was charged and anxious to begin, 'follow me, come on Ed, chop chop.'

He was out of the kitchen and had moved quickly up the main stairway before Ed had even had the chance to gather himself together.

HR followed them from the kitchen and stood watching from the bottom of the stairs. He tapped one skeletal finger on the wall next to him. Seeing the light that shone from both of them, he stopped in his tracks. He flinched, eyes narrowed, heart sinking. What was happening to him? He felt drained, exhausted and was almost ready to give up. He hoped to Darkness that Ed wouldn't take up Albotain's love and forgiveness idea, that would finish him off for good.

Ed followed Albotain up to the top of the stairs. The old man walked past Ed's bedroom and the storage rooms. He headed towards the staircase at the end of the hall that led up onto the next floor. Ed had never bothered coming up here before, Mrs P had said it was just an empty attic room. He managed to catch up with the old man and they climbed the steep, unpainted stairs together, Ed getting more than a little out of breath, his trainers catching on the rough wooden steps.

At the top Albotain went through the open doorway and turned on the light. It flickered apathetically for a few seconds before gracing the room with a dingy yellow glow. Ed found himself in a large, low room that was desperately in need of some TLC. An ancient armchair sat next to an old battered table, which stood in the centre. The table was almost completely covered by piles and piles of yellow, brittle looking papers and a thick layer of dust coated everything. Ed moved a little closer to the table and wiped one of the papers with his sleeve. Clouds of dust threatened to choke him and the paper crackled, but, as the air cleared, he could make out a little more of its content. However, this proved to be entirely unhelpful as the writing on the papers was unintelligible, consisting of strange symbols and odd–looking patterns that could have been anything. There were also what looked like circular charts and tattered drawings strewn carelessly all over the floor.

Ed picked one of the charts and peered at it under the gloomy light. He frowned, he could he thought recognise a few of the symbols, but wasn't sure enough to say anything to Albotain. The old man was sitting at the table, picking up various bits of paper and blowing the dust from them, clouds of debris darkening the room even more. He was happy though, he sang a little tune to himself as he carried out his work. Despite the dinginess of the room, none of the light had gone from him. Just like Tinkerbell, someone believed in him and he was alive again.

At last Ed spoke, 'so, what is all this? I can't make head or tail of it. Is it something Lance did?'
'Oh yes, this is Lance's handiwork – can't you tell from the mess?' Albotain chuckled, 'your uncle decided in his wisdom a few years ago, that I and the Talisman weren't enough for his needs. For all of his adult life he had used the Talisman's power at its lowest level. Mercury in Aquarius brings about great knowledge and truth if used properly. However, at its lowest expression, it can be used for purchasing merchandise, selling and buying material goods. Lance had a strongly

placed Mercury, but he decided not to use at a highly developed level. When he was young, my nickname for him was 'the Glistener'. He was shiny and attractive, but held no real substance. He was also articulate and intelligent, but he coveted all things for the sake of ownership, not for the good of others.'

He continued, 'some of my subjects before Lance also used the Talisman purely to better themselves, to prosper. As Mercury governs speech, these individuals were able to use their verbal eloquence to persuade others to do what they wished, to persuade them to lower their prices or give away that which they wished to keep. I called them the Silver-tongued Messiahs, I had no choice but to stand back and let them do as they wished.'

He continued, 'anyway, despite using the Talisman this way, Lance was still missing some artefacts, objects that he had coveted for many years. In order to complete his precious collection he decided that he would try to obtain them through the study of astrology. He had asked me to teach him, but I just couldn't bring myself to. His motives were purely selfish and I couldn't be party to helping him further. He already had use of the Talisman and I wasn't willing to give him anything else. However, he thought that if he learned this ancient art, he could find the answers that he wanted.'

Albotain shuffled through the papers, grimacing at Lance's obviously terrible attempts at calculating astrological charts.

'Before that he'd tried to make his own Talismans. He even bought the raw materials and the equipment, the metal press and engraving kit. Needless to say, he gave that up before he even began. He at least had the sense to realise that it was well beyond his capacity. It was shortly after that he turned to studying astrology.'

'Did he manage to achieve anything at all?' asked Ed curiously.

'No, no Ed. The power that allows understanding of the planets is granted to but a few men. It's about motives you see, they have to be pure. You have to want power for the right reasons. I should know all about motives and what happens when you try to take from the universe without giving,' he grinned wryly, 'I've made many mistakes Ed, which I have hopefully learned from. However, I had to sit back and watch Lance attempt to harness the power of the universe using astrology, through these charts you see around you. I knew it would never work. It was like watching a child trying to navigate a spacecraft. He was such a clumsy soul and he had no idea what he was doing. However, what was more detrimental to his progress than his complete ineptitude was the fact that his motives were not pure. He wanted gain and profit and that is just not possible to use astrology this way.'

He shuffled through a pile of papers in front of him, tutting irritably as he worked his way through them. After a short while he stopped and laid them back on the table.

He continued, almost as if talking to himself, 'all of spirituality, including astrology, is based on faith and trust, the ability to give away your personal power, to place yourself in the hands of the Light, of God. The astrologer must understand absolutely and completely that his role is to give freely and without self–interest, purely for the good of others. True astrology is used to help and guide, to provide a light that illuminates the awareness and heightens the consciousness, to bring out the highest potential in your subject. Lance, in his usual way, grasped too hard.

Consequently it slipped out of his hands and he failed dismally.'

Albotain smiled as he carefully selected the relevant papers and books from the chaos before him, 'However, he has at least left me the tools of the trade so that I can show you what a wonderful instrument astrology can be if used correctly.'

Ed frowned, 'but isn't astrology just what people read in the papers...*You're a Capricorn and so you will have another awful day ending in the usual set of disasters*...that stuff is all rubbish isn't it?'

Albotain looked up and stared hard at Ed as he spoke, 'my boy, astrology has been used by Mankind for over seven thousands years.   Today's astrology that you read in the newspapers is as close to the true art as graffiti is to Renoir. It is no more than meaningless scrawl designed to entertain the masses.'

'But how did Lance think it could help him get the pieces of his collection?'

'He tried to use something called horary astrology. This is an ancient technique that sets up a chart, one that contains the answer to a specific question. It can help with queries such as where to find something that you need or have lost. It takes many years of practice to read and understand the chart accurately.   As you can see from this mess, Lance drove himself mad with frustration and anger. He couldn't even construct the charts accurately, never mind read them.   He also, by not having pure motive or intent, brought some rather nasty energies into his life.   This is what slowly drove him towards the breakdown and in the end contributed to his death. His heart attack was bought on by fear and stress.'

Ed looked at Albotain, his eyebrows raised. Feeling decidedly nervous he asked, 'what exactly do you mean by 'nasty energies'?'

'Well, whenever anyone enters into spiritual work for the wrong reasons, for their own gain or to increase their personal power, they open themselves up to a whole new world. This world, however, is one where many living entities exist. Some are solid such as you and I. However, many are nebulous and indefinable creatures, ones that live somewhere between here and the higher astral planes. A good number are benign beings, happy to guide and help people. However, those that lie on the lower levels of existence are often angry and spiteful. They are without soul; they lack purpose and so enjoy taunting unwitting individuals who wander onto their path. By misusing astrology, Ouija boards or tarot for example, ignorant and foolish people attract these darker creatures that feed off them. They drain their life force and weaken their spirit. This, of course, causes many problems and is exactly what happened to Lance.'

Ed gulped, 'sounds scary. How do I know that we won't be doing the same here if you show me this stuff?'

Albotain smiled, 'when used correctly, astrology can bring great inner progress and wonderful transformations on many levels. When an astrological birth chart is produced for one who has requested the help of an astrologer, it carries the vibrationary rate, the level of goodness of the individual who casts it. I have worked very hard over the last eight centuries to purify my soul once more and to ensure that whatever I do is for the right reasons, for the good of all. You, Ed, are a naturally clean soul; you will only ever do what is good and true. I know that probably even better than you do. Therefore, as you and I are of pure intent, then our work will be clean, free of negativity or dark energies. We are safe Ed, I promise you.'

Ed replied, 'I'm really nervous of all this stuff, I had a couple of horrible dreams before you came. They really shook me up.' He stopped suddenly, a little surprised to hear himself being so open with Albotain.

'It was your fear of the Talisman that brought the darkness to your dreams. I was trying to contact you at the time through the Talisman, but you were so consumed and weakened by your terror that we couldn't connect. Fear becomes a real, tangible enemy when we give our power to it. What you actually experienced was a part of yourself.'

Ed didn't know what to say to this, he just pinched the bridge of his nose with his fingers as if trying to squeeze some sense into himself.

'But what about HR..?' he started to say.

Albotain laughed, 'he's nothing but a lost being who needed someone to cling onto.'

'I feel sorry for him in a way.'

Albotain smiled and nodded, `yes, you are learning already.' He continued shuffling through charts and papers adding, 'don't worry, you're safe now that you're with me. I can promise you that.'

HR, lurking at the bottom of the stairs, shuddered. He didn't know what was going on, but he did know that he felt terrible. He felt like he had lost something, only he wasn't quite sure what it was. He did suspect that change was afoot though and he didn't like it one bit. He sat quietly on the bottom stair pondering his fate.

Once again, Ed was lost for words. If he tried to think about everything that had happened, he felt as though his head was going to explode. He gave up and tried to focus on what Albotain was saying.

'Now let's have a look at your birth chart Ed, let's see what we can find out about you!'

'What exactly is a birth chart?'

'All of the planets in our solar system move slowly through the sky and through the zodiac signs. The birth chart is a picture of the position of each planet at the moment of birth and it's depicted using ancient symbols.' He paused, 'each planet's position is calculated using degrees, minutes and seconds.'

'Sounds complicated,' Ed replied, 'is this a good idea do you think, looking at my birth chart? '

'Absolutely! Come on, sit down – relax.'

An odd thought occurred to Ed, 'how come if you are so old, you speak like a modern person?'

Albotain smiled, 'the Talisman has allowed me to be part of history in the making. It has in a sense given me a window into the world and so has allowed me to witness the changes that man has undergone. Whilst caring for Daniel's descendants, I have seen wars, plagues, death, magic and miracles. I was with Lance for years and before that I was with others who obviously spoke in modern tongue, well more modern at least than 13th century English! As my students learned from me, I also picked up their colloquialisms and ways of speaking.

Albotain then asked Ed for his date, place and time of birth.

'5th January 1987 in Erlington, Birmingham, at about one in the morning I think. Mum always complained that I ruined her night's sleep. Why do you need to know the date and time?' queried Ed.

'I need the date and time to know exactly where the planets were – which zodiac signs they were in as you were being born into this world. The place of birth tells me the longitude and latitude. I use this book here called an ephemeris to calculate the positions of the planets. This book is quite different from the charts I used in my time at the castle, for a start, it's much more accurate. However, in essence it's all much the same. Through teaching my students, I have kept up with the progress that has been made over the past few hundred years. I understand the principles of the more recently discovered planets. I also use the new approach, the circular chart not the old geometric layout. You see,' the old man winked, 'I have moved with the times.'

'Now, down to work.' He picked up a pencil and referring to the book in front of him began to write down numbers on a blank piece of paper. Then he drew a circle, which he began to split into sections from the centre, like a pie chart, Ed thought.

'I use something called the Placidus system to divide the chart into twelve sections, which are called houses. Placidus was a 17th century Italian monk and a brilliant mathematician. He devised the system using an original 13th century Arabian text.'

Ed was curious, vague memories of a history book read a long time ago coming back to him slowly, 'how come this guy was an astrologer and a monk? I thought the church was against astrology.'

'Yes, that's true now but in the past the two were inseparable. The church separated from astrology centuries ago. Many of your more recent ancestors have been horribly persecuted for their beliefs. They often had to go into hiding, especially after the witchcraft act of the 18th century, 1735 to be precise. This essentially banned all forms of the art.'

'But back then in the 17th century Placidus was both a monk and an astrologer and that was ok?'

Albotain continued, 'Absolutely, Monks practiced astrology as part of their academic requirements. Throughout history, even doctors were expected to be experienced astrologers. Doctors today take the Hippocratic Oath. Hippocrates himself said, "he who does not understand astrology is not a doctor but a fool".'

'Why don't people believe in it now?'

'Beliefs are like unfashionable clothing, give them enough time and they come back round. Man will see the merits of this ancient art again before long,' said Albotain tolerantly.

Ed frowned at the mass of lines and symbols on the paper in front of him and said doubtfully, 'so, that's my birth chart. What exactly can you tell me about myself?'

'Wait just a minute,' Albotain replied good–naturedly, I need a while to finish calculating it and then time to digest it. It takes a little time as I have to consider all of the planets, the Sun, Moon, Mercury, Venus and so on. I have to consider which of the twelve zodiac signs they fall in and which house they are found within. I also have to look at how many degrees, minutes and seconds there are between each planet. These are called aspects. I'll explain more later on. Don't worry, although to be honest it takes years to perfect the art of astrology.' He returned to his work, looking pensive as he drew more strange symbols on the paper.

Unsure as to what he should do whilst Albotain was working away, Ed wandered about the attic room. He picked up books and papers, disturbing the dust as he did so. He could hear the man muttering odd, unintelligible words, 'now, let look at the aspects…Mars and Venus trine, lovely. Moon, Ascendant quincunx…poor lad, his mother must have been a bit of a trial. Good old Saturn's challenging the Moon and Jupiter, that's what I like to see!!'

To be honest, Ed was too curious about what Albotain would find to concentrate on anything else. Despite the fact that he was still telling himself that Albotain was either a lunatic or a charlatan, he had to admit that the old man certainly seemed to know what he was talking about.

Eventually he sat back down at the table to watch the astrologer do his work. Albotain seemed completely absorbed, but every now and then would explain to Ed what he was doing. 'I'll teach you all of this very soon. However, astrology is something that you will probably use every day of your life for one reason or another. It reveals what is hidden and clarifies what is unclear. It does *not*, however, take away your free will,' he said very firmly. 'Astrology only shows you what you have been given to work with, your Life Tools if you like. You make of yourself what you can with what the stars endow you with using your own conscious Will. You can lie in bed for the rest of your life and do nothing, or you can try to save the world. That is the essential choice that is given to every single human being.'

After a while, the man sat back and looked at Ed very seriously.
'Good!' he announced finally, throwing his pencil down.
'That's it, that's all you can tell me?' asked Ed.
Albotain smiled, (a little *too* smugly Ed thought, considering he was technically still on trial).
'Your Sun is placed in the sign of Capricorn. You probably know that already. What you perhaps don't know is

that there are many other planets that influence your personality and life–path. It's not just the Sun that affects you. The Sun does give a general picture of you though. For example, the Sun in Capricorn shows us that you are introverted, cautious, modest and can be a tad pessimistic. I think we can both agree on that!'

Ed smiled properly for the first time that day, 'maybe. What else does it say?'

'Your Ascending sign shows us how you express yourself to the outside world, your façade if you like. The zodiac sign that is coming up over the horizon at the minute of your birth is the Ascendant, or Ascending sign. Yours is in Libra. '

'What's that mean?'

'Libra is a gentle and unassuming sign. You are a romantic and you fall in love very easily, although you perhaps find it difficult to express your deeper feelings to others. You are one who dislikes conflict; you will do anything to maintain peace and harmony. The Ascendant governs to a certain extent our physical or external mannerisms and actions. So, you will alter your behaviour to become what you feel pleases others. This is possibly a pattern that stems from childhood experiences.'

'Ok. I can go with that,' Ed agreed reluctantly, absentmindedly drawing patterns in the dust on the tabletop.

'We will look at your chart in more depth when you begin your studies. I must just mention your Moon sign though. You are Moon in Pisces. The Moon governs the inner self and the emotions. It is one of the most important parts of the birth chart. If you look at your Talisman you will see the symbols for the Moon and the zodiac sign of Pisces is intertwined in the centre.' Albotain pointed to the two relevant symbols on the chart in front of him so that Ed knew what to look for. Ed fished in his pocket and brought out the Talisman. He squinted as he peered at the disc. What had seemed previously to be indiscernible squiggles took on a new, meaningful form now.

Albotain continued on, 'this particular Moon sign is highly influential regarding the development of the spiritual self and an understanding of the deeper aspects of human existence. It is highly appropriate for the bearer of the Talisman to have his Moon within this sign.'

'So what does that mean for me?' Ed asked.

'This Moon sign shows me that you are highly sensitive, a natural healer. You are also very good with animals and children, as you have a natural connection with them. Where your Moon is placed and the influences that it receives from other planets gives me some information about your mother. The Moon in quincunx aspect to the Ascendant in Libra shows me that she is not someone that is easy to get close to. The quincunx aspect is formed when two planets are about 150 degrees apart and is a challenging influence. I would assess that perhaps you feel as though she has never been emotionally constant or reachable. You probably experienced a great deal of discordance and confusion as a child as a result of her influence.'

Albotain stopped and, frowning, took up his pencil once again. He began to make more notes, drawing strange lines and symbols on a scrap of paper in front of him. 'Very interesting. Tell me, when you were about eight years old, just over actually, did you experience some health issues?'

Ed frowned, 'I was really ill with allergies and asthma then. I also had some kind of virus. I was in bed for months with swollen joints. I remember not even having the energy to read. How did you know that?'

'After the moment of birth, the planets continue their journey through the sky and through the zodiac signs. In mid–1995, Saturn and Mars put tremendous pressure upon your birth chart, possibly indicating a time of ill–health and of a challenge that was both physical and psychological in nature.'

'Well, I was ill as I said,' he stopped, thinking back for a moment, 'but I think it was triggered off when me and my mum went to live with my gran and her family. They were horrible to me and I just couldn't cope.'

'That was obviously a difficult time for you Ed. However, it was a test, a time whereby you developed an inner strength. You overcame the challenge and it only served to make you stronger in the end.'

'I suppose after that I stopped trying to be like them and just resigned myself to being alone. Books became my life after that. Thinking about it, I suppose I didn't quite suffer as much after that. At least they stopped bullying me quite so much.'

Albotain turned his attention back to the chart in front of him, 'you have a great many talents and abilities that you have yet to develop. You are also a great deal stronger than you think you are and I think that you will grow from strength to strength as you mature and progress.'

'Thanks,' replied Ed a little morosely, 'not sure about the talent bit though.'

Albotain smiled, 'We will discover them together Ed. You'll be surprised at what you can do. I will begin by teaching you the art of astrology.'

Ed was slightly concerned that Albotain might be sorely disappointed when he realised that he, Ed, had absolutely nothing that could be even remotely construed as talent. He thought that it was more likely that Lionel could learn to ride a bike.

'What if, by some miracle, I do become an astrologer? People are going to think that I'm a loony if I tell them.'

'People are, of course, entitled to their opinion about astrology. However, it is at this present time in history considered acceptable to reject this ancient art without consideration or even understanding.'

He continued, 'Remember, to be open to new ideas or concepts is indicative of genuine intelligence. To choose to abandon something that you have studied carefully is a sign of discernment. However, to reject something that you have not even considered is outright ignorance.' Then the old man yawned and stretched. 'It's been a long day, I think it might be time to turn in, don't you?'

Ed couldn't have agreed more. He was absolutely exhausted. It had been a long, traumatic day and he could do with some time alone to think. His body ached and he felt like he'd been run over by a truck. Even his teeth hurt.

They went back downstairs to the floor below and said goodnight. Ed called Lionel who had been waiting patiently for him in the main hall. Albotain put his hand on Ed's shoulder, which he squeezed tightly.

'You have no idea what this means to me. I may be able to teach you, but you have already taught me something that is invaluable, something that I never understood. You see Ed, I have never really cared about anyone before. I have spent hundreds of years developing my mind, expanding my knowledge and carrying out my duty to the boy's family. I never knew the joy that truly caring for someone else could bring' he smiled sadly, 'I also didn't know what pain it could inflict! Nevertheless, for that I am grateful. After all, every emotional experience expands the soul, brings to it another, higher dimension.' The old man looked away, seemingly embarrassed at having revealed his feelings so readily. He turned away and went downstairs to his bed.

Ed didn't know what to say. He was touched by what he had heard and felt ashamed that he still wasn't sure if he could trust Albotain. He wanted to believe him, but was still very afraid of being let down. He heard the old man sigh heavily as he closed his bedroom door.

Chapter XIV

Ed lay awake in the darkness. Lionel slept at the bottom of the bed, snoring gently and twitching, chasing rabbits in his dreams. Thoughts span round and round in Ed's head, he didn't know where to begin. Like a ball of string without an end, he just couldn't unravel the events of the day into any semblance of order. One incident bothered him though, really bothered him – the voice on the beach and the stones. How was that possible? The rest of the story he could put aside, label everything somehow with something logical and understandable. He could understand that it was all down to a strange series of coincidences. Either that or the old man was just mad and deluded. But the voice, that was weird, more than weird. If he accepted that that had actually happened, then he would have to accept that everything he had been told was true.

A part of him wanted to believe Albotain though, wanted to maintain the friendship. He realised though that by believing that he had heard a disembodied voice, he was accepting that reality did not exist the way he thought it did and that was scary. He wasn't sure if he was ready to walk into another world, one where anything was possible, where he could become a different person. Although Ed knew he had never been really happy, he at least understood the cage that he had built for himself, he was comfortable with the limitations that he had allowed life to exercise over him. Familiarity was frustrating and deadening, but at least it was safe.

As he was falling asleep, he realised that if he was to decide to believe that all of this was real, then he was going to have to let go of what he knew himself to be. Ed the unemployed loser, the no hoper, was going to have to take a back seat. That night he dreamt that he was walking out of a dark, damp cave into bright sunlight.

The morning broke bright and clear, the gulls crying out to one another across the bay. Ed sat up in bed yawning. He felt well rested and surprisingly optimistic. He trundled downstairs, Lionel at his heels. He went into the kitchen to find Albotain sitting at the kitchen table, shoulders slumped, his sparse white hair flat and dull against his head. He looked tired and worn out. Ed was immediately concerned and asked him what was wrong, but the old man just smiled and told him not to worry. Then he got up from the table and went into the lounge. Ed followed him and found him sitting in an armchair, staring out of the long window. He was obviously deep in thought, his eyes not looking at the outside world. Instead, he seemed to be seeing something that was within him. He obviously didn't want to talk about whatever was bothering him and so, unsure as what to do, Ed decided to leave him in peace and went upstairs to carry on packing up the boxes.

That evening, Ed asked the old man again why he was so quiet. Albotain looked up at Ed, his blue eyes soft with sadness 'I don't want to burden you Ed, I don't want to take away the happiness that we may have. You have given me the chance to make amends and I want you to be free from misery and sadness.'

'But why are you so unhappy? I don't understand.'

'Remorse, Ed, remorse. The events here and my relationship with you have caused a deepening of my soul.

There has been an illumination of my consciousness, one which has shed light upon the darkness of my past. I can see now what I have denied both myself and others. I never received love and I certainly never gave it. It is a terrible thing to realise what you have lost, what you cannot regain. I will never have the chance to apologise to all those that I turned away. I rejected others because I felt that love and affection were a waste of my time and energy. I could have married and had children of my own. I never knew the joy that it could bring just to care for another. I could have had a son Ed. Perhaps,' the old man smiled sadly, 'he would have been like you.'

Ed's heart ached to see Albotain so unhappy. He really couldn't imagine that anyone could fabricate this depth of feeling so convincingly. He had to accept that his friend was telling the truth. It was the only way forward, the only way to keep the friendship alive and to also perhaps change his life for the better. He sat down at the table facing Albotain.

'There is nothing even you can do about the past, but you can change the future. We can change the future for the better. If we succeed, then you'll be free again, you won't be tied to the earth or the Talisman any longer and I might be able to find my dad.'

Albotain smiled and reaching over, patted Ed's hand softly, 'thank you. Yes, you're right of course. We must focus on what is good and positive. Tonight we will sit together and talk and I will answer any questions you may have. I have always thought that the great planet Saturn is too strong in my chart. It gives discipline, steadfastness and focus, but unfortunately it is not called 'melancholic' for nothing. Its influence can bring gloom and pessimism, which can be hard to overcome.'

They spent the day working in the warm, green garden first and then they moved into the house to pack up more boxes. In many respects, it was just like old times. The sun shone and slowly but surely Albotain began to lose some of his sadness, the beautiful weather chasing away some of the clouds from his heart. Ed lost himself in his work, enjoying the brief respite from his own thoughts. Towards the end of the day, he and Albotain went into the kitchen to make some food. They sat in silence as they ate, the only sound breaking the silence was the cutlery clattering on the plates. After they had finished Ed said, 'There is something that I'd like to ask you. How was it possible for me to hear the voice on the beach?'

'Everything is an illusion, Ed. Men are restricted by their senses. Just because something cannot be perceived does not mean that it doesn't exist. Man's ego has grown to such an extent that he believes that the universe contains only that which he can see or hear. I contacted you by thought projection. Once I am familiar with a person's energy, I can change my frequency, my vibration, to that which matches theirs. My mind can then act like a radio transmitting its messages for the other to receive. The Talisman helps to strengthen the flow of the energy and ensures that the message is as clear as possible. It's simple really once you know how.'

'Yeah, sure. Simple,' replied Ed, taking a slurp of water from his glass, 'I'm sure I could do that, easy peasy.'

Albotain chuckled, 'you may scoff my boy, but you would find it very easy indeed I can assure you.'

'Ha. It sounds like a very useful thing to be able to do, but I wouldn't know where to start. '

'Well, let's see what you can see when you hold the Talisman.'

'Now?'

'Good a time as any I'd say.   Right, now, hold the Talisman in your hand.'

Ed retrieved the Talisman from his pocket. He was feeling very nervous.

'First of all you must connect with the Talisman and feel its energy. Just hold it in your hand, close your eyes and tell me what you see and feel. Remember, it is your friend.'

Ed did as he was told. The Talisman felt warm in his hand and his arm tingled. It felt a little like static electricity, but with a stronger energy, pulsating waves travelling up his arm to his neck. He gulped, more than a little scared, but still he held on tight. He couldn't see anything at first, just the insides of his eyelids. Then, slowly, colours began to emerge, strange forms swirled in front of him like graceful dancers, merging and blending to create intensely beautiful colours.

After his initial surprise subsided, he became mesmerised by the kaleidoscope in front of him, lost in the vibrant clouds. Then the colours began to take form. Slowly he saw a blue and green dragon with golden eyes in front of him, it looked directly at him and then changed into a silver eagle, its regal head held high, wings outstretched. The eagle then became an Angel, white and shimmering gold, its face as perfect as anything Ed had ever seen. The purity of this vision took his breath away. He was almost afraid to look at her too closely, as if he would taint her beauty with his humanness, his imperfections. He didn't know how he knew this, but her name was Aurelie. Then he heard the word 'faith', a whisper deep inside his mind.

The pictures faded and Ed was left with just soft grey, the Talisman cooled in his hand and the energy subsided. He opened his eyes.

'Wow,' was all he could say.

He felt as though he had been transported to another realm, had travelled light years to an unknown universe. The room looked odd to him, unfamiliar, the shapes too jagged, the colours a little too harsh.

Albotain smiled, 'I take it that you and the Talisman are becoming acquainted?'

Ed told him what he had seen and the old man seemed very pleased indeed. He also mentioned the word he had heard.

'Those are the highest manifestations of the Talisman's energies, the most elevated conscious entities that reside within it have shown themselves to you. The fact that you have been told the angel's name is a sure sign. You are honoured. I sent the word 'faith' to you and you heard it clearly. I knew that you would be good Ed, and I am happy that I was correct! The Talisman will help you progress, possibly even more than I can. This is so very exciting! You must practice holding the Talisman every day and noting what you see. It will help you develop.'

'Develop what exactly?'

'Your psychic ability if course!'

Ed was nonplussed, 'What psychic ability? I'm no more psychic than Gideon.'

'You are very psychic indeed. How do you think that you are able to see the dark entity that haunts you? You have in your birth chart all the pointers that show me that you are one who is able to tune into the other worlds. You are connected to much more than this reality. I know that you have, all your life, felt and seen things that you cannot explain. Although you have shut yourself off from that which frightens you, you cannot avoid the fact any longer that you are destined to see more than others. You will come to understand that which most people cannot even begin to contemplate.'

Ed interrupted, 'about HR, why did he choose me?'

'HR attached himself to you because you emit an energy that he can use as nourishment, food if you like. Until now he has been able to feed upon your latent psychic energy to empower himself.'

Ed thought about what Albotain had said about him being psychic. He couldn't deny that he had always been subjected to strange thoughts and sensations. That was why he withdrew so much into books and fantasy; it was a way of blocking it out. He had never even considered that he might be psychic though. He just thought that he had an overactive imagination and was possibly a bit unstable. His family, of course, were not the sort of people that you shared these kinds of thoughts with and so he had just learned to deal with it in his own way. Despite the fact that he now felt strangely comfortable with the Talisman, he was more than a little nervous at the prospect of further developments. He relayed these thoughts to Albotain.

'Of course you are concerned Ed, and rightly so. In fact, if you were blasé about the whole matter, I would have to rein you in a little. Whilst courage is an admirable trait, it is wise concerning these particular matters to exercise caution and restraint. We know what happened to poor old Lance don't we?'

Ed felt a chill run down his spine when he thought of Lance. He could picture him sitting at the table in the attic room, panicking, sweat poring down his face as he struggled to find the answers to his problems in the illegible charts in front of him. Strange dreams haunting him at nighttime and his days shrouded in fear and worry. Ed could clearly see the grey, shadowy shapes surrounding him, sucking his energy until there was nothing left in him to fight them. He shuddered.

'You have nothing to fear Ed. You have no badness, no evil within you for anything powerful to attach to. However, your particular enemy is your own fear and that is a demon that you alone must conquer. If you allow fear to dominate your thoughts and actions then you most certainly run the risk of lowering your vibrational rate to one that corresponds with the Lower Planes of Being. If that happens then another weak entity may attach itself to you and feed off your vital energies.

'Is this where HR came from?'

Yes, he is a little different as he is a more physical than most. He has manifested so strongly because you have connected so intensely with him. You have given him far too much power Ed. You may not even be aware of it, but this kind of entity, whilst they can't do you any real harm, can bring lowered moods and an inability to see the light, the good in your life. I don't want to scare you Ed, but you must be aware of this. Once you have conquered your own fear, once you have found your faith, in yourself and the power of Goodness, then you will find that you develop very quickly indeed. The more you develop, the higher your vibrational rate will become and the more elevated you will be above the greyness. Essentially the safer you will be.'

'How do I stop feeling afraid?' Ed asked, feeling a bit panicky and, he hated to admit it, more than a bit scared.

'Keep the Talisman with you at all times. It cannot stop you being afraid, but will help you to overcome your fears through the lessons it shows you. It is your guardian, but most of all it is your teacher. You must show it that you are ready and willing to let go of any negativity that lives within you.'

He continued, 'now, I think that is enough for this evening, I don't want to overwhelm you! He yawned and stretched. 'I'm going to go to bed.'

Ed said goodnight and stayed at the table for a while longer. He picked up the Talisman. It was cool to the touch, obviously it has finished for tonight he thought. Strangely enough, he didn't feel as frightened as he thought he should. If six months ago someone had told him that all of this was going to happen, he would have given them a wide berth and told them to see a doctor! How he got to this point, believing in other worlds, spirits, magic and astrology, he had no idea. The only thing he was sure of was that his life would never, ever be the same again and that had to be a good thing, he decided finally.

As he lay in bed that night, just before he fell asleep he imagined sending positive energy to HR. Once asleep he dreamed of the caves again, except this time he wasn't afraid, he carried a huge flaming torch and walking next to him was the Angel.

HR watched Ed peacefully sleeping from the top of the old wardrobe, his feet clicking impatiently on the side. He was bored. He was also worried and confused. He had tried to dodge the Light that had come from Ed towards him, but suspected that he hadn't been completely successful. Now, much to his disgust, he was feeling different about Ed and that worried him. He didn't want to devour the lad's energy any more; it just didn't seem to taste the same. Changes were obviously afoot and perhaps it was time to move on for good. But where? Again, there as this awful feeling of someone sending Light to him. He shivered as if a ghostly hand from beyond had touched him.

Suddenly he had a thought...he would find someone new to torment, some poor, unsuspecting soul to relentlessly feed upon. There was a whole world out there, full of vulnerable people. What was he waiting for? Oh, how exciting, a new adventure. Then his heart sank as he realised dejectedly that he just didn't have the passion any more. The fire in his belly had well and truly gone out. He just couldn't do it and was at a loss as what to do next. He tried to conjure up pictures of suffering and misfortune and all it did was make him feel queasy. Drat! Drat! Double drat! He'd been more affected by the Light sent to him than he realised. He hated to admit it, but he didn't want to hurt anyone. He really had no desire to attach to some poor, innocent person, after hadn't most people suffered enough?

He tried to snigger evilly, failed sadly and drooped down from the wardrobe in a heap. He had no incentive, no evil intentions left and so he had no future as a dark entity. He'd been got at. He took one last, slightly regretful, look at Ed and decided it was time to find something completely different. He left with ideas of perhaps haunting a few politicians. He might enjoy that and surely it could *almost* be considered as working for the Light.

Chapter XV

The following days passed without incident. Ed and Albotain worked as per usual on the house and the garden and in the evenings would discuss various matters. Ed learned to use the Talisman's power to help him overcome his fears. Albotain taught him how to draw up astrological charts. It was a difficult task and Ed struggled with the maths. He persevered though, enthralled by the magic that lay in the birth charts and driven on by the secrets that they revealed. He found that despite his initial problem with the calculations he learned the principles of the art quite easily and enjoyed the language of astrology. The symbols and their meanings brought him a sense of calm and contentment, as if they were old friends. His world was opening up and he was grateful to Albotain and to astrology. He learned so much about himself and was inspired by the positive messages that his birth chart gave to him. He grew to understand that it was only he who had previously limited himself. He had refused to see the power that lay within him and had denied himself anything positive or good. Through his birth chart he found that he was loving, loyal, affectionate and a natural healer of both people and animals.

Ed also learned to heal using just his hands. When Albotain first suggested that he lay his hands on Lionel's arthritic back, Ed was more than dubious. The old man explained, 'the power of thought is what lies in every space in the universe, from the vast stretches of darkness that lie between the planets, to the minuscule, quantum space between each and every atom. Our consciousness guides that

159

power and it can be directed towards good or evil. Using the power of consciousness, of thought, every human being possesses the ability to heal. They just have to want to.'

Ed sat with his hand over Lionel's back feeling more than a bit stupid. At first, nothing happened, but as he practiced the method that Albotain had shown him, something began to take place. Visualising golden energy coming through the top of his head, through his body, down his arms and out of his hands, Ed began to feel heat and tingling. At the same time he tried to picture the bones in the dog's spine receiving the energy and focused upon thinking about how much he wanted the old dog to feel better. Lionel had responded by shuffling about and licking Ed's hands. He persevered and to his surprise after a few sessions, he began to notice that the dog was moving more easily.

One day Ed and Albotain were in the attic poring over some old papers they'd found tucked away in a drawer under the table. Whilst Albotain seemed to be quite excited by their find, Ed couldn't make head or tail of the scribbled symbols. They were different from the astrology symbols he'd been taught. He became a little bored and drifted off. He became lost in his own thoughts for a while when a thought suddenly occurred to him.

'How did you get the name Albotain?'

'Medieval astrology honours a method called the Mansions of the Moon. My Moon is placed in Aries. However, when I was born the Moon was found within the second Mansion, called 'Albotain'. Hence my name, chosen of course by my astrologer father. There are 28 Mansions of the Moon, all of which have different meanings. Albotain is connected with the finding of lost treasure.' He grinned at his friend, 'the Talisman could of course be considered treasure. However, as I have found you Ed, my own treasure, I believe that I have now fulfilled this prophecy given to me in my birth chart.'

Ed smiled and replied, 'where is my Moon, which Mansion is it in?'

'Your Moon is in the 28th Mansion, 'Arrexhe', this placing promises a long and fruitful marriage. It also brings protection when travelling. However, it is said that it can also cause lost treasure and until now you have indeed been without your treasure, the Talisman.'

'So,' said Ed deep in thought, he was strangely fascinated by this subject, 'that must have meant that I was destined to be without the Talisman, if that's what it said in my birth chart.'

Albotain frowned slightly as he thought about this for a moment, 'perhaps on some higher level nothing is ever a mistake. Perhaps you were indeed not destined to inherit the Talisman from your father and you and I were meant to take this path together, who knows? Even though I have not been able to restore the Talisman to your father, I am only glad that I could bring your treasure back to you.'

As the weeks went by Albotain and Ed talked together every night, often into the early hours of the morning. Ed heard tales of magic, spells, Angels and the spiritual planes. Albotain taught the boy how to protect himself from negative forces using the Talisman, by holding it and allowing its energy to surround him like a force field. Ed also learned how to call upon his Angel for strength using the ancient language of the Angels. He began to use astrology in its truest form, to cast charts and connect with the astrological symbols at their highest, purest level.

Ed also grew stronger physically and emotionally. His skin was clear, his eyes sparkled and he moved with new confidence and ease. Gone was the grey, defeated pessimist, here was the new Ed, a vital, strong and happy being. However, what had really changed him was not just what Albotain had taught him, but it was also what the man showed him. Through living with his friend, Ed learned that goodness, true goodness, was not boring, it was not humourless or lacking joy. Goodness was funny, intelligent, quick–witted and enthusiastic. Goodness took life on with full force, with courage and integrity; it defended the weak and supported those who needed help. It was never selfish, nor was it a weak, sappy victim of life or circumstance, yet it understood the value of self–preservation. Ed drank in this energy and it nourished him in every way.

The two friends also practised thought projection and Ed quickly became very good at receiving Albotain's messages. There were a few disasters, nothing too major though. One day Albotain was working upstairs and sent Ed a 'thought message'. Unfortunately, at the same time downstairs Gideon had decided to steal Ed's socks, so the young man was distracted and misheard the message. Albotain could not understand why when he came downstairs that he was presented by Ed with a large, battered Aboriginal hunting weapon (courtesy of the former Aussie gardener). Albotain explained to Ed that he had actually asked for one of Mrs P's rather individual cakes from the larder – one of her famous 'blue meringues.' Ed listened more carefully after that.

As the weeks went by, the weather became warmer. Every day when Ed woke up in the house, the sun was shining in through the bedroom window and when he opened his eyes, he still felt as though he was dreaming. As time went by, he grew to understand Albotain, both the man and the magician. Although he still found it hard to accept what he had been told, in his heart he knew that his friend wouldn't lie to him and he had to trust him. Albotain seemed to grow younger every day, the happiness shone from him as he pottered around the garden talking to Ed about all manner of things. They spent hours in the attic room, drawing up charts for them both to study.

However, Ed was finding it difficult to reconcile his two lives, the life he had left behind so suddenly in London with the life here in Guernsey. This showed itself in his dreams, confused and jumbled images came through as his mind tried to work through everything that happened. Often he would dream of the bedsit and of his old job. He would wake up with a start, relieved to find himself in the old double bed, the sunlight flooding into the large bedroom.

There were other dreams though. Strange, lucid events that weren't just dreams. 'Astral travelling' Albotain called them. He taught Ed that it is possible to separate the soul from the body temporarily and to travel to different, non–physical dimensions. He reassured Ed that it was safe as long as care was taken that the physical body was not moved whilst the soul was elsewhere.

It took Ed some time to perfect the technique. Whilst in bed drifting off to sleep, he had to remain aware of his intention to leave his body and to return safely. Albotain told him that often imagining that one was walking out of one's body was an effective method of leaving the physical body behind. Ed soon got used to the strange sensation of leaving his body. His body would vibrate and hum, a rushing sound would fill his ears and he would feel as though he were being sucked into a sandstorm. He could then see a bright light and shortly after that would 'wake up' in another reality. Albotain did warn Ed however, that this was not a game and that it should not to be done for entertainment. Again, as with all spiritual practice, the motive had to be pure. If one wished to seek enlightenment and knowledge, then protection was guaranteed. However, selfish or low level motives could result in journeys to the lower astral planes, which were not at all pleasant and could result in some nasty experiences.

After a while, Ed was able to consciously connect to Albotain so that the two could travel astrally together. Travelling with Albotain, Ed saw other worlds, cities and lands populated with strange beings, some human–like and others totally unrecognisable. The two men flew together during the nighttime, yet it wasn't dark in their world. The sky above them was bluer than cornflowers, the grass a vivid green and the sun shone like a golden jewel in the sky. They travelled across lands Ed didn't recognise, golden temples and bridges made of diamonds forming the skyline. However, he knew he wasn't dreaming and was consciously aware that his body was in bed asleep. He could feel the wind on his face and the touch of Albotain's hand as the man guided him though the skies. During these experiences he could speak and think clearly, more clearly than when he was awake and in his physical body, he often joked to his friend.

The two friends discussed their experiences and Ed was surprised that Albotain also remembered their journeys together clearly. He asked the man how it was that he felt so alive and vibrant when they were on the astral planes. The old man explained that man is spirit encapsulated by his body and so is weighed down by this physical vehicle. Consequently, everyone is restricted by the limitations of the five senses. 'In spirit,' he said, 'we are free to be all that we truly are.'

Ed wondered why most people didn't experience astral travel. Albotain told him that it was simply due to lack of belief in anything other than man could see, feel or hear that stopped him experiencing the joy of the other realms. The astrologer said that he hoped in the future that technology would allow man to move beyond the boundaries of his sensory limits. He grumbled at Mankind's ignorance, 'dogs cannot see colour and yet man knows it exists. So, if other species are limited in their perception of reality, how can man say that the world is only made up of what he is able to perceive with his own eyes and ears?'

He went on, his frustration evident as his voice quickened, 'before the invention of the microscope, illnesses such as Black Death were thought to be caused by supernatural forces, punishment from God. Now we know that disease is result of bacteria, a form of life so small that we cannot see it without the aid of technology. Spiritual beings and entities also exist, it's just that they operate at a frequency that is so fast, their density so light, that the naked human eye can't see them. That doesn't mean that they don't exist!'

He sighed, 'man is just discovering that multiple universes exist. Even science is questioning that possibility, so we are someway there. The spiritual laws are closer to science than anyone could ever imagine. Einstein himself suspected strongly that there was more to physics than his formula $E=MC^2$. Through his study of quantum physics he recognised that different laws govern the smallest particles. When life is examined at this minute level, neither time nor distance exist, as is so in the other realms. I just hope that soon the human race will finally realise that they have so much to learn and that just because something can't be seen doesn't mean that it doesn't exist.' He smiled wryly at Ed and said, 'today's supernatural is just waiting to be discovered by tomorrow's science.'

During their nighttime travels, Ed and Albotain met with people. However, these creatures were not just people, they were more like gods or angels, Ed wasn't sure how to describe them. They were purer, clearer and more beautiful than any ordinary person. They were also warm, loving, tolerant and kind. They spoke of things with Albotain that Ed could not comprehend, of other dimensions, races, worlds and names that he couldn't recall once he was awake, no matter how hard he tried. They spent what seemed like weeks, (but was actually only one night), with a Native American Indian called White Feather. He was a beautiful soul with eyes that held the secrets of the earth, dark, warm and full of love and compassion. He cared for humanity, the world and tried to protect man from himself. He flew with them over the earth and showed them what man was doing to his world, how he was destroying his own home. Afterwards, Ed had hung his head in shame on behalf of his race. When they said goodbye, White Feather held Ed close in his strong arms. He felt as though he had been touched by God.

Some of the worlds that they travelled to were absolutely beyond Ed's comprehension. One night they came upon a being that Albotain told Ed was called Zammereth. An Angel of gold, he was huge, at least forty feet high. He stood statue–like upon the towering walls of a great crystal city. At the foot of the gates to the city sat a multitude of tiny cherubim, golden children of the Heavens. Ed asked Albotain what the huge Angel was doing there.

Albotain replied, 'he is the father of the cherubs. They guard the city from the negativity of Mankind and Zammereth watches over them. When they shed tears, he knows that it is man's wrong doings that are the cause of their misery. He flies onto the earth and cools the heat of man's wrath with his great golden wings, so salving the pain of his children.'

Sometimes at nighttime in another world, Ed would find himself without Albotain, often in some strange half–lit reality. He would find himself in a familiar room in the house, thinking he had woken up, only to find later that he was still asleep in bed. The rooms would look the same, but often something would give it away. A door would be in the wrong place, or a strange piece of furniture would confuse him. Occasionally an unfamiliar person would be present, or Gideon would be cute and fluffy, (then he knew for sure that it was an astral dream!). When he asked Albotain why the house seemed the same but wasn't, Albotain told him these other earthly realities were an astral manifestation, created by the power of thought.

'They exist as a mirror of your familiar, solid reality. However, as they are formed from the flowing energy of thought, not solid atoms, then they shift and distort as you move through them. So, you unwittingly alter them with the power of your mind.'

Ed found that these realities could indeed be transformed just by willpower or desire. He soon learned that he could change his surroundings the way he wanted, sometimes to conjure up gateways to other realities within this astral version of the house.

By this stage when out of his body, Ed could almost fly on his own. Well, it was actually more like a slightly raised stumble. Albotain told him that he would be able to fly higher soon; it was his fear and lack of self–belief that made it difficult for him to leave the ground properly. It would come with time, reassured the old man.

Once Ed was awake the astral dreams faded quite quickly. However, when they were actually happening Ed found it hard to tell if he was awake and in his real body or whether he had left his physical self behind asleep in bed. Albotain told him that if he could see his own hands in front of him, then it was not a dream but an astral experience. Ed eventually worked out how to tell if he was in or out of his 'real' body by stretching his fingers with the other hand. If he was still asleep and it was his 'astral' or spirit body, then the fingers would stretch painlessly to whatever shape he pulled them into. However if the knuckles cracked and he felt intense pain, then he knew he was awake and in his physical body!

Chapter XVI

One night Ed found himself travelling alone. He knew that he was on an astral plane, but it was not a mirror image of the house, or any part of his reality. He found himself in a strange land, but he didn't recognise where he was at all. The sky was not blue; it was steel grey and charcoal clouds floated across the moonless sky. However, it was light enough to make out the old stone buildings that surrounded him. The small courtyard where he stood was flanked by low walls and an old iron gate led to a dense, dark green forest just beyond. At the edge of the courtyard, circular towers stretched into the sky, they were dressed in dark ivy and the black leaves rustled in the cool breeze. He was obviously in some earlier time. This, he knew from Albotain was possible, as the astral planes can hold time still in certain places. They kept a point in history as it was, safe from the ravages of the years in a kind of cosmic bubble.

He breathed in the night air; it was cool and smelled of wood smoke. A flock of crows took flight from a nearby rooftop, the sound of their beating wings filling the air. Strangely though, Ed wasn't afraid. The place was eerie, but not frightening. The grey light was gentle and it felt oddly comfortable, like dusk in your own garden. He began to explore, the earth beneath his feet soft and moist. To his left there was an ancient graveyard, small irregular stones marked what Ed assumed to be the graves. Ahead, a small stone building stood in front of him. It was windowless, faceless apart from a small wooden door, no higher than he was. Ed tried the door and it swung open, complaining only softly.

Not knowing why he was drawn to the building, Ed stepped inside. The door swung shut with a clunk.

He found himself in quite a large, low room, a small oblong window along the back wall grudgingly allowed some light in. The room was empty of furniture; a dirt floor and rough stone walls greeted him. Ed began to feel a little nervous, his stomach did a gentle flip as he sensed there was something with him in the room. Telling himself it was just his imagination he turned to leave. He put his hand on the old iron handle and the sensation that he was not alone grew stronger. Beginning to panic now, Ed turned to look behind him. He thought he could see a shape, a silhouette in the window. It looked like a man. He gulped and wished Albotain was with him. Feeling suddenly claustrophobic, he tried to open the door. His heart was pounding and he felt like he couldn't breathe. As he turned the handle, he felt two arms enfold him. He struggled, sure that he was about to die. *'Without my body..how would that happen?'* came the errant and totally unhelpful thought. Then not knowing what to do next, he stopped struggling. The arms around him relaxed and Ed realised that he was no longer afraid. The arms felt strong but soft, not aggressive in any way. They released him. Now that he had stopped panicking, the room seemed to be full of peace and was totally calm. Ed turned to face whoever it was.

The man in front of him was dressed in a dark robe, his face pale in the dim light, eyes luminous with curiosity. 'Who are you?' asked the stranger in no more than a whisper.

Ed didn't know what to say, indeed in this world who *was* he? He hesitated and then answered as truthfully as possible.

'…I suppose we're two spirits from different times.'

He was surprised to see the man's eyes widen with shock and he took a step back quickly away from Ed as if afraid. Ed realised that the man was genuinely scared and obviously did not understand what was happening. Ed tried to reassure him and calm him down.

After the man had recovered from being so frightened, the two talked for a long time. They stood in the dark low room, neither of them moving from the spot. Face to face, they shared their stories. Ed found out that the man did not know that he was on an astral plane. He had had no idea that he was no longer physical, no longer alive in the usual sense. He told Ed that he was a 'warrior monk,' a knight who was also committed to God. He had given himself to the Crown and to God at an early age and he did not know what to do once the King had died. He had known nothing else but to serve those he loved. So, he patrolled the graveyard, protecting the dead from looters and making sure that those who travelled through were safe. However, all of his friends were gone and he had no one to keep him company. He was desperately lonely and unhappy. He explained that this was why he had approached Ed in the way he did. It had been a heartfelt plea for human contact. He had restrained Ed simply to stop him leaving him.

Ed's heart went out to him. Despite the fact that he was a committed and loving person, this poor man had never had a proper life, one that had given him love or any future. Ed talked to the knight about his own past, about how he had also trapped himself in a life that was grey and bleak, in a prison of his own making.

'You can be free as well,' he told the knight, 'you don't have to stay here. You are a free sprit now. You need to leave and explore the world. Now that you understand what has happened, you can experience being the man that you should have been, not just a monk or a knight.' The man nodded, looking thoughtful and then retreated into the shadows. As Ed went to leave, he asked the knight his name....

The next morning Ed woke, the dream fading as reality clumsily replaced it. He tried to recall all of the details. He was convinced that the whole experience had been real until he remembered the last thing the man had said. He remembered clearly that the knight had said his name was Katie. How can a man be called Katie? I must be losing my marbles, he decided.

Later on that day Ed told Albotain about the dream, laughing about the fact that he had thought it was real until the man told him his name. Albotain put down the book he'd been reading, rolled his eyes to the ceiling and looked at Ed.

'Firstly, *Catie* in times past was also a man's name and secondly, you have just completed your first spirit rescue on your own. Well done!!' The old man beamed at Ed.

Ed couldn't think of anything to say to that.

A few days later, the two were talking in the kitchen. Albotain said, 'I think, Ed, that you need a bit of a break from all this. You have done so well, but you really should have some time to live a normal life. Have you any friends of your own in Guernsey?'

'Well I met a lad on the ferry called Martin and he introduced me to his mate Sparrow. They gave me a lift here the first night I arrived. They gave me a phone number, I'll have to see if I can find it. I think they spend most of their time in the pub though and I'm not much of a drinker,' said Ed looking a bit worried. He knew Albotain was right, but he didn't like to admit that he found it difficult to make the first move with people. He was always waiting for them to reject him. He decided to wait a bit until he thought about contacting them.

Every now and then Ed would 'dream' about Catie. The first time the knight came to him, he thanked Ed for helping free him from his lifeless world. He promised that as a token of his gratitude he would always protect Ed. The young man just had to call him and he would be there. He was Catie the Man now, not just the Knight or the Monk. His world was as it should have been. He told Ed that he travelled the astral planes freely. He hunted and fished in the crystal clear lakes of the Aqua Moon and walked upon the sandy shores of the Twilight Sea. He had friends and companions now. People he thought he had lost were found once again, comrades from the army and members of his long dead family, his parents and sisters. He was whole at last and the joy shone from his eyes as he spoke. Ed was pleased that he was so happy and also felt honoured that he had a protector from another time.

It wasn't just Ed's nighttime reality that altered though; his days were very different as well. As he developed and grew stronger psychically, so he began to see other worlds, ones intertwined with his waking reality.

Walking in the woods with Lionel one sunny day he looked up at the tree line. He blinked as he saw swathes of white looping up above the trees and then seemingly float back down into the woodland. He walked towards the forest and into the depths of the trees; the shadows were cool and dark. There it was again, a flash of light. It wasn't physical, but it was most definitely there. As Ed approached the trees, he saw a misty figure standing next to a large oak tree. It was

173

huge, at least thirty feet tall and translucent – glowing white in the soft light. Taken aback, he stood back a little and watched it. Lionel grumbled low in his throat and tried to hide behind a nearby bush.

Ed was puzzled, *what* was it doing? Its huge arms seemed to be pulling something from the top of one particular tree, a long, white length of something. Ed had no idea what it was.

After a little while, the figure turned and looked down at the boy and the dog. Ed looked back, not exactly afraid but a little hesitant; after all, this was a *very* large spirit. The being smiled, a gentle smile that lit up the skies around him. Ed looked up at him, his head tilted up. The spirit looked back at Ed and Lionel like someone watching tiny kittens, compassionate, protective and more than a little amused.

The being's eyes were the palest, purest blue that Ed had ever seen and he was overawed by this magnificent creature. However, he eventually plucked up the courage to ask him who he was and what he was doing.

'I am Arazynth. I am a Light Retriever.' His voice was a whisper, but one that seemed to fill the forest. It was an impossible combination of gentleness and power.

Seeing Ed's puzzled expression, the great spirit, through tender words and beautiful visions, explained to the young man that the forests and woodlands were a wonderful source of Light energy. This energy was useful not just for the earth, but also for other worlds and other dimensions. The earth held within it a potent combination of physical and spiritual energy. This force was a catalyst for the production of the most powerful known energy in the physical Universe – Light. This is why the earth had been created. Arazynth told Ed that the earth is a Light Reservoir, a source of energy for a multitude of other worlds. He also told him that he came from the Rainbow Dimension. As a Light Retriever it was his task to harvest the Light from the trees and return with it to his own world. In the summer, the Light Retrievers harvested the tree's energy. In the winter, they allowed the trees to rest from their work whilst they protected them. This great spirit was one of many beings that worked in this manner with the forests of the world. Ed was dumbfounded at the knowledge that poured from the being. As Arazynth spoke Ed felt as though he were standing under a fountain of coloured crystals. Brilliantly coloured spheres of light tumbled down and rushed through him, bathing him in images and feelings.

'Man is also potentially a Light producer,' Arazynth explained, 'his desire to fight the Darkness is what makes him special. Each man's physical energy and spiritual essence struggles constantly to combat the lower energies of physicality, the negative energies that exist everywhere in the universe. It is this desire to fight evil that creates a spark of Light, of pure energy. Every time a human being holds a good thought within him, or carries out a good deed, this energy creates a better world. This brings positive energy to himself and to his world. However, the light that shines from him also positively affects the other dimensions. Look down at your feet child, look up to the sky.'

Ed looked around him and felt that he was seeing the world clearly for the first time. He gazed at the wild daffodils blowing in the wind, the golden celandines glowing like stars in the grass, the wide swathes of purple blue bells mixed with the white wild garlic. The clear, vibrant colours of nature took his breathe away.

Arazynth continued 'Look at the beauty which is your world, your God and your true heart. Make Light boy, move through the world and illuminate the Darkness. This is your mission.'

The entity faded slowly back into the forest, leaving nothing behind but the rustling of the trees and the sound of the birds. Ed stood still for a while trying to absorb what the spirit had told him. The sunlight flickering through the trees made him blink as he squinted in the light, trying to bring back the image of Arazynth. But the great being had gone. He felt lost, as though someone had turned out a light and a sense of sadness overwhelmed him. However, he also felt a sense of awe and was incredibly humbled by what he had learned. He turned and made his way back to the house to tell Albotain. As Ed walked home, he noticed that the world looked different; it shimmered and shone as if it had been cleansed somehow.

The fine weather continued and one Saturday afternoon, as Ed and Albotain were about to go upstairs to pack up boxes, there was a loud knock at the front door. The two men jumped, they weren't used to visitors. Mrs P had popped around a few times and luckily, she had never run into Albotain. However, they knew this time that it couldn't be her at the door. She was away for the week on a shopping trip to Jersey with her sister. Albotain quickly scooted up the stairs as Ed answered the door.

It was Martin, small, wiry and more than a bit spotty. He was dressed in the same tatty jeans and old leather jacket as when Ed last saw him. He greeted Ed enthusiastically, 'Hello mate, long time no see! I meant to call round earlier but you know what it's like,' he said and shrugged nonchalantly, grinning widely at Ed.

'You remember Sparrow and this,' he inclined his head slightly to his left, 'is our mate Anna.'

The girl standing next to Martin smiled at Ed. She had short, dark, spiky hair and large, dark, brown eyes, ringed

with thick, black eyeliner. She was wearing black leggings, a
baggy yellow top and on her feet were black pumps. Ed
noted that despite the fact that she was not the most feminine
of girls, she was very pretty. He experienced the familiar
lurch of self–consciousness landing in his stomach.

'We picked up Anna and as we were coming past your
house, we were wondering if you'd like to come for a spin in
the car and then to the pub?' continued Martin, oblivious to
the effect that Anna was having upon Ed, who was
momentarily lost for words. There was a long silence.

'Well,' said Martin eventually, 'can we at least come in
then? This place looks very cool and I wouldn't mind a bit of
a look.' Ed stood back to let the three of them in, trying very
hard not to stare at Anna. He was at this moment in time
completely incapable of forming anything resembling a
constructive sentence.

He took them through to the kitchen, amidst cries of,
'wicked place,' 'cool!' and 'lucky boy.' He bolted upstairs to
find Albotain. The shock of seeing Martin and Sparrow, not
to mention the very attractive Anna, had put Ed into a panic.

'What should I do? Is it ok to go out? I haven't seen the
outside world for so long, I'm probably agoraphobic!'

Albotain replied, 'You need company, young people of
your own age. Go on Ed,' he smiled, seeing Ed's worried
expression, 'I'll be fine, honestly. Go!'

Reassured, Ed went back to let his friends know that he
would be joining them. They were gathered around Gideon,
who was, thankfully, being very well behaved. He was even
refusing to repeat the dreadful swear words that Martin was
trying to teach him. He was showing off a bit in front of the
youngsters though, crooning and preening his feathers like an
aged rock–star revelling in the limelight. Ed could have

sworn that the bird was holding his belly in as he swaggered up and down his perch.

Chapter XVII

The four of them left the house and got into Sparrow's old car. Ed remembered just how smelly it had been and so was prepared this time for the terrible odour. He held his breath as he climbed in. He sat in the back next to Anna. He stared fixedly out of the window. He kept his head turned away from her, just in case she thought he was looking at her, which of course he was. He stole furtive glances in her direction, only when he was sure that she wasn't looking though. Martin, Sparrow and Anna chatted to Ed about life in general. Martin told Ed that Anna worked as a waitress in a local bistro on the west coast. Ed listened as Anna explained that she'd just finished her 'A' levels and wanted to go to Art College. Although she'd been accepted by a few good ones, she wasn't sure which course she wanted to do and so was taking a year or so out. She didn't seem too bothered about her current situation though. She told Ed, (who found it easier to stare at the view just behind her head rather than directly at her), that she liked not knowing what was happening next, leaving everything to chance. She came across as a very independent girl, one who obviously enjoyed life to the full.

As they drove towards town, Sparrow at the wheel, Ed became even more fixated with Anna. He listened as she talked about her love of travelling and her desire to see the rest of the world. Despite her young age, she had already been to many far away and very exotic places. In the summer break last year she'd gone backpacking with a friend and had travelled by train down to Spain and then over to Morocco. She was so confident and full of life that Ed felt like a pale shadow in comparison. His heart sank as he decided that a girl like Anna wouldn't look twice at him. She was pretty, outgoing and talented. He eventually summoned up the courage to speak to her directly, asking her where she lived.

Sparrow chuckled and spoke for the first time, 'Anna lives in a German bunker on the common. It's from World War Two, it's in her parent's garden. Apparently, it's haunted. You wouldn't get me sleeping in there on me own I can tell yer.'

'Yeah, but I'm not a chicken like you Sparrow,' Anna grinned at her own terrible joke. Sparrow gave her a dirty look in the rear view mirror.

'I don't mind at all. I sometimes hear voices and footsteps, but I'm kind of used to it now. I call him Herman the German. Sometimes I tell my dad his yacht is haunted, just for a laugh!'

Ed was further humbled when he realised that Anna obviously came from a well off family.

Anna told Ed that her mother was a landscape garden designer and her father was an architect. She said that her parents were very laid back and really let her do her own thing. They were bit bohemian, kind of free spirits and encouraged Anna to 'express herself.' Then she asked Ed a bit about himself. However, as he was still paralysed with shyness, he could only mumble 'yes' and 'no' answers. She eventually gave up and turned her attention back to Martin and Sparrow.

They drove onto the coast road towards the west coast. This part of the island was much flatter and Ed was transfixed as he stared out at the sweeping bays and miles of golden sand. Tiny cottages and impressive mansions stood side by side looking out to sea, their windows glistening in answer to the movement of the waves breaking on the ragged rocks. Ed watched the seabirds strutting jaggedly across the sand, their beaks poised as they searched for food. Anna pointed out her place of work, 'The Fisherman's Bistro,' to Ed and he took a mental note of the name.

Gazing at the beach, Anna said, 'did you know there is a petrified forest on the beach that you can only see at very low tide?'

Nobody responded, so Anna shrugged and turned away. Ed, however, thought that this was an amazing fact and wanted to ask her more about the prehistoric woodland remains. However, his desire to fit in with the boys overcame his curiosity and so he also said nothing.

At Ed's request, they stopped briefly at a kiosk so that he could buy a postcard for his mother. Even though he doubted she'd be very interested, she was the only person in the world who might be even remotely curious to know his whereabouts. Marlene was currently living in Portugal with a retired paper products salesman called Geoff, a florid man with alopecia. Still, Ed supposed, his mother was no spring chicken and whilst Geoff was certainly no oil painting, life in sunny Portugal had to be better than a dismal half–life in Erlington.

They turned inland and travelled past more houses and tiny farmsteads. The sheep and cows turned to look vacantly at them as they passed. Eventually they reached the town of St Peter Port. They drove along the front, past the shops and taverns that looked out into the marina where the sailing boats swayed slowly in tune with the rising tide.

Sparrow parked the car on one of the piers and they all made their way over the main road, which was along the sea front. From there they went towards a large, beautiful church. Its spire dominated the sky above; the grey granite walls were austere and imposing even in the sunlight. Baskets of brightly coloured flowers, like glorious jewels on a grand old lady, bought life to the stately building.

'This,' said Anna, who seemed to have appointed herself the official tour guide, 'is the Town Church, this is the Town Square, and the old Market is just behind it.'

Ed saw granite buildings, cobbled streets and a glorious view of the seafront. A large seagull sat soaking up the sunshine on the slipway next to the little ferry office offering trips to the nearby island of Herm. It was idyllic and Ed wanted to stay there forever. He thought that the wonderful view combined with the presence of the beautiful Anna was enough to keep him happy forever

Next to the church was their destination, a small pub called the 'Tartan Bar'. Anna said to no one in particular, 'this is the nearest pub to a church in the British Isles.' Ed, however, was taking careful note of everything she said. Partly through a genuine interest in the island, but also because he just wanted to be able to recall every word she said.

Inside the pub it was very busy and the air was heavy with the smell of stale beer, old leather and warm bodies. A group of bikers were crowded around a table in the far corner. Pint glasses, some full, most empty, covered every inch of the surface. Heavy rock blared out of the duke box and a couple of biker girls stood next to it dancing apathetically, glasses in hand, the tassels on their leather jackets twitching lethargically in time to the beat of the music.

They made their way to the bar and Martin bought the first round. Ed, bravely, ordered a local beer, something called 'Hanois'. It looked very inviting indeed. However, he told himself that he must drink it slowly, or he took the risk of looking like a complete idiot in front of Anna. Beer had a habit of going to his head very quickly. Sparrow drank juice, but that was because he was driving so no one commented. They made their way over to one of the vacant tables, Sparrow collected the dirty glasses that had been left by the previous occupants and took them to the bar.

On the way back he was greeted loudly by the bikers, 'alright me lad? How's your dad?' they laughed uproariously, obviously finding something very funny.

Unfazed, Sparrow grinned as he sat down with his friends. 'They're taking the mick out of my dad. He's a taxi driver, but he's always wanted to be a biker. He only bought his first motorbike last year. It's flippin' embarrassing, he's too old. You should see him all dressed up in his new leather gear, lurching around our kitchen, knocking stuff off the worktops. My mum goes mad. This lot here think he's the funniest thing they've ever seen. He keeps turning up at their meeting place at the beach kiosk at Vazon, hanging around them like he's one of them. It wouldn't be so bad, but he's only got a 100cc, he can't even keep up with them!'

Ed glanced over at the leather–clad group. 'Isn't he a bit nervous of them? They look like they could be mean.'

Martin replied to Ed, 'naaaah, this lot are as soft as mud. Most of them have never even left the island. Their idea of causing trouble is feeding the seagulls too many sandwiches. Gives 'em wind apparently – the seagulls that is, not the bikers,' he added. 'That bloke over there,' Martin inclined his head at one of them, a big chap dressed in heavy black leather from head to toe. He had frizzy brown hair trailing down his back and a long matted beard. Ed thought he looked like an extra from a scary movie.

Martin continued, 'he's Big Mickey, their leader. I know he looks like he could do you some damage, but his day job is driving around old people in a mini bus and he lives with his gran. Also,' he lowered his voice and put his mouth to Ed's ear, 'it's rumoured that he keeps guinea pigs in his back garden. Nobody's ever seen them though. Apparently he dotes on them, they're all called after old movie stars, Errol, Grace, Marilyn, etcetera etcetera, but you didn't hear that from me.' he chuckled slyly.

They spent the afternoon talking and drinking beer. Ed, however, was very careful and sipped his slowly. Anna made them all laugh with stories of how, when she was a child, the house was always busy with people staying over. Many of them were artists or writers, passing through on their way to some exotic destination. Her mum was very unconventional, she dressed mostly in flowing kaftans and wore flip–flops even in the winter. She was also very sociable and had held some very remarkable dinner parties. The most embarrassing time was when her mum became friendly with a couple of young naturists and her dad had decided to bring his elderly boss home for dinner unannounced. That was a very interesting meal,' giggled Anna.

Obviously, they had very different childhood experiences thought Ed ruefully. Anna's life seemed to be full of excitement, bursting with warmth, love and material comfort. If he hadn't liked her so much he could have been a bit envious. He also noticed that she and Martin seemed to be very close. They shared drinks and he kept poking her in the ribs to make her choke on her beer. Ed desperately hoped that they just were close in a brother, sister kind of way. He felt physically sick as he admitted to himself just how much he liked this outgoing, funny, gorgeous girl.

184

After a few rounds they left the bar. Martin announced that they should take Ed for a walk around the town and so they did. They wandered around for a while, it had been raining and the air was damp with a light sea mist. The sun was coming out, the air was fresh and clean and smelled of the sea. The shops were closed by now and the streets were more or less deserted. They walked up the High street, the cobbled stones echoed with the sounds of their footsteps. Antique shops sat next to new boutiques, huddled comfortably together like old friends. A beautiful old granite building announced grandly that it was the 'Moore's Hotel'. The large old building stood the end of the High Street like a graceful galleon, its coloured flags reaching out into the azure sky.

Ed was surprised to see no burger bars or take out cafes, just quaint bistros nestling amongst the buildings. The peaceful slumbering town made him feel as though he had gone back in time. He felt strangely safe and protected in Guernsey, comfortably removed from the harsh world. The old and new seemed to live side by side without friction or discord. Even in the harbour, the old fishing boats lounged contentedly next to the shiny white gleaming yachts.

They drove home in silence, all lost in their own thoughts. As they made their way up the steep, winding road from Town, Ed looked at the gorgeous woodlands that rose up in front of him as the old car climbed the hill. The dappled woods were cool and soft, bluebells, snowdrops and pink campions blanketing the floor beneath the mossy trees. He sighed, how could the world be so different? London and its dingy streets couldn't possibly exist in the same reality as this world of colour and beauty. At that moment he realised that Anna was watching him. When he turned to look, she quickly looked away. He decided he'd imagined it.

185

At the top of the hill, they dropped Anna off to see a friend. Ed hoped desperately that the friend wasn't a boyfriend.

'Night then,' she called as she left the car without so much as a backwards glance. Regretfully, Ed watched her fade into the darkness. He wished he'd said something to her, anything to let her know how he felt.

Albotain was waiting for him when he got home. 'Good time?' he asked hopefully.

'Great thanks, really good,' Ed heard himself saying.

Over the next few weeks, Ed saw his new friends regularly, visiting the pub with them every Saturday afternoon. Often if the three of them felt a bit jaded from a heavy night partying before, they would call for Ed, just to go on a walk on the beautiful cliffs near the house to clear their heads. Ed never went out with his friends in the evenings though. He wanted to stay with Albotain and continue his training, which was, even if he were to say so, going pretty well. He told them that he couldn't leave Lionel and Gideon at night and luckily they believed him. During their times together, Ed studiously avoided Anna, not making eye contact and making sure he never got too close physically. He was petrified that she would realise that he was besotted with her. The rejection would be too much for him to bear.

Ed kept this part of his life separate from his world with Albotain. He treasured both lives and feared that if they collided, then they would both disintegrate and he'd be left with nothing. Of course, he also had to ensure that Albotain was safe. Martin, Sparrow and Anna came into the house occasionally, but Ed was careful to warn Albotain so that they wouldn't meet. The astrologer wasn't even supposed to be in this world, this physical reality. If his friends were to come across the old man all sorts of karmic repercussions could occur. He was also careful that Mrs P didn't accidently meet his friend. Ed knew that Albotain encountering anyone besides him could affect the fabric of fate and the delicate weave of destiny. So, he had to make sure that his two lives remained separate.

Despite the fact that Ed led in a sense two different lives, he was happy. For the first time in his life he wasn't downtrodden, criticised or laughed at. The greyness that had been so much a part of him dropped away. Like a snake shedding its skin, he was a shinier, more vibrant version of the boy he had been in London. He couldn't believe how much his life had changed. He felt like a different person. He wasn't afraid any longer, he was full of enthusiasm, excited about life and happy to be alive.

Ed had sent off the postcard to his mum. A reply from her came a week or so later…

'Dear Edward,
What are you doing stuck on a godforsaken island in the middle of the Channel? Your uncle had no money, so if you're hoping to cop for an inheritance you're out of luck. I tried years ago to get him to part with some of his cash and all I got was a big, fat nothing.

Geoffrey and I are building an extension onto our house here in Sao Pedro. We're not spring chickens any more you know, so we could do with a bit of help with the drains (if you're not too busy doing nothing, that is). The plane ticket is attached. See you next week (and don't bother bringing your flipping books either, you'll be too busy to read).
Mum

*Ps. could you pick up some waterproof body glitter for me?
'Discoball Purple' if you can find it. I can't get any of the
waterproof stuff over her and Geoffrey's complaining that I'm
clogging up the pool filters – as if I don't have enough stress
already.'*

Ed read the letter at least four times, hoping that he had
missed some token of affection, some semblance of loving
expression. He just wanted to find *something* tucked away
hidden behind the lines that showed his mother actually gave
a flying fart about him. Nope, nothing, zilch. He looked
blankly at the plane ticket, holding it gingerly. He felt as if it
were detailing a rite of passage to the nether regions of Hell,
which in a sense it was. As he went upstairs to pack up some
more boxes with Albotain, he dropped the letter and the ticket
in the bin.

Later that afternoon in one of the storage rooms, Ed was
searching through some piles of rubbish on the floor. This
was the last room that they had to pack up and Ed was, to be
honest, stringing it out a little. In a few short weeks they'd be
finished and he really, truly didn't want that, not yet anyway.
He sifted through what was obviously some of Lance's old
mail. Electricity bills stamped with red greeted him, letters
from the bank detailing huge overdrafts and unpaid loans. It
was all quite depressing. Then Ed discovered a small black
diary. Curious, he opened it. The scrawl was practically
illegible, but he gasped when he saw a familiar name and an
address.

*Blyte Ivan. 23 Llannelli Lane, Lanceter, Ceredigion, Wales,
U.K.*

Strange, he thought, that's no travellers site – that's a proper address. Frank Arvil obviously hadn't known this or else he would have been able to contact Ivan. Ed's heart lifted – his dad lived in a house. Maybe he wasn't the loser that he'd been led to believe. Ed smiled and shoved the book into his back pocket. Later on, he put it carefully in the bottom of his rucksack. You never know, he thought to himself as he made his way downstairs to join Albotain for dinner.

Chapter XVIII

A few days later Ed and Lionel were taking their usual walk to the corner shop and were on their way back to the house. The weather was gloomy, the sky threatened rain and Lionel seemed reluctant to keep going. Eventually, the old dog stopped on a corner of the lane and refused to go any further. The stubborn look in his eyes told Ed that he was planning to stay put. As Ed was trying to talk some sense into him, a black four–wheel drive careered around the corner, nearly hitting both of them. Ed leapt out of the way, followed shortly by a suddenly mobile Lionel. The car swerved and came to a stop a little way away from them, scraping its bumper on a granite wall as it did so.

Ed leant over and checked Lionel to make sure he hadn't been hurt. Reassured that they were both in one piece, he looked up to see the driver marching toward them. She was small, very slim and wearing high boots with the jeans tucked in and a beige, mohair jumper. Her long, pale blonde hair was pulled back in a ponytail. Despite her small frame and feminine appearance, Ed noted that she looked very, very angry.

Her pale blue eyes glared at him, 'what on earth do you think you were doing you idiot?' she shrieked.

She was obviously well to do; her accent was typical British upper class. She pronounced earth, 'aarth'.

'Look what you have done to my car.'

Despite the fact that he was taken aback by this tirade, Ed was enraged that she could have injured an innocent animal.

'You could have killed us. My dog could have been badly hurt.'

'Do I look as though I give a hoot about your mangy mutt? He looks about ready to be put down anyway. Just look at my new car, it's ruined,' she gesticulated wildly at the vehicle and, despite the fact that she appeared only to be a couple of years older than Ed, added, 'you stupid boy, you should have more respect for road users.'

Ed replied, 'and you should have more respect for people's lives. You were going too fast!'

At that she glared at Ed, then turned and stomped back to her car, leaving him incensed. As he walked back to the house, he felt absolutely furious that the woman not only almost killed the two of them, but also had spoken to him as if he was nothing, a nobody. He wondered angrily if she ever took the plum out of her mouth. She obviously had more money than manners. Although he was a much more positive soul than he used to be, he was still tired of people thinking they could treat him how they liked.

Once inside Ed relayed the story of what had happened to Albotain, who was in the lounge sitting on one of the leather sofas reading. After he had finished, his friend was in no doubt as to just how angry he was about the incident.

'What would you like to do to resolve this, what would make you feel better? '

'I don't know. Maybe if I saw her again I could tell her how I feel, how fed up I am of people thinking they are better than I am,' he answered bitterly.

'So is the problem this particular lady, or is it that she triggered something off within you? '

Ed thought about this for a moment. 'Both, I think. She was so rude to me and very cruel about Lionel. But,' he sighed, 'it wasn't just her voice I was hearing when she was shouting at me. It was all the people in my life who have treated me like I'm nothing but a punch bag, someone to take things out on.'

Albotain patted the space beside him on the sofa, 'sit down next to me. Hold the Talisman in your hand. I can show you something that will help you to overcome your feelings of inadequacy.'

Puzzled, Ed did as he was asked. Albotain continued, 'as you have met this lady, you can tap into her energy field. I am not asking you to read her thoughts, that would be morally and spiritually wrong, I'm just asking you to witness the reality of her existence. I want you to see not what she wishes to show the world, but who she really is.'

Ed closed his eyes and concentrated, the familiar tingling moving up his arm. In his mind's eye, he pictured the woman getting back into her car and driving off. He saw her pull into a long, sweeping driveway, stopping in front of a large white Georgian house. He watched her as she went into the house and then into a large, modern kitchen with a glass roof. *Definitely well off,* he thought resentfully, the bitter draught of anger still bubbling away in his stomach. She walked towards a cupboard and took out a small bottle of pills. Swallowing two, she went to the fridge and took a plate of fruit from it, already chopped up. *Bet she didn't even have to do that for herself,* Ed grumbled to himself as he watched her. She took a bite from a piece of apple, then walked over to the bin and threw the rest away.

The images were becoming clearer by now and Ed was surprised to see that she was crying. Tears were streaming down her face as she scraped her plate. Her shoulders shook and her hands visibly trembled as she sobbed. His anger subsided a bit and he felt a little guilty at his harsh judgement of her.

He opened his eyes and turned to Albotain, 'why is she crying?'

'Because Ed, the person you encountered doesn't really exist. That hard–faced lady is just a child in adult's clothing, as indeed we all are. She presents her front, her armour to the world in an attempt to protect herself. She uses possessions and money as part of that façade. The more unhappy she feels the more armour she builds up around her and the more possessions she accumulates. The more she does this, the more unhappy and isolated she becomes. So, in an attempt to show the world that she doesn't care she collects even more possessions, so creating more distance between her vulnerable self and the outside world. It's a vicious circle and an entirely miserable existence.'

'How do you know all of this?'

'Despite my personal lack of experience when it comes to human emotions, I've spent centuries studying people. I can see into their hearts and souls and so I know what sorrowful creatures most are. I also remember how desperate I was in the castle to cling onto what made me feel safe. It was, of course, an illusion, the possessions and adoration I received were the merchandise of false gods. Those people in my life were ready to strike me down the minute I revealed any flaw, any imperfection or vulnerability. I know now that to live in fear is certain death for the soul.'

The old man stopped for a moment, lost in a time long gone, his blue eyes seeing far beyond the confines of the room. After a while he took a deep breath and continued on,

'I can see this particular lady because I am able to connect to her through you. I can tell you Ed that she is crying because she hates herself, she despises what she has become.

She takes medication to block out her emotions, to numb her heart and soul. She hasn't eaten a proper meal in years for fear that what she sees as the ugliness within her will show itself in her body. She fears that it will expand and become gross and unattractive, a reflection of how she feels inside. If she does not appear to be perfect then she believes that she will not be wanted by the world, the world that she tries so hard to impress.'

Ed was speechless, this was not at all what he expected and he felt terrible about his response to her behaviour.

Eventually he asked, 'hasn't she got anything good in her life?'

'She has extinguished everything that could potentially be good, for fear that it will expose her flaws. She is afraid that the shining light of joy will just reveal her to be the monster she fears she is. She is also desperately afraid that her husband will be angry with her because of the damage to the car. He is no happier than she. He is exhausted and numbed by his endless quest for money and belongings. He is someone who also masks his feelings with a drug, except his drug is alcohol. These two poor creatures live in the same house moving about one another. Like reversed magnets, they avoid touching or making contact. They are repelled by one another's misery and fear.' He paused before asking, 'now do you still feel angry at her and inferior to her?'

'I'm not sorry that I was angry at her. What she did was wrong. I am sorry though that she is so unhappy. But, no, I don't feel inferior to her any more. We're all just people aren't we?' Then he asked, 'everyone can't be like this inside this surely?'

'No, not everyone is quite as unhappy as this lady, she is an extreme example. I suspect you were led to her by the Talisman to give you a lesson in opening your eyes and your heart. There is a saying that only the very poor and the very rich truly suffer.'

'But the poor are that way because of circumstances that are beyond their control. But the very rich, how can they all be unhappy?'

'The very poor are not necessarily just those who come from materially deprived backgrounds. I am referring to those that are unhappy because they envy the rich. They feel that they have lost a birthright. They believe that they should have what others have and so they resent anyone who has more than them. They are able to move from this desolate place, this low vibrational rate, once they recognise that abundance comes from within. Once they accept responsibility for their attitude, they then find that they possess within themselves an endless source, one which gives them all that they need.'

'And the rich?' Ed queried.

'Only the very unhappy are driven to accumulate great wealth. Like the lady you met today, they feel that they have nothing within them that is valuable or lovable, that their souls are empty. They build up their armour, or perhaps armoury is a better word, so that others will admire them, or at least be afraid of their power. They are to be pitied as much as the poor I think. They can, however, also change. They can elevate themselves once they recognise that they lack love and faith within themselves. They suffer from what I call 'a hole in the soul,' one which they attempt to fill with the debris of the material plane. What they really need is unconditional self–love and absolute self–acceptance.'

'Isn't there anyone who is rich and happy?' asked Ed hopefully. He was struggling to accept that money equalled misery in every case.

'Some of the very new souls, those who are just forming, can live life on a very superficial level. These souls are just playing at earthly life and, yes, I suppose they are happy. However, they will experience a more challenging reality as they develop. It is true that we are only given what we can truly cope with.'

He continued, 'on the other hand, not all material wealth is a result of spiritual immaturity or malnutrition of the soul. There are also older, wiser souls who are granted material abundance. However, this happens only once the individuals concerned have cleared their Karmic debts and are able to live life on a wholly selfless level, helping others with their financial means.'

Ed considered what he was hearing, 'but the poor and the starving do suffer terribly. How can that be right?'

Albotain sighed, 'the world is far from perfect I'm afraid. Man's greed has got the better of him and consequently many, many people experience unnecessary hardship and loss. What I do know, however, is that those who suffer without becoming embittered are granted much when they pass over. Those who do not lose faith or love for their fellow man will be rewarded when they move to the next world. They will truly experience Heaven.'

Ed thought about what he had been told. It opened up a whole new world for him. Whilst it certainly didn't make him happy to know that there was so much pain and suffering being experienced by people, he at least knew that it wasn't in vain. There was a reason for everything and that ultimately everyone was treading the same path, he thought.

As time went by Albotain felt as though he were growing younger every day. Although he was still bothered a little at nighttime by the dark shapes, they didn't seem to be getting any stronger. He had decided that ignoring them was the best option. Despite the fact the he was, (physically anyway) over seventy years old, he felt very well indeed and moved about the house with ease. He loved to keep the house clean and whistled tunefully as he swept and mopped the floors.

If Ed couldn't believe the change in his friend, this transformation from the old doddery gardener to a man full of vitality and life, then Mrs P also couldn't believe the change in the level of cleanliness in the house. She was so impressed with what she thought were Ed's newly developed talents that she didn't even bother coming into clean up anymore. The only thing that did puzzle her on the rare occasions that she did venture into the house was the amount of food that Ed seemed to go through. She and Ed had a chat and a cup of tea one afternoon and she took the opportunity to gently ask him whether he was ok for money, considering that he had 'such a healthy appetite.' Ed reassured her that he was fine. He explained that he had an overactive thyroid and so had to eat a lot. (This wasn't true in the slightest, but he was put on the spot and had to think of something fast.) She was also amazed at the rate that Ed was progressing with packing up the boxes. However, she put that down to the thyroid problem as well, so she didn't say anything more.

As she walked quickly across the driveway to her house, Mrs P remembered that she'd had an aunt with the same condition. A few years ago, they found her dismantling her husband's Audi at two o'clock in the morning. One Christmas Eve she made three hundred feet of paper chains in an hour and a half, at the same time preparing Christmas dinner for twelve people. This was all well and good until in her haste she stuffed the turkey with coloured paper by mistake. That was not a good combination as the dye from the paper ran into the cooked fowl, dribbling grotesquely from the foil wrapping. Mrs P could still see the revolting green and blue tinged bird in her mind's eye. Actually that turkey looked a bit like Gideon, she mused, smiling just a little maliciously to herself at the thought of the nasty old parrot being served up for lunch.

One night a few weeks later, the two friends had just had their evening meal. Ed had cooked and Albotain was busy clearing up. The old man buzzed around the kitchen tidying and wiping down the surfaces efficiently. Once Albotain had finished, Ed decided it was time to broach the subject of Anna and his distinct lack of progress regarding this area of his life. If anything, she was becoming more distant as time went on. To make matters worse Martin mentioned something about her seeing some mechanic bloke from L'Eree, an area on the west coast near where she worked. Ed thought his head was going to explode at this dreadful news, he couldn't stand the thought of Anna with someone else. He'd been trying to pluck up courage to speak to Albotain about this for a while and tonight seemed like a good time. His three friends were coming over tomorrow afternoon. Ed was going to cook lunch for them, afterwards they were planning to go for a walk. Albotain had suggested this idea, telling Ed that he needed to spend more time with other people.

Albotain sat at the table listening patiently and nursing a glass of water.

'I want her to like me, but I feel like such an idiot when I'm around her,' he told him.

'Well Ed, I'm sure she does like you,' he replied encouragingly.

'No. I mean I *really* like her. I..,' he flushed embarrassed, 'I want her to be my girlfriend,' He composed himself quickly and continued on, 'I know in my birth chart that the Mansion of the Moon promises happiness in relationships, but I just don't know. I do know, however, that she's out of my league. I've got no chance.'

'You have a very good chance Ed, you have a lot to offer a young lady.'

'Yeah, right. Not many girls like spindly idiots. Maybe in your day my sort was chased by hoards of damsels. Nowadays girls want strong, muscle–bound blokes with flash cars and big wallets. I've got none of that.'

'I may not have had direct experience of romantic love, but I can tell you that whilst there's certainly always been call for the more masculine types,' said the old man tactfully, 'each person needs something different. Maybe you suit Anna.'

'I doubt it, I doubt it very flipping much,' grumbled Ed. 'Why can't the spirits help? I do all this studying and work and I try really hard to understand everything. Don't get me wrong, I am grateful to you and them, in fact, I don't know where I'd be without all of this. But I want to feel, well, *normal*, not like some kind of freak in a castle.' He stopped. 'Sorry, I didn't mean that, you know I didn't.'

Albotain smiled, 'I understand Ed. Firstly, the spirits are not here to provide answers. I learned a long time ago that their job is to raise the questions in order to stimulate us towards finding our own answers. If they provided the solutions, man would not have the opportunity to exercise free will and so could not progress spiritually.'

'Well, what do I do? Am I supposed to have a relationship?'

'Of course you are. As you mentioned, your chart shows this. Also, I'm relieved that you ask. This means that you won't make the same mistake as I did. The fact that you want to experience love, shows that you are treading a different path than I. I'm glad that you will have more balance in your life, it will make you a better teacher.'

Ed was beginning to get frustrated, 'so if that's right, then why can't I make her notice me. Why can't I ...I don't know, cast a spell, make a Talisman or do a chart or something to help make it happen? I know you won't be here forever and I don't like to think about that, but I have to face facts and I don't want to spend my life alone.'

Albotain replied, 'you can't cast a spell to make someone love you. Well, actually you can, but it never works in the long run. True love is eternal. Love that comes as a result of a spell is like temporary glue holding two people together. Sooner or later it comes unstuck and then the people concerned are even more lost. They've wasted their time and have often missed their true love, bypassing soul mates that were meant to come their way if only they'd had faith and waited.'

'So, how do I know that Anna is the one?' Ed was getting desperate now.

'You don't, that's why it's called faith,' came the somewhat unhelpful reply.

Ed left the table and stomped upstairs to his bedroom feeling angry. He had to admit it though, he was more than a little ashamed at his rather unspiritual response to Albotain's advice. Lying in bed, he calmed down and decided to try to accept the 'faith theory'. He would see what happened tomorrow when Anna and the others came for lunch.

Chapter XIX

The day broke warm and sunny and despite last night's conversation, Ed awoke feeling excited and more than a little nervous. Albotain said that he would spend the day out of the way in the top room drawing up charts and studying the remnants of Lance's work. He told Ed that he was prepared to carry out this rather tedious task, 'just in case there is anything at all of value in it, although I doubt it very much.' He went off slowly up the stairs, balancing a cup of tea and a plate of sandwiches precariously on top of a half a dozen modern astrology books he'd found in the downstairs library.

After talking with Albotain the night before, Ed wasn't at all sure what he should do about Anna. He decided just to act normal, (whatever that was – because the more he thought about it the less normal he felt). They arrived on time, a hot, sweaty bunch gasping for breath. Sparrow's car had a flat tyre and so they had decided to walk to Ed's from Town which was uphill most of the way. Anna had stayed over last night at the boys' flat in St Peter Port after being out in Town. Ed hoped fervently that she hadn't been with the mechanic bloke.

Martin had, as usual, brought some lagers, which they all slurped from the cans as Ed finished preparing lunch. He'd made pizza and salad, nothing special. They were all starving, so it disappeared quickly, washed down by the beer. They left the dishes and wandered off down the lane towards the cliffs. A tiny stream ran down the side of the lane, its banks covered with a multitude of wild flowers. The lane was flanked by high grassy banks. The sun sped across the sky, sporadically beaming out from a cloud, blessing the trees with her warm light, only to suddenly disappear again leaving the sky grey and cold.

Ed and Sparrow were in front, Anna and Martin followed behind. Ed was at a complete loss as to what to do. Anna had been very quiet at lunch and had hardly said a word. She hadn't even looked at Ed, never mind spoken directly to him. His heart felt like it had been stamped on. His mood was flat and he just wanted to run away and hide.

They reached the cliffs and made their way along the path. The sun valiantly fought with the clouds for ownership of the sky and the noise of the crashing waves seemed to fill the air. The cliffs were green and lush, yellow gorse gleamed at their feet and a soft breeze played with their hair as they walked along the narrow dirt path. Despite Ed's ever increasing feeling that his love life with Anna had as much chance as a snowflake in a microwave, the scenery lifted him. The expanse of the blue and white tipped ocean made him feel free and alive and the call of the seabirds still gave him a thrill, even after all this time. He heard the sea pulling longingly at the shingle and when he looked down, the golden sands were so clean and vibrant that they almost seemed to glow.

He turned to speak to the others behind him, Sparrow was there but Anna had gone. Ed strained his eyes and could just see her in the distance, a small black dot. When he looked at Sparrow, eyebrows raised, the lad just shrugged his shoulders. Obviously he had no idea why she had turned back.

Ed was about to carry on walking when something surged up inside him. No, it was *not* going to end like this. Bugger fate, he was going to try; he wasn't just going to give up like some spineless wimp. Martin and Sparrow were obviously taken aback as he turned around, broke into a run and charged down the cliff path towards her. She had practically disappeared by now and so Ed had to run as fast as he could to reach her.

He rounded a corner and there she was, he could see her clearly now. The problem was he was so out of breath, his chest felt like it was on fire and he could hardly draw breath. He came to a stop about fifteen feet behind Anna, almost collapsing on the spot. He tried to speak, 'where..are…you…going?'

Anna turned, the look of surprise on her face was quickly replaced by a noncommittal stare. 'Home. Why?'

Ed had caught his breath by now, 'I thought you were coming for a walk.'

'Well,' she replied, her lower jaw jutting out slightly, 'I changed my mind.' Her face softened a little, 'seeing as I'm not wanted round here. I may as well not exist.'

Ed gawped at her, 'what do you mean? I don't understand. You're the one who hasn't been talking.' He was getting annoyed now. She'd been really rude all afternoon and now she was turning it around on him.

To his utter amazement, Anna began to cry, tears streamed down her face as she tried to turn away from him. He lunged forward in an attempt to grab her arm to stop her, but his legs were still so weak that all he did was manage to pull them both over. They both landed in a bush tangled up in a heap. Ed got up quickly and put out his hand to help the girl up.

However, she had stopped crying and was glaring up at him furiously.

'*That* is the closest I have ever got to you and that was only 'cos you fell. Two seconds of accidental body contact hardly constitutes a passionate snog now does it?' She had raised her voice even more now to try to drown out the sound of the waves and the cries of the seabirds. Ed was so surprised that he let his arm drop down by his side. He left her sitting on the ground, bits of bush and twigs dangling in her hair.

'Oh, just great, now I have to pick myself up, obviously you've had quite enough of me already!'

'What *are* you going on about?' he was becoming more confused by the minute.

'You, you idiot. I'm sick of hanging around like a loose end in the pathetic hope that you notice me. You never speak to me or even look at me. I've had enough!' her voice was getting louder know, even the seagulls had given up competing with her. 'Ed, cool flipping Ed from *London*,' she said derisively. Ed just stared at her, his mouth hung open. He felt like his whole body had gone somewhere else and he was just a large, gaping hole hanging in mid air.

But she hadn't finished... oh no, she was on a roll and her face became redder and redder as she continued on. Ed noticed nervously that she managed to do this seemingly without even breathing.

'Ed,' she almost spat out the word, 'Mr I–live–in–a–big–house–on–my–own.'

She scrambled up, the leaves and sticks falling off of her as she tried to regain her balance. Her hair became even spikier as she ran her hands through it distractedly.

'Well, I might just be from Guernsey and I might live with my parents, but so bloody what. What's so wrong with that, you pompous git?' she challenged. Ed couldn't even begin to think of a reply. Although, if he was honest with himself, he did think that he actually preferred the crying to the shouting, it was less scary.

Anna turned and walked off, striding up the cliff path like a major general. Ed, gobsmacked, just watched her go. It was one thing to try to talk to her, but he was not, was definitely not, going after her. She'd eat him alive. He thought he might actually be in shock, he couldn't feel his legs at all, (unless that was just the exercise). But what was she going on about? He tried to recall everything she'd said, well, yelled more like. Did that mean she liked him or that she hated him? It sounded about 50/50, but she couldn't like him and hate him at the same time...surely? He shook his head, brushed the dirt off his trousers and turned to catch up with Sparrow and Martin.

'How'd it go?' asked Martin, a little cautiously Ed thought. He didn't reply and so his friend went on, 'you know Anna's not like you think she is. I know she's my mate an' all, but I think it's only fair to warn you that she's got quite a temper and boy can she shout!'

Ed just stared at Martin and nodded mutely. Not knowing what to say was becoming something of a habit, he thought hazily. As they walked home, he was in a daze. His head felt like a fairground, spinning, whizzing with coloured bulbs popping and fizzling. Strange shapes lurched around his head like drunken visitors colliding as he tried to form some kind of understanding, as he tried to work out what had just happened.

That night in bed, he tried again to sort it out in his mind. At times, he decided she liked him, only to then remember the names she'd called him. Then he decided that, yes, she definitely hated him. Then he'd think that maybe she had liked him before and now hated him. Or maybe it was the other way round? Just as he dropped off to sleep, he concluded that she must hate him to shout at him like that.

He woke up the next morning with a banging headache. He didn't think he could put all the blame on the beer.

Albotain knew something was wrong as soon as Ed came into the kitchen. His t–shirt was on inside out for a start and he still had his toothbrush in his hand. However, he wisely decided not to say anything – from Ed's facial expression he could see that the lad wasn't exactly in the mood for conversation. Albotain put down a plate of eggs and bacon in front of Ed, who stared through it like it wasn't there. Eventually he picked up his fork and began slowly picking at his food. They ate breakfast in silence, Ed looking more and more morose as time went by. Tactfully, Albotain said that he had some unfinished work in the attic. Apparently, Lance's work wasn't quite as diabolical as he had feared and he wanted to have a better look at some of his notes. Ed just grunted and played with his breakfast, (which by now looked like pulverised mush). Albotain sighed and made his way upstairs. Lionel followed him, looking more than a little bit lost. His beloved master had ignored him all morning and he wasn't about to stick around where he wasn't wanted. Ed watched the two of them go. It was ridiculous, he admitted to himself, but he felt left out and more than a little bit rejected. Even the dog couldn't be bothered with him, he grumbled to himself.

As the days went by Ed reconciled himself to the fact that he would never have a relationship. Nope, no girlfriend, nothing. They were far too complicated; he had no idea what Anna was about and he really didn't care. He decided that for now he would stick to his books and packing up the boxes. It was so much easier with him and Albotain, no complications, (other than the fact that the man was an eight hundred year old astrologer who had pretended to be a gardener, but that was kind of by the by). Between them there were no hidden agendas, no shouting, all nice, calm and peaceful. Yes, that's what he wanted...peace and quiet. His relationship with his mother should have forewarned him, women were absolutely impossible, selfish, aggressive and nasty. He almost convinced himself...almost. He knew he hadn't quite talked himself round though because he still felt depressed. Also, he often found himself staring at his own reflection in the bathroom mirror, as if looking for a clue, a reason why he wasn't quite good enough, not up to scratch in some way. Despite Albotain's attempts to cheer him up, he just couldn't lift himself out of the doldrums.

Albotain continued to try hard to brighten Ed up and this included him serving up a full medieval feast, complete with snails in pastry shells. He couldn't find proper leeches he explained, as he happily tucked in to what looked like a plateful of warmed up mucus. After tentatively tasting them, Ed decided that molluscs weren't going to be an addition to his staple diet. It took him days to get the bits of shell out of his teeth.

The weeks went by and the summer decided not to bother arriving. The clouds hung grey and heavy and the wind brought in a cold mist from the sea. The weather was at least compatible with Ed's mood. He too was grey and felt chilled inside, like a fire had gone out. He did his daily tasks, packed up the boxes, tidied the garden and worked with Albotain, but deep down he felt empty and hollow. The old Ed, the no hoper, the pessimist, had woken up once again and was whinging feebly in his ear. He didn't like this Ed. He wanted the other one back, the one with a spine and a sense of humour.

One night Ed and Albotain sat talking. Ed tried to explain to Albotain about how he felt. He knew he was depressed, but he just couldn't seem to reason himself out of it.

'You know Ed, depressed feelings can bring benefits.'

'What do you mean? I can't imagine how feeling like this could possibly be helpful in any way, shape or form.'

'Well, sometimes if you just accept that you feel down, then you can experience a new level of being. Part of the problem with depression comes from the fear of the feelings you're experiencing. Be kinder to yourself, be loving, not harsh or derogatory. You wouldn't kick someone with a bad leg, so why be cruel to yourself when you're feeling down?'

Ed reluctantly agreed that his friend was talking sense. Albotain continued, 'just let go of the fear and you'll be amazed at how much more quickly you'd recover. Believe me, I've had plenty of experience of this kind of state. Over the years I have come to think of melancholy or depression as a kind of 'pearl diving'. Let yourself sink down through the pool of emotions. This pool is a safe place, after all its part of you. Allow yourself to float gently to the bottom of your mind or heart and you may be surprised at what you find. Often lying quietly, just waiting for us, is the answer to our problems – a new perspective or philosophical understanding. These are the pearls that can help us recover. They are what help us find the strength to rise to the surface – to feel the warm sunshine once again.'

Ed thought about what Albotain had said for a while. Over the following weeks he followed his friend's advice. He visualised moving down through a calm, dark pool and allowed himself to sit quietly on the bottom. After a few sessions, he found that he began to feel a little better. He would often emerge from the pool of his emotions holding some truth, some ideal that led to a better understanding of himself and of his current feelings. As he grew stronger, he began to experience glimpses of sunlight. He began to realise that he was stronger than he realised.

He saw Martin and Sparrow a few times, but there was no sign of Anna. No one mentioned her, Ed didn't ask and the two boys seemed to be studiously avoiding the subject of the cliff path incident. After a few meetings with his two friends, Ed decided that he would have to get over it, pull himself together. After all, his life was so much better than it was, why should he let a girl ruin it all for him?

A couple of days later he left the house and took Lionel on a long walk. The bad weather had lifted, the fog had cleared and the sun was shining as he took the path into the woods. The birds were singing and the air smelled fresh and green. He and Lionel took a long, circular walk that lasted about and hour or so. Ed had begun to feel better lately, not so down. The meditation, or 'pearl diving' technique, had really helped him. He had even begun to study new areas of astrology with Albotain.   He was slowly but surely getting better at interpreting the masses of handwritten symbols that the man presented to him.

He made his way back to the house through the leafy lanes, the sun glinting through the branches of the trees. Lionel, however, was not at all keen on returning home and began to drag behind, stiffening his legs in an attempt to halt Ed's progress.
'Come on boy,' smiled Ed, as he pulled harder on the leash. Lionel eventually gave in and begrudgingly walked alongside Ed with his head hanging down sulkily.

'Sorry mate, but I have to get back and carry on working. It's alright for you, all you've got to do is crash in your basket and sleep.'

Lionel looked up mournfully, as if to let Ed know that he had no idea how hard it was to be a dog. Ed patted him in response and they made their way down the drive together.

They were almost at the front door and Ed stopped suddenly. Leaning against the wall was a battered black pushbike. He inhaled quickly, he had no idea whose it was, but whoever it was, they were certainly not welcome. Albotain was alone inside. Due to the distinct lack of presence regarding the owner of the bike, Ed could only assume that they were also in the house. He started to feel panicky, if anyone saw the old man then there could be real trouble. Perhaps if he could find the intruder quickly then he could get them out of Albotain's way – if it wasn't too late already.

He decided not to go in the front door, just in case Albotain hadn't realised that there was someone in the house and came to greet him. He didn't want to alert the unwelcome visitor. He crept around the rear of the house and went through the back door. Lionel tagged behind looking decidedly unenthusiastic. Ed carefully turned the handle.

Slowly, he crept past Gideon, who just turned his back on him as usual, blatant disregard shimmering off of every feather. Ed went through the kitchen and the smell of coffee assailed his nostrils. Puzzled, he moved into the second part of the L–shaped room.

As he turned the corner, there at the table drinking a cup of coffee was *Anna*. What's more, sitting opposite her for all the world looking like he was a normal, everyday person was Albotain. They looked up, surprised to see Ed peering around the corner towards them. Anna did have the grace at least to look a little embarrassed. She squirmed uncomfortably, twiddling with her silver necklace.

Albotain, however, just grinned, 'hello Ed, what are you doing sneaking in the back way, forgot your key did you?' He winked at Anna who just stared at Ed like he was a reptile–man from another planet. Ed didn't answer. His stomach had turned into a cement mixer and his head was suddenly completely empty. He wasn't sure which was worse, the fact that Anna was with Albotain, or that it was Anna. Personally, he couldn't have thought of a worse scenario if he'd tried.

'I..err,' was all he could manage in the way of an answer.

'What's happened, parrot got your tongue?' Albotain began to chuckle so enthusiastically at his own joke that he had to put his coffee cup down before he spilt it all over himself.

Once he had got that little quip out of his system and recovered his composure, the old man glanced at Anna and then at Ed. Getting up he said brusquely, 'right, ok, I'll leave you two to it. I have lots to be getting on with and I can't sit here all day. He gathered up a couple of old, unrecognisable books that were lying on the table and left the kitchen, leaving Ed and Anna alone. Thanks a bunch, thought Ed, he's just basically scarpered and now what do I do?

Chapter XX

There was silence in the kitchen. Not the peaceful, gentle kind that you can fall asleep to though. No, this was the thick, treacly stuff that seemed to stick in your lungs and glue your belly to your back. This kind of silence lets you know without doubt that things are, well, awkward to say the least.

Ed stared past Anna at the kitchen door as if it were an escape hatch in a rapidly descending plane. Anna seemed to be transfixed by her necklace, squinting at the tiny silver star like she'd never seen it before. The seconds ticked by, the silence broken only by the occasional whine from Lionel. After a while, the old dog gave up and left Ed's side. He trotted through the kitchen and plonked himself in his wicker basket by the back door with a long sigh. Obviously, he wasn't going anywhere else today.

Ed tried to pull himself together, he leaned against the kitchen unit, arms folded.

'So, you ok then?' that was about the extent of his vocabulary at this point in time.

'Yeah, I'm fine…you?'

'Good, thanks.' He was starting to feel annoyed now. He wished she'd just tell him what she wanted and then bog off and leave him alone. Funnily enough, he wasn't in the mood for another barrage of insults.

'Your granddad's nice – Bert isn't it?'

Oh, flipping hec, what had Albotain told her? Ed put his hand up to his face and tried to think quickly. This wasn't easy, as his brain had completely frozen and it felt like it

215

needed a reboot. He decided that going along with whatever she said was the only option for the moment at least.

'Yes, kind of,' was his feeble reply.

'Is he staying for long?'

'What? Oh yes, he's helping me with packing up the house.'

'Strange you never mentioned him before. He reminds me of my granddad, he died ages ago, about five years ago, I think.'

That's nothing, thought Ed, *this one died nearly eight centuries ago.* However, he replied as casually as he could, 'Well, he only arrived a few weeks ago and I haven't seen you to tell you.' *Phew, that was pretty quick.* He breathed a sigh of relief.

'I know I haven't been around, sorry.'

'Doesn't matter to me. You obviously had more important things to do.' He couldn't quite stop himself sounding just a little resentful on that last part, a teensy weensy bit ticked off. He just couldn't help it.

'No, well, I mean yes, I have been busy, lots of shifts at the Bistro. But,' she looked down, 'I figured that you wouldn't want to see me anyway.' At this, tears welled up in her eyes and she looked as though she was about to start crying.

Oh no, last time she started off crying, I got it in the neck shortly afterwards. Ed wanted to leave, to run, to turn away so, so badly. But he didn't. Instead, he found himself handing her a bit of clean kitchen roll and sitting down opposite her.

'Don't worry I'm not going to shout at you,' came a muffled voice behind the tissue.

'Well, that's a relief,' Ed relaxed slightly, (not too much though, you just never know with girls). 'What's up then?'

Anna blew her nose, (in a very unlady–like manner, Ed noted), and then stuffed the hankie up her jumper sleeve.

'I'm an idiot that's what. I get worked up and shout and lose my temper and muck everything up. I've always done it. My mum and dad used to lock me in the car when I was little I was so bad. I had tantrums that would go on for hours. It nearly drove my mum insane. That's probably why they don't really like me now. I'm just too much trouble.'

Ed tried to digest all of this, 'but you always sound so happy. I don't understand, you've got everything.'

'Happy? Happy? I've never been happy!!' her voice raising. Ed slid his chair back a fraction ready to bolt. She continued on, the words spilling faster and faster.

'Everything? Huh! I'm nearly twenty years old, I live in a bunker in my parent's garden for God's Sake. I've travelled a bit, but always with a credit card and a pre–booked itinerary, not exactly roughing it. I've always lived in Guernsey. I hate cities because they scare me. I'm too afraid to leave and go to Art College so I keep putting it off. My parents are too busy being successful and having stupid dinner parties to even notice me.'

Ed was stunned by all of this, 'but I'm sure they love you.' He cringed inwardly at his own ineptitude.

'Yeah, right. They never even wanted kids, I was an accident. They avoid me most of the time. They never set any rules when I was little because they thought that free–thinking was what mattered. If I misbehaved, they would just walk away from me, tell me to sit in my room and think about what I'd done and make up my own punishment. I pretend I'm alright to everyone because that's what I do at home. I've tried to talk to my mum, but she just books me a Reiki session or buys me yet another stupid flipping fake healing crystal from the internet.'

Tears were running down her face now and her shoulders shook. Her voice trembled as she said, 'and now, because of my stupid temper, I don't even have you as a friend.'

Ed sat in stunned silence. He breathed in and out a few times slowly, trying to get a grasp of what she was saying. *Why did girls have to use a hundred words when ten would probably do the job?* he wondered.

Something was creeping back into him though. It had been there before but had left shortly after the cliff path incident. It was a little furry creature, all soft and doey–eyed. It was crawling sneakily back into his chest, nestling snugly in his heart and purring happily. He knew what it was. It was called Romantic Hopefulness. Ed thought seriously for a moment about turfing it out on its cute little ear. Trouble was it was nice, comforting and sweet. It made him feel happy and sick inside all at the same time, like too much ice cream. His head felt fuzzy. Then, something came up from inside him, a strange sense of not being quite in control, of being overwhelmed by a force bigger than him.

'I am your friend. I'm actually more than your friend, if that's ok. I mean I want to be more than your friend...I mean if that's what you want.'

What just happened? I just blurted out everything. What an idiot. RH was quite at home now, stretched out comfortably and snoring sweetly.

There was silence once again. This time though it wasn't the treacle silence, it was like the space between church bell chimes at Christmas, a silence that was filled with excitement and promise. Anna stared at him. Ed stared back. Anna smiled, (a beautiful smile that could light up the whole world he thought). Ed smiled again, unsure but actually pretty hopeful. So far, she hadn't even called him a horrible name.

'Are you asking me out? ' the smile disappeared and was replaced by a worried look. She stopped and thought for a moment, 'why? Do you feel sorry for me?'

Ed gasped in amazement and let out a short laugh, 'sorry for you? No. No definitely not. Actually the only reason I think you would ever, in a million years, go out with me is because you feel sorry for *me*!'

Anna laughed, 'why would I ever feel sorry for you?'

Ed replied, 'because I'm a loser. I've never done anything, never achieved anything. My mum doesn't even like me and I don't even know where my dad is.' He stopped to draw breath.

'You have everything! You're cool, good–looking and you've lived in London. You're so independent; anyone can see that you don't need people. You have this air of aloofness, like you know something that no one else does. As for people not loving you, well you have your granddad. He loves you a lot, I can tell by the way he talks about you.'

'Listen,' Ed interrupted her, 'about him, my granddad, it's not that simple and I have to talk to you.' He paused, 'but not now – later on.' He had no idea what he was going to say, no idea at all. He knew that he needed to stall for time right now.

'Oh, ok.' She sat for a second and then said, 'anyway, you're not a loser at all. But we do seem to have quite a lot in common.' She stopped again, 'so,' she swallowed hard, 'will you go out with me?'

'What about that other bloke, the mechanic?'

'Who? Oh.' She blushed, 'I told Martin that because I knew that he'd tell you. Pathetic I know, but I just wanted to know if you liked me. Sorry.' She smiled sheepishly.

Ed was so relieved that he just laughed in response.

'So, do you want to go out with me?' she asked again.

'God, yes.' said Ed, 'yes. Definitely, yes.'

'Was that a 'yes' then?' laughed Anna.

'Oh yes,' was all Ed could say again. RH snuggled deeper into the soft recesses of Ed's heart, dreaming of pink flowers and little fluffy white clouds.

Albotain came down a little later on. He carefully opened the kitchen door to see the two of them holding hands across the table, talking and laughing softly. He quietly closed the door and went upstairs. He smiled as he climbed the stairs, his heart bursting with love and pride for his boy. He looked up at the ceiling thankfully. It was all going to plan – at last. As he reached the top of the stairs, he frowned and brushed the side of his face, as if he were sweeping away a dark shadow.

The next morning Albotain busied himself in the kitchen. The house was quiet, too quiet and he wondered where Ed was. About ten minutes later the boy came into the kitchen. He was beaming from ear to ear as he made a cup of tea for the two of them. Then, he sat down at the table smiling and humming quietly to himself. Albotain noticed that he was looking out of the kitchen window as if he was in a trance. If he hadn't been so sure that this was girl–related, the old man would have sworn that Ed had lost his mind. As they sat at the table together, the man thought he heard the front door close with a soft click and possibly the sound of a bike going across cobbles.

'So,' Albotain said eventually, 'how are you this fine morning?'

Ed's grin was so wide that it looked like his jaw would drop off.

'Fine. Great.' He paused for effect, his impossible grin widening even further, 'I'm going out with Anna.'

'Oh, that's wonderful Ed, I'm very happy for you,' replied Albotain trying his very best to look surprised.

Ed's smile lessened a little and a small frown appeared, 'the only thing that's worrying me is that she's met you and well, you've met her....'

Albotain looked unimpressed at this last statement, 'yes, very observant Ed.'

'Why did you let her in? You could have just ignored the door.'

'Yes I could have done, but I knew that you would want to see her.'

'But,' Ed was starting to look exasperated now. He put his tea down, lifted his hands, palms upwards, arms outstretched to the side, 'you're not supposed to be seen by *anyone.* What about mucking up fate and messing up destiny and all that? I mean this could be serious, couldn't it?'

'Very succinctly put but, yes, I see what you mean.' The old man looked thoughtful, but still not unduly concerned. To Ed's surprise Albotain still didn't seem to be catching on, either that or he was being deliberately obtuse.

Eventually Albotain spoke, 'well, Ed. The only answer I can give you is that sometimes there is a plan within a plan and in that case, things we think shouldn't happen are actually ok.'

Ed looked confused, 'what do you mean?'

'Perhaps you are meant to be with Anna and it's not important that she's met me because she is already following her destiny.'

'Oh, ok, now I'm getting really muddled up,' complained Ed.

'If what is happening between you and her is destined, then if I'm a part of it, it won't alter anything. I'm incidental.'

'How do you know its destiny and not some fluke, yet another cosmic mistake like Ariadne and Hector's death?'

'Because the planets in your birth chart are telling me so, that's why. There is presently a lovely sextile aspect from

Saturn to Venus influencing your chart. This has to signify
your relationship with Anna. So it is obviously fated and I,
my boy, am in the clear!'

Ed thought about this for a little while and then the smile
reappeared, 'so nothing bad will happen from you two
meeting? Even better, Anna and I are meant to be together?'

It was Albotain's turn to smile now, 'yes, all is in order.
The weave of this event is too strong for my presence to
disrupt. Now relax and just enjoy being in love. She and I
can be friends. As long as no one else gets involved it will do
no harm.'

'That's good, that's really good. The three of us can be
friends. That's brilliant.' He stopped, 'I suppose we have to
keep the granddad story going? That makes me a bit
uncomfortable, but I guess we have no choice?'

'I know that it's difficult for you Ed, but telling Anna really
would start to complicate matters. We don't have to lie, we
just have to not say anything about my background.'

Ed sighed, 'I hate all of this dishonesty, but I do
understand. I can't see her accepting the truth anyway
somehow.' He grinned suddenly, 'hey, if you're my
granddad, does that mean I get pocket money?'

'No, it doesn't. I'm your *penniless* granddad, remember.'

The weeks passed and Ed and Anna grew closer and closer.
Romantic Hopefulness had grown, he had metamorphosed
into something else. He was a more mature, defined creature.
He had become stronger and more solid nestling in Ed's heart,
thriving in the fertile soil of the boy's love for his girlfriend.
This creature had now become True Love. TL liked his new
grown–up identity and so decided that he would stay forever.
Ed still studied with Albotain, but the two of them waited
until Anna was not around. Neither of them discussed telling
her the truth. It was their guilty secret.

Love had transformed Ed's world. He knew though that it was love for all things that mattered. It was his love for Albotain, for Anna, for the trees and plants and the ever–changing sea, for the majestic cliffs, even for old Lionel. It was all forms of love and it made him very happy. He felt free and whole and yet part of everything around him. This was a new Ed.

Ed and Anna spent most of their free time together. During the long summer days they explored Guernsey, often with Lionel tagging along behind them faithfully. Anna was proud of the island, her beautiful home. She loved to have the opportunity to be able to show her beloved Ed her favourite haunts. First, they visited the numerous Neolithic graves that were dotted around the island. She informed Ed that some of the sites were more than seven thousand years old. Ed was fascinated by the 'La Varde Dolmen', the largest above ground burial site on Guernsey, situated on the wild and unspoilt L'Ancresse common.

He was curious though as to why so many of the names of places were French. He was told by Anna that they were a reminder of the fact that Guernsey had once belonged to France. They spent nearly a whole day at Le Creux es Feies, known locally as the fairy grotto. In the past, the locals had believed that this tomb was the entrance to fairyland.

To Ed the ancient structure seemed to hum with energy. Having worked hard with Albotain to develop his psychic powers, he was still surprised to be able to see ghostly figures at the entrance. One such apparition, a bearded man dressed in a dark orange robe, seemed to be guarding the narrow entrance to the large stone tomb. He was obviously from a time long ago. He greeted Ed with a smile and showed him how the land had been thousands of years ago. Visions of a primitive encampment flooded Ed's mind. People milled everywhere dressed in simple robes, some holding spears, others carrying baskets of fruit and vegetables. Some people were working, making tools or pots and others were building fires. Low, round structures made of wood littered the land as far as he could see. He couldn't believe that it was so clear, so real to him. He was almost sad as the vision slowly faded to be replaced by reality once again. However, the view that greeted him was just as stunning. The lush, rolling landscape leading down to the blue, blue sea which stretched as far as the eye could see. Anna was, of course, oblivious to what Ed had seen and he felt a little disappointed that he couldn't share his wonderful experience with her.

They sat on the headland holding hands, Lionel sitting at Ed's feet, looking over to the tiny island of Lihou. Anna told Ed that the nature reserve had previously been inhabited by an order of monks and also by seaweed eating sheep. Ed was confused at first as he thought she meant that the poor sheep were devoured by seaweed, like some kind of oceanic triffid. Anna explained that it was the sheep that ate the seaweed, not the other way around.

Afterwards they walked around the coast to the Le Trepid near to Le Catioroc. Ed was transfixed as Anna told him that Victor Hugo, the famous writer, had claimed that this was haunted by the cries of dead women waiting for the devil, whom they considered to be their lover. It was quite a disturbing thought; visions of deranged women floated around Ed's mind. But he didn't mind, he loved to hear Anna talk. He loved everything about her.

Chapter XXI

A few weeks after they had begun their relationship the couple decided to visit the gorgeous stately home, Sausmarez Manor in the parish of St Martins. The gentleman that owned this wonderful old house was a Peter de Sausmarez. He was an elegant and articulate character with more than a touch of the eccentric aristocrat about him. Anna had called the house earlier and had organised for her and Ed to take part in one of the famous Sausmarez Manor Ghost Tours.

As they walked up the tree–lined driveway towards the stunning granite house which was nestled amongst the trees, the windows glinted at them as if acknowledging their presence. Ed felt as though it seemed to somehow know that they were coming. He felt as though they were being watched. The evening sun was sinking beneath the trees, its final rays casting an ochre glow on the path before them. In the dimming light, Ed was sure that he could see figures at the windows. He assumed the tour had already begun.

However, when they arrived, the tour had not only not begun, but Anna had arranged a private viewing for Ed as a special treat. Ed was perplexed, who were the figures at the windows? His question was answered shortly after he walked into the beautifully ornate Tudor style entrance hallway. Peter led them almost immediately up the dark, carved stairway and they entered a small room at the top. As they did so, strange phantom–like shapes gathered around Ed, whispering to him quietly. He had expected some spiritual activity, but there were so many of them. At first it was quite overwhelming and he instinctively drew back. This was much to the surprise of Anna, who had no idea what was happening to him. He told her that he had mistakenly thought that he'd left the door behind him open.

He gathered himself together and began to communicate with the spirits silently through the power of thought. One, the spirit of a lovely old lady, told Ed that she was so happy that she could communicate with someone in the Living World at last. She told him that all of the spirits in the house had known that he was coming before he even arrived, that his highly evolved vibrations had permeated the air like a psychic call. They had all been waiting for him, she said. Ed realised that that was who he had seen at the windows earlier.

Anna and Peter wandered into the next room, chatting amicably. Anna had known the man for years and was very fond of him. Ed was sure that they would be talking for a while. He moved quietly into a corner of the room so that he wouldn't be seen.

The lady explained to Ed that when she had been alive, she had been a children's nanny for the family that lived in the house. They had had many children and she had devoted her life to looking after them. She knew that this was not a natural state, but she did not wish to move on to the Other Side. She was happy to stay where she was. She loved the people that lived in the house now and saw it as her duty to protect them. She also took care of all the many other spirits that chose to stay on in the house. However, she had been waiting years to be able to talk to someone like him. She needed his help to move an earthbound spirit onto the Other Side.

She informed Ed that she could not move this spirit on herself. She needed the strong presence of a medium from the Living World to provide the energy for this process. She moved aside then and Ed could see the figure of a small boy in front of him. He looked no more than ten years old. The nanny explained that when she had been alive she had cared for the child as a baby. She was very fond of him and when she passed away, she stayed with the family and continued talking care of him and the other children. As a spirit, she watched him grow and had protected him as much as she could. When the little boy became ill and died, it was only natural that he came to her. The two of them had been together for a long time and they had indeed been very happy. The nanny realised though that the boy could not develop further as an earthbound spirit. The lady was actually very knowledgeable and seemed to be quite a highly developed soul. She told Ed that she knew that when a spirit is trapped on the earth plane, that it is stuck in time. The deceased are often aware that they have passed on. However, they become stuck in a habitual response to their physical environment. Consequently, they are firmly attached to their past life for better or for worse and it can be difficult to move them on.

The old lady knew that the boy needed to move to the Other Side. Once there, he could be reunited with his now deceased family members, his parents and siblings. There, she explained, he would be able to grow and develop in the spirit world more or less as he would have done in the physical world.

Ed wasn't quite sure what to say, but the little boy spoke first, 'can you take me to my mother? Nanny says you can.'
'I can try. What's your name?'

'I'm Thomas Edward. I'm scared though. What will you do?'

Ed thought back to what Albotain had taught him. He knew it was the power of thought, of consciousness, that allowed spirits to move onto the Other Side, to Heaven, or whatever you called it. He, Ed, just had to visualise a stairway and it would be there. However, first he had to reassure the child that all would be well.

'Your parents will know that you're coming and they will be waiting for you. I'll show you a staircase, a bit like the one here. You just have to go up it to the top.'

The little boy looked doubtful, 'what if they're not there. Can I come back down again?'

'Of course you can. But you'll be fine I promise.'

The little boy stood at the bottom of the stairs. He looked quite lost and was holding the lady's hand tightly. They both looked very sad. Ed felt for them both. The nanny's love for Thomas shone from her though as she looked down at him fondly. 'Go Thomas, go on now. It's time.'

Thomas let go of the woman's hand reluctantly and begun to climb the staircase. It did indeed look like the one in the Manor, except that it shone with a golden, translucent light. At the top it faded away into a beautiful silver mist. As Thomas reached the end of the visible stairway, a hand reached out to him and a pale, delicate arm swathed in chiffon emerged from the haze. A soft voice said, 'Oh Tommy, my Tommy. Its Mother darling. I've missed you so much. Come on, we're all waiting for you.' Thomas took one look back at them. He smiled, his face shining with happiness and the scene faded away.

Ed opened his eyes and returned to the room with a start. He hoped that no one had seen him standing in the corner apparently sleeping on his feet! There didn't seem to be anyone around luckily, well anyone living anyway. He hurried to catch up with Anna and Peter de Sausmarez who had moved downstairs again. As he went to leave, the nanny put a gentle hand on his arm and with tears in her eyes thanked him for his help. The other spirits withdrew respectfully and allowed Ed to move forward.

'Where have you been?' queried Anna as he rounded the corner in the hallway.

'Just looking around. It's an amazing place isn't it?'

Anna seemed content with his explanation and they continued on with the tour. Ed enjoyed the ensuing spirits' activities immensely. He noted that they played their part perfectly, opening doors, clanking pipes and generally making their presence known. They would smile and wink at Ed as they did so, obviously enjoying their job. Anna was half laughing and half hysterical by the time they got to the end. She admitted though that she really enjoyed it. Whilst she believed in ghosts, she hadn't quite experienced anything like that before.

Late in the day, Ed and Anna would often be found sitting outside in the evening sunshine, with Ed reading and Anna sketching the scenery. They were inseparable and, (to the absolute disgust of Martin and Sparrow), the two were obviously in love. The two boys really couldn't come to terms with this new arrangement, Ed and Anna being so enamoured with one another. So, they resorted to calling them names like 'soppy gits' and 'love–birds,' together with much rolling of the eyes and dramatic sighing. Secretly, Ed thought they might be a bit envious, but he also tried to make sure that they didn't feel as though they'd lost either himself or Anna as friends. The problem was really that neither Martin nor Sparrow had ever really had a girlfriend. This was not for want of trying though, particularly on Martin's part. He could often be found in the 'Tartan Bar', begging some poor, unsuspecting girl to let him buy her a drink. For the first time in his life, Ed felt quite mature and sophisticated.

Albotain and Anna got on like a house on fire though. Anna seemed to have adopted the old man and was forever bringing him little gifts, like homemade jam from the market, or she would pick up some eggs from the farm near her own home on the way to the house. Her old black pushbike was often found leaning up against the wall by the front door. That was until Albotain made a bike rack for her out of bits of granite, complete with a cover made of an old tarpaulin. Ed would come in from walking Lionel to find them at the kitchen table, drinking mugs of tea. They would often be eating cake Anna had brought with her, like two naughty children. Ed could have been a bit jealous, but the truth was that he was so happy that his two best friends got on so well, there was just no room for him to feel left out. He would play up though, pretending to be hurt that they'd finished the last of the cake, or petulantly accusing them of ignoring him. They would just laugh and Anna would get up and hug and kiss him, reassuring him that she still loved him. Ed lapped up the exaggerated show of affection and revelled in her phoney apologies. Albotain smiled gently as he watched his two favourite people teasing one another and laughing.

There was something wrong though. Albotain knew it. Ever since Ed and Anna had become close, the shadows and dark shapes in his room at nighttime had become stronger, more powerful. It was as if his previous, exclusive relationship with Ed had protected him. Now that the young man was besotted with Anna, Albotain seemed to be more vulnerable. The old man did not, could not, begrudge his friend's happiness, no matter how it affected him, but he knew he was in trouble. Deep down Albotain knew why the Darkness was coming closer and if he was honest with himself, he had half expected it. He had hoped though that the three of them could just continue as they were, but knew in his heart though that this was not possible. He knew it was going to get worse. And it did.

He realised that the aim of these dark beings was to finish what they'd started hundreds of years ago. They wanted him. He was familiar to them and they had quickly known where to find him once he had physically incarnated again. They had left him alone whilst he was in spirit form. He was powerful then and under the direct protection of the Higher Council. But they sensed that he was weak and was so much more vulnerable than before, now he had returned to live as a man.

This time though it was much more than personal. Oh yes, this time they were after more than just the soul of one paltry human being. This time it was more than just wishing to plague Albotain, to weaken and influence him to turn back towards the Darkness. He knew from their whisperings that their plan was to stop the Talisman going to Ed. Albotain also sensed that somehow the change in Ed's life threatened them. They wanted to make sure that the work Albotain had done to destroy the destiny of the world continued to disrupt everything. They had thrived on the spiritual carnage and mayhem that had ensued since Albotain had betrayed the Light. The Darkness had held so much power since Daniel, the Sapphire Soul, had lost his way and they weren't about to give this up without a fight.

At nighttime these grim beings seemed to crawl into his skull and pick at his brain. They feasted upon his thoughts and devoured his increasingly sickly spirit. What he knew, they knew, he was sure of that and this gave them even more power over him. He tried to block them out, to stop them, but each time there seemed to be more and more. These were his old friends, creatures of the lowest planes, from the Mud Slopes of Hell and the Dark Pits of Depravity. In the castle they had formed an attachment to him, binding to the very fibres of his soul. Now, during the night, they crawled across him on their bellies. Deformed jaws and hideously elongated limbs brushed his skin, their fetid breathe upon his face making him feel nauseous and disorientated. They whispered and hissed in his ear. They cajoled him and promised him eternal life, wealth and power if he came back to them. They threatened him with torturous punishments that made him shudder. Sometimes he fought them. Sometimes he sobbed quietly with fear, ashamed of his weakness.

Anna and Ed were of course oblivious to all of this, the haze of love colouring their days rose pink and clouding their vision. They saw only each other, the rest of the world was just a comfortable blur. Albotain was an extension of this rosy love–tinged world and so to them he was also happy and contented, what other state could there possibly be? If Albotain seemed a little distant, they put this down to him understanding that they needed time on their own. He would often wander off with a pile of books under his arm. Anna assumed that he read in one of the spare bedrooms upstairs. It never occurred to either of them that he was suffering in any way.

However, as time went by it was Ed who was the only one out of the three of them that was completely oblivious as to what was happening. This was because in order to protect the boy, Albotain had deliberately blocked Ed from connecting with him on a psychic level. So Ed was totally unaware of what was happening to the old man.

However, Albotain vastly underestimated Anna's perceptiveness and after a while the young girl became aware that something wasn't quite right. As she cycled home one morning after spending the night with Ed, her mind began to wander into places that she had been trying very hard to avoid. These past few months she had never been happier and she didn't want anything to change. However, recently she'd begun to wonder what was actually going on. Ed had asked her not to tell anyone about Bert. He told her that he was a very private man who couldn't cope with too many people around. He made her promise not to divulge Bert's existence to anyone. He told her it was nothing to worry about, but that it was very important. Of course, she would have agreed to anything for Ed. Only, there were some things that didn't quite make sense. For a start, Bert never talked about himself. It was one thing being a private person, but what bothered her was that he never even mentioned any other family, where he came from, his past or indeed his future. She had asked him, but he'd always managed to avoid answering her. She'd toyed with Bert being a runaway, a prisoner, a mental patient or perhaps a witness to some heinous crime. None of her ideas fitted though.

There were also the dreams, strange, hazy imaginings that came to her at night when she was half–asleep. In each one she was sitting with Albotain at a table in a small room she didn't recognise. The table was strewn with papers and books. What was clear though was the fact that in these visions the old man looked terrible. He was painfully thin, withered and frail, his skin and eyes were yellow. He would be begging her to do something, but she couldn't quite hear him. There was a gushing, roaring noise that drowned out the sound of his voice, like he was behind a waterfall. Whenever she awoke she felt uneasy, as if there was something in her room with her, something nasty.

Also, another thing was bugging her. A few weeks before this she had decided to sketch Albotain. She had had to do it from memory, as he hadn't seemed keen on the idea of sitting for her. She thought she'd surprise him with a framed portrait as a thank you for the bike shelter. The odd thing was that she had had to redo the drawing at least five times now. This couldn't be connected to the dreams she was sure, but it was still very odd. First of all she couldn't find her paper, then she broke all of her pencils. She brought some more to the house and began to sketch outside in the garden, but a sudden heavy downpour had ruined her work. The second time she sat in the kitchen, she left the half–finished piece on the table and Gideon had stolen it. The soggy, tattered bits of paper that she rescued from the bird were not even recognisable as a portrait. The next time she managed to finish one at home in her own bedroom, only to have the wind tear it out of her hand as she took it out of the basket on the front of her bike at the house. She never even saw that one again. The remaining two times they had just disappeared. Both times she recalled putting the unfinished work in her artwork folder, only to find that it simply wasn't there when she went back to it. She had almost given up by now, but was still nevertheless very puzzled as to why this had happened.

As she rode along, the cool wind breathed new life into her, clearing her thoughts and lifting her spirits. She decided to leave it all alone. She wanted to continue feeling happy and carefree and in love. Her mother always said that she never knew when to stop, when to leave things as they were. So, she thought, I'll forget it for now. It's not my business and I'm not going to create problems where there aren't any. She smiled to herself as she made her way homeward through the leafy lanes.

Chapter XXII

For Albotain, as time went by the dark shadows that haunted him became stronger. Recently, they had begun to seep into his daily life. Like ink spreading slowly on blotting paper, they threatened to colour all of his waking moments with a thick blackness. Some were his old acquaintances, the blackened souls of hatred and malice who had waited nearly eight hundred years to find him again. Some were recent additions however, different creatures with an intelligence that allowed evil to take on new meaning. Embodied within them was a power that allowed evil to be so much more than just a brute, violent force. These latter creatures were not as disfigured as the others. They were more human in form, but it was their eyes that gave them away, gaping hollows that spoke of hopelessness and of a deep, dark void greater than the universe. They watched him day and night, carefully waiting for the right opportunity, the right time to make their move.

He was greatly weakened by their presence. They knew what he had been and now that they wanted to stop him from doing his job. They wanted to block him from bringing Ed into the Light. In the castle, they had initially fed on the man's fear and greed, as do all things negative. Now it was his physical weakness that was his downfall. He felt unable to stop them. Worse, he knew somewhere deep inside that they were still part of him, the man who had done wrong, the one who had betrayed the Light. He was ashamed, but he knew he had to stop them, somehow.

One Sunday afternoon, Anna found herself alone in the house, Ed had gone for a walk with Lionel and she had decided to stay behind to make them all some homemade chicken stew. Albotain had gone for a nap, he had looked exhausted all day and so Anna had decided to let him have a rest from the cooking. She was worried though, he seemed to be tired quite a lot lately. But, she supposed, he wasn't getting any younger and it was usual for older people to sleep in the daytime. She chopped up the fresh vegetables Ed had brought in from the garden just before he left. She tried not to think about the strange dreams where Albotain had looked so ill.

The house was completely quiet. Anna was comfortable though. She felt very settled nowadays. She'd also lost her defensiveness, her tendency to speak first and think later. Her relationship with Ed had softened her. He was so sensitive and loving she smiled to herself. She was also becoming a right sop! Her mum would have had a fit to see her cooking for two men. She'd never so much as made toast for anyone at home. Six months ago she'd have been more likely to have challenged them to a drinking game. She chuckled to herself at the idea of Ed and Bert playing 'Ring of Fire'. Ed could hardly drink one solitary beer without feeling sick and she'd never even seen Bert drink any form of alcohol at all.

She had just finished preparing the meal when it began to rain, large round drops splattered the kitchen window. She peered out, the sky was black and heavy with rainclouds and she hoped Ed wouldn't be too long. She knew that Lionel hated getting wet, so she was sure that they would be back shortly.

As she was just about to sit down and look through a magazine she'd brought with her, she heard a noise. It was just a very faint clunk, so she decided to ignore it. She sat at the table and picked up the glossy publication. There it was again, she tutted, turned the page and carried on reading. The noise carried on faintly, intermittently, but becoming very annoying nevertheless. Sighing, she put the magazine down and decided to go and see what it was. As she entered the large hallway, she could hear Albotain snoring on the other side of the lounge door, so it wasn't him then, she thought. There it was again. It was louder than the rain that was falling heavily onto the roof now. She went up the stairs, ears pricked. Reaching the landing, she listened to see of she could tell where it was coming from. *Clunk*. It was really annoying her now. She frowned and hoped the stew would be ok for another few minutes. She checked Ed's bedroom – nothing in there. As she softly closed the bedroom door, she heard it again. She looked to the end of the hallway at the stairway to the next floor. It sounded like it came from up there. She'd never really bothered about the next floor up before, she figured it just went up to the attic. *Clunk*. 'Ok, ok,' she said to herself, 'I'll have a look up there and then if I don't find anything, I'm going back downstairs.'

She clicked on the light switch. She was no coward, but she didn't fancy going up to the attic in the semi–darkness. The stairs creaked as she climbed them, her socks catching slightly on the rough wood. She could still hear the beating of the rain interspersed with the irritatingly repetitive clunking, which was getting louder by the second. At the top she found that the door was closed. She tried the door handle, it creaked, a token complaint and then turned. Anna pushed the door open, she could see nothing, it was pitch black. A little light filtered in from the hall light, but only enough to illuminate the first couple of feet in front of her.

She groped around the inside of the room and flicked the light on. As her eyes adjusted to the shadowy light, she froze, her heart leapt into her mouth. She put her hand up to cover her mouth. She thought she would faint or vomit, or both. Before her was a small room, in the middle stood a wooden table, covered in papers. Books lay open on the floor beside it and even the spare wooden chair next to her bowed under the weight of yet more paper. She stood for a few moments, trying to work out what it meant. *This was the room from her dreams.* No mistake, right down to the table and the old armchair next to it. She shook her head, trying to remember if in fact she had been up here before and had just forgotten. No way, she was a bit forgetful, but she wasn't completely barmy. *Clunk*, she nearly jumped out of her skin this time. Pulling herself together, she looked over to the other side of the table, the window was wide open, the wind was blowing through the room and the rain spattered heavily on the wooden floor. She went over to close it.

As she crossed to the window, she heard the noise again and she looked down. One of Bert's jackets was hanging on the back of a chair, its pocket swinging heavily. It was hitting the table leg noisily as the wind blew it from side to side. She noticed that it was damp from the rain coming in through the window and so she picked it up to take downstairs and dry off. Phew, it was heavy, no wonder it was making such a racket, she thought. It felt as if there was a ton of iron in the pocket. She reached into the jacket and drew out it contents carefully. In her hand were at least a dozen large, circular, metal objects. Each was a slightly different size. She peered, squinting at them in the gloom. She could just make out the strange markings that covered each one.

Some were familiar, like the astrological symbol for the Moon, the Cross and the Star of David, others were completely alien to her. However, she did recognise a few of the symbols as being the astrological glyphs that represented the other planets and zodiac signs. A year or so ago her mother had decided that Anna and she needed to bond, to spend some quality time together. She had booked them into a workshop with a visiting astrologer from the UK. Her mother was always taking part in some new–age course or alternative therapy lecture and this time, somehow she managed to drag Anna along with her. The astrologer was a sixty something 1970's ex–commune inhabitant, with a huge beard, a voice like an original Shakespearian thespian and a belly to match. Surprisingly, she had enjoyed it and had learned quite a lot. She knew she was sun sign Taurus. She was amazed to learn that her Moon sign was just as important as her Sun sign. This was placed in Scorpio, which apparently was a strong indicator of the state of her relationship with her mother.

However, astrology hadn't been something that she wanted to follow up, more to make a point to her mother than through any aversion to the subject itself. She didn't want to be badgered into attending any more courses. The last one her mother took part in was called '*Rebirth, find your spiritual placenta,*' by a woman called Autumn Heredyke–Magganity. Anna thought this sounded disgusting, (the workshop, not the woman's name). She had no desire to encounter any kind of placenta, spiritual or otherwise. Whilst Anna was far from closed, regarding the deeper, more spiritual, aspects of life, she didn't feel that workshops and courses were a suitable replacement for a loving healthy parent, child relationship. She felt that it was like trying to ice an uncooked cake, there was no solidity or stability to it.

She had met many of her mother's friends over the years. Some were wonderful people, clear, clean and genuinely loving and compassionate about life and people. Others, however, were clearly trying to present a façade, to wear the cloak of spirituality in order to cover up their deep–seated and unresolved issues. Anna was intelligent and intuitive enough to know the difference. It was quite easy to tell who belonged to which group. The former exuded a calmness and joy, an acceptance of both their strengths and weaknesses. The latter expressed a nervous anxiousness, an inner tension that leaked out through unconscious words and actions. She felt sorry for these people, instead of being happy to express themselves freely they tried to shut away what they felt were the 'bad' or 'negative' aspects of their personalities. This created a split as they tried to show the world a different person than the one that they believed they were inside. She couldn't understand why they just couldn't love and accept themselves for who they really were, faults and all. She had the feeling that her mother suffered this way. She had always seemed unhappy, unsettled – seeking something from the outside world that, even Anna knew, could only be found within her.

Anna was so disillusioned by her relationship with her parents that she hadn't even bothered to introduce Ed to them. Her mother had visions of her marrying some kind of aid worker or therapist and Ed was, well, just not alternative or different enough.

Returning her attention to the coins she turned them over in her hand one by one and put them on the table in front her.

What are they? She gazed at them, noticing that the charts and papers in front of her contained many of the same symbols. She recognised the birth charts and an ephemeris, a book of planetary positions. With a jolt she recognised Ed's handwriting, just notes on the top of charts, but it was very clear to her that he had been helping Bert. She had no idea exactly what the two of them had been doing up here, especially considering the strange discs. She didn't even know Bert was familiar with astrology, which is what she assumed all of this was. She felt bad actually, a bit guilty at snooping through his things, even if she hadn't meant to. Perhaps this was why Bert was so secretive. Maybe he didn't want to risk people ridiculing him, they could be so narrow-minded. Even Anna realised that the commercial rubbish in the papers turned discerning readers away. Bert obviously didn't want her to know what he'd been doing. She didn't want him to know she had been up here either, she decided and she wasn't going to mention it to Ed. He was obviously part of it and also didn't want her to know. She didn't want to risk breaking the beautiful love bubble they shared by upsetting him. She carefully placed the jacket back on the chair and put the coins back into the same pocket. She slammed the window closed and left the room, hurrying as she remembered the stew on the stove. As she descended the staircase, a dark shape watched her, its breath staining the air with a rancid smell.

Despite the fact that Anna had decided not to mention the attic room and the things she had found there, she felt strange. She was uncomfortable with the fact that Ed and Bert were, or rather had been, hiding something from her. To be honest, she felt a bit hurt and from that point onwards sensed a wall between her and them. They didn't seem to be aware that anything was wrong though and life continued, on the surface at least, in much the same way. However, Anna did spend less time at the house, saying that she had work at the Bistro. This was partly true, but the fact was that she still felt wounded that neither of them had shared Bert's secret with her. She was also worried that she was in the way and that by being at the house she was stopping them doing what they wanted to. She was used to feeling as though she was just a nuisance and it was more habit than anything that drove her to remove herself from the house. It was strange, but the dream about Bert never happened again after she visited the attic room.

Albotain's dreams had not stopped though. At night he was tortured and by day he was plagued. He found himself shutting himself away, away from Ed and also from Anna when she was there. He also avoided the outdoors, staying out of the sunlight. He neglected the garden and left Ed to do the work, telling him he was unwell. He was unwell though, that was no lie. He was deathly ill, his limbs ached and he felt as though he was being poisoned. Toxic thoughts and feelings flowing around his body, tainting his heart and deadening his mind. He knew he deserved this. It was his punishment for all the badness he had brought into the world all those centuries ago.

Albotain continued to fight to protect Ed from them and from himself. He sat, late at night in the attic room studying charts. Using Lance's equipment, he created more Talismans, intending to use them to protect his protégée. He hid them from Ed though, fearing that his friend would ask too many questions. Albotain drew up more and more astrological charts hoping for a glimmer of information and he prayed fervently each night to the Angels. But it was no good; he was a carrier of evil, a vehicle for the damned and even his magic turned away from him in disgust. He gave up trying to save himself. His skin grew yellow and his hair was dull and matted. His blue eyes seemed to be fading to a pale grey. These monsters were cunning and were not about to be outwitted by a mere mortal. They tainted him, pried open his soul with their claws and bared his belly to the cold air. They showed him his weaknesses whilst cackling with glee. He was made to re–live his worst moments, to suffer the sins that he had inflicted upon others. Night and day merged into one, there was no respite. At times he would think that he saw the Angel Micha, only to look closely and see that it was one of them playing sick games with him. He sat and gazed into the blackness, too drained to even feel.

But somewhere deep inside he still fought them, allowing them to do their worst, to drive him insane, but he would not let them near Ed. The boy was so much stronger now and if the worst did happen Albotain prayed that the boy would be immune to them.

By now, Ed was worried and more than a little scared. His friend was changing before his very eyes, shrinking, shrivelling up like the life was literally pouring out of him. He tried to talk to him, but the old man just shuffled off muttering incoherently. Nowadays he no longer taught Ed, nor did he venture up to the attic. He lay on the sofa in the lounge on top of his blankets, staring at the ceiling. There was also a strange smell about him, like rotting earth, dank and moist. Ed, frantic by now, spoke to Anna on the telephone about his concerns.

She responded by bringing homemade soup, carried carefully all the way in her bike basket. The sun was setting over the house as she arrived, its golden rays flooding the driveway. In the lounge, on the old settee, they spoon fed him together. Ed propped up Albotain's head whilst Anna gently fed the soup into his parched mouth. But the old man didn't manage very much before he fell asleep, twitching fitfully as he did so. Afterwards they went into the kitchen together to talk.

'What shall I do?' pleaded Ed to his girlfriend. 'You've seen him, he looks like he's dying.'

'You must call the doctor out Ed, he's too sick to go to the surgery.'

Ed looked as though he was going to burst into tears, 'I can't. You don't understand.'

Anna glared at him, outraged, 'Ed, I know you said he's a private person, but this could be life or death.' She went on. 'For goodness sake, being an astrologer isn't exactly a crime nowadays. I don't think they've burned people at the stake for a while!'

She stopped, realising that she'd said too much as usual. She had blurted it all out in a rage.

Ed frowned, 'you know he's an astrologer?' Despite his frantic worry about his friend, he was still incredulous. He thought for a moment. 'How much *do* you know?'

Anna, leaning against the kitchen table, told Ed about the Sunday afternoon when she'd been left in the house alone, about the attic and the papers.

Ed sat down at the table, he stared into space, his hands resting on top of his head. His head was spinning and he just didn't know what to say or do. All Anna actually knew was that Bert was an astrologer. That was ok, that wasn't a problem in itself. The real issue was that now his friend was sick and both of them needed help. Ed needed someone else to understand, he just couldn't manage this on his own. A lump came to his throat, he felt so useless. Once he tried to explain exactly why he couldn't call a doctor out, he was probably going to lose Anna as well. His whole world was falling apart and he was powerless to stop it.

Meanwhile Anna was lost in her own thoughts. Why wouldn't Ed call a doctor out? There must be something else they could do. She knew that the answer had to be in the attic, she was sure of it. That was obviously where Bert kept his papers and valuables. Maybe she could find some contact information or something that might tell them what was wrong with the old man. After all, it was obvious that Ed didn't know anything about Bert's medical history and they needed something to go on. Perhaps if she found something that gave a clue to the problem, Ed might be willing to call a doctor. She left the kitchen saying something about looking for information that might explain why he was so ill. After a while, Ed followed her. He also hoped that the answer to helping Albotain was in the room upstairs, only for very different reasons.

He climbed the stairs and found Anna sat at the table poring over the papers. She hadn't found anything of real value so far and in desperation had picked up an astrological birth chart and was studying it intently.

'Can you read that?' he asked.

'Yes a bit. I did a course with my mum,' she replied absently as she tried to decipher the chart in front of her. She frowned, 'I don't understand this birth chart, it's for a date in 1169.' She peered more closely at the paper, 10th of September at 4.00pm. Why would you two be interested in that and who's Al..bo..tain?'

Ed moved the papers from the chair opposite Anna and sat down, head in hands.

'You wouldn't believe me if I tried to explain,' he replied, although he knew in his heart that he was going to have to try if there was to be any chance of saving his friend.

'Well, whoever it is, I don't think a birth chart can help us, its not exactly medical records.' Anna put the chart aside and continued searching through the papers. Ed kept quiet. She got up from the table and continued searching the room. After about ten minutes, she sat down again.

'I don't understand, I can't find anything about him anywhere. I know there's only his bed in the lounge and a few clothes, he doesn't even seem to have a bag. There's no passport, no identity papers – absolutely nothing up here. It's like he doesn't exist.'

Ed also realised that there were nothing in the room that could help them. He knew from Albotain that astrology could be used to find the source of illness or disease. However, he just didn't have enough knowledge to be able to find out what was wrong with his friend.

'Anna, I have to explain something to you. Bert's not my granddad, we're not even blood relatives. What I'm going to tell you is going to be hard for you to understand. But once I've explained it all, I'll let you walk out of here and never see me or Bert again. If that's what you want. I won't stop you.'

Ed started at the beginning, about Albotain, his time in the castle and the Talisman. He told her the story of Micah the Archangel, the High Council and Daniel the Sapphire Soul. He recalled how he, Ed, had come to Guernsey, his life before and how it had changed. He detailed his time with Albotain and how at first he also found it hard to accept the truth. He talked about how he had studied with the astrologer and how now he, Ed, was a different person, a stronger better man than he ever would have been without Albotain.

He opened his heart to her and said how much she meant to him. He told her how he needed to save his friend and so needed her to trust in him, to accept what he was saying. He pleaded for her help. He had never poured his heart out so completely to anyone in his life. By the end he was exhausted and almost in tears.

After a very awkward silence, Anna's first words were, 'I thought my mum and her cronies were barmy…I think…'

However, before she could go on, a blood–curdling scream filled the house. The two of them simultaneously leapt up and raced downstairs, their hearts filled with fear and apprehension. They stopped outside the lounge door. It was deathly quiet and they were afraid to go in. Ed felt sick as he opened the door. He couldn't breathe properly and it felt like there was a ton weight on his chest. He prayed that Albotain was still alive.

Chapter XXIII

The room was glowing with a sickly yellow light, as if the light bulb was failing. There was a smell that reminded Anna of death and decay and she put her hands over her mouth to block it out. Albotain's bed was empty, the blankets were half dragged off the sofa and the pillows were strewn haphazardly across it. There was a sound though, a tiny noise coming from the corner behind the other sofa, a whining, mewling, pitiful squeal, like an injured kitten. Ed took Anna's hand and they slowly crossed the room together, afraid of what they were about to find.

There on the floor was Albotain, the great magician, the powerful astrologer. He was curled up in a ball in the corner, crying like a small child. Ed thought that his heart would break. He went to lift him up, to put him back into his bed, but the old man cowered and shuffled further back into the safety of the wall, his breath wheezing and rasping.

Anna tapped Ed on the arm. He turned to look at her. She was looking behind him. She was deathly pale, her eyes wide with terror. Ed turned to see what it was. His eyes strained in the semi–darkness, he brushed his hands over his face as if to clear his vision. He could make out shapes in the far corner of the room, strange forms, vaguely man–shaped, dark and shadowy. They were there, but they weren't there. A chill travelled down his spine as he realised it wasn't so much what he could see, it was what he *felt* that really scared him. A hard, cold hand reached into his stomach and twisted his guts viciously. He found it hard to explain to himself as to what exactly was happening. It was as if all hope had been sucked from the room, all light extinguished. It was so cold. All love had been suffocated with hatred, leaving a void that drained the soul of everything good, everything clean. A dark grey haze lingered in the room like cigarette smoke and the dark shapes floated slowly towards them.

From the look on Anna's face, she felt the same, the hideous energy was affecting her as well. In the dim light she was almost green and looked as though she was going to collapse. Ed had something of an idea now what he was dealing with, what was making Albotain sick. Anna, however, was totally unprepared for this, mentally and physically. Ed was seriously worried that she wouldn't make it, that she would break down completely. He really didn't know what he'd do if both her and Albotain ended up in the same state.

He held her up, his arm around her waist, her legs buckling underneath him. They both stood still, Ed trying to shield Albotain from the shadows. He frantically tried to think of what he could do. He and Albotain had discussed dark entities for weeks on end, but all he could think of doing now was running away. But he couldn't leave Albotain, no way, these foul entities were obviously about to devour him.

The opposite of love is not hate, its fear. That was the only thing he could remember. Well, right now all he could feel was fear – real, solid, muscle paralysing, stomach wrenching fear. He knew he had to overcome it and to do so he had to use the power of Love. Not just weak, watery half–hearted love. If Albotain was to survive, he had to summon the real thing. Pure, Real Love, the force that ruled over all of the goodness in the universe had to manifest here, in this room.

Then he remembered that he had the Talisman in his jeans pocket. He reached in and closed his hand around it. He forced himself to think about Albotain and Anna and the love he felt for both of them. He tried desperately to connect with the heart of the universe, with the essence of God and the core of Goodness that resides within every living being.

The warm tingle was faint at first, like a bird singing softly in a storm, but it was there. Then he called upon the Knight Catie and his Angel, Aurelie. He willed with all his might for the energy of the Talisman to get stronger, and it did. The heat travelled up his arm, slowly flooding him and Anna with a bright, white Light. Ed felt calmer, clearer in his head and in his mind's eye, he sent out the Light, projecting it towards the shadows. The entities stopped, pausing as if contemplating their next move. Ed saw his chance, and although Anna looked practically catatonic, the Light seemed to have helped her a little. At least, she seemed to be standing on her own now. He dropped his arm from around her waist, reached down and scooped up the frail, weightless Albotain. He lifted him up gently and put him over his shoulder. Then he grabbed Anna's hand and they crossed the room quickly. Once out of the room, Ed let go of the girl's hand and slammed the door shut tight. He knew though that a wooden door would not stop these evil, vaporous monsters. He didn't know what he was going to do next.

Ed carried Albotain upstairs to his bedroom, cradling him now like he was a baby. Anna stumbled behind him, obviously still in a daze, small sobs escaping from her every now and then. He did notice that she was slowly coming back to life though, she had the presence of mind to turn over the blankets so that Ed could put his friend into his bed. Albotain was semi–conscious now, shivering and lashing out feebly

253

with his arms. He was trying to talk – garbled words that didn't even sound human, never mind English.

Ed and Anna watched him for a while. Then Ed took command, 'we need to protect him somehow. They'll be back very soon to finish what they started if we don't do something. We need more power, something that carries the correct symbols, ones that'll protect him.'

Anna looked blankly around, 'I don't know..I don't know.' She turned back to Ed, her face pinched with fear and shock, 'what was in that room back there Ed?'

Ed hugged her close to him, 'its part of the story I was telling you. I told you about Albotain in the castle and how he turned to the Darkness for power and so attracted some pretty nasty energies. Demons, bad spirits, whatever you'd call them. Anyway, I've realised now that he's back in a physical body they want him. They want what they believe is theirs.'

Anna swallowed, trying to absorb what Ed was telling her. Her mouth felt paper dry and her head hurt like she had a hangover. She was also still badly shaken and her legs felt as though they could give way any moment. She sat carefully on the edge of the bed. Albotain was asleep now and she didn't want to disturb him. She must be going mad to even consider that any of this was real. She'd wake up any minute and find out it was just a nightmare. Then a thought occurred to her.

'When I was in the attic room that Sunday, I found something in Bert's, I mean Albotain's, jacket. I'm not sure what they were. They were circles with symbols on.'

'Like this one?' Ed pulled the still warm Talisman from his jeans pocket and held it in front of her.

Anna looked at it, 'yes, like that but a bit smaller and with different markings engraved on them. There were quite a lot, about eleven I think.'

Ed put his Talisman back in his pocket, leant down and kissed her firmly on the cheek. 'You're amazing. Wait here, I promise I'll be thirty seconds.'

Anna sat frozen with fear as Ed dived out of the room. She could hear him running quickly up the attic stairs and almost immediately stampeding down them once again.

He burst into the room, Albotain's jacket clutched in his hand. He drew out the Talismans and placed them on the large dresser in front of him. He recognised some of the symbols, the astrological glyph for the Moon, the Pentangle of Solomon and the Cross, all powerful symbols of protection. He had had no idea that his friend had been using Lance's equipment to make these. Ed could only conclude that Albotain had known that he was in trouble long before now and wished with all his heart that his friend had told him that something was wrong.

Through the mush that constituted what had been, (a short while ago), a relatively active mind, Anna watched him. She was mildly impressed, he definitely seemed to know what he was doing.

Ed, however, felt very differently. His conscious mind had no idea, no idea at all what to do. He reckoned he'd have had more of an inkling if he'd been asked to pilot a spacecraft. However, some part of him that he was unaware even existed, was obviously much better informed. He began to work automatically, rearranging the Talismans until they were in the correct order. Or rather until they *felt* like they were in the correct order. He took his own Talisman from his pocket and placed it in the centre of the others. He held his hands over the discs and called upon his Angel and Catie once more. A tingling shot through him that was so strong it hurt and a searing heat came from him. Even though his whole body felt like it was on fire and his eyes were watering so hard he could hardly see, he stood there for a few moments. After a while, the heat subsided and he put his Talisman away again. He needed to keep it with him to protect Anna and himself, to keep them safe.

He put the remaining Talismans around Albotain, placing them equal distances apart around the man's lifeless form. He prayed for protection whilst he did this, for everyone and for the strength to help his friend.

When he'd finished, he turned to Anna, who by now was shaking so hard she could hardly talk, 'is he, I mean, will he be ok now. Shouldn't we stay with him?' she asked.

'I hope so,' came the reply. 'I can't do any more than I have. There's no point staying with him. He's got as much protection as we can offer him.' He put his hand out and gently squeezed her shoulder, 'come on, let's go and get a cup of tea. You look like you could do with one.'

Anna smiled weakly, 'think I'd prefer a vodka and lime actually.' They left Albotain quietly sleeping and went downstairs.

They walked together, moving quickly past the lounge door. It was deathly quiet, too quiet though, like something had sucked out the very spirit of the house. The air was thick with a sickly tension and Anna jumped at every slight movement and flickering shadow. They sat together at the kitchen table, both with large mugs of tea. Lionel leaned heavily against Ed's leg. Anna was opposite to Ed and they held hands over the tabletop. Anna was gripping onto Ed as if she was about to fall off a cliff. She was still very pale, with dark shadows under her eyes. They were silent, both lost in their own thoughts. The only noise to be heard was the gentle hum of the refrigerator.

Anna was struggling to fit everything together. Her rational mind was drowning, thrashing about wildly in a sea of images and sounds. She was exhausted though and after a few moments, she stopped fighting the waves that threatened to overwhelm her and let herself sink into the abyss of confusion.

Strangely, as she did this she felt herself relax and a sense of calm came over her. The debris that whirled dizzily around her started to slow down a little, to come together. It began to make a kind of sense, (if she discounted any of her own previous perceptions of reality, that is). Bert's lack of history, belongings and family connections, his secrecy and immense knowledge regarding the past. It was all starting to fit, even if the answer was unbelievable. Her attempts at drawing a portrait of Albotain also crossed her mind, the fact that she could not create tangible evidence of the man's existence.

Also, despite the undercurrents of animosity that existed between her mother and herself, Anna had been brought up to believe in the spiritual aspects of life. Ok, so it was mainly pseudo–beliefs wrapped in eco–friendly paper, sold as the answer to middle class inertia, but Anna had still been exposed to it from a young age. Even though she appeared to reject it all, that was mainly because she was stubborn and hated to be told what to do. But this was a just defence mechanism, a way of proving that she was her own person. If she was honest with herself, it was also a way of provoking a reaction from her parents, to express her anger indirectly at their emotional neglect of her.

She had grown up in a world where crystal therapy and Reiki were considered more powerful than conventional medicine.   As a small child she had had multi–coloured dream–catchers hanging in her bedroom window.   Lavender bags and semi–precious stones were placed under her pillow when she had nightmares.   Still, what was happening now was a long, long way from that safe, cosy bubblegum world that believed in fairies and sprites.   Her previous experiences were about as similar to this current situation as a fast food burger is to a living, breathing, extremely bad–tempered cow.

So, although Anna was confused, she kind of understood that what Ed had told her was true.   She also needed to believe him.   She had never loved anyone the way she did Ed and she wasn't going to let a little thing like mundane reality get in the way of that.   She also knew full well that what had happened to them earlier was real, very real.   She shuddered, she had never felt so afraid, had never experienced such terror in her whole life.   That was the deciding factor in all of this.   She had had direct physical evidence of the effect of those horrible creatures and also of Albotain's heart–rending response to their attack.   She gripped Ed's hand even tighter and he yelped in pain.

'Sorry,' she apologised.

'S'ok,' replied Ed, rubbing his bruised hand.   'I've been thinking,' he continued, 'these things are after Albotain we know that, but why now? Why have they managed to become so powerful? '

'I don't know, perhaps the longer he's in his body the weaker he becomes,' she replied.

'Yeah, probably,' Ed thought for a while. 'Those Talismans will protect him for now. They form a shield around him, but he can't stay like that forever. It's the first time I've ever done anything like this before and I don't know how long the power will last.'

'We have to find a way. Perhaps we should wait until he wakes up and ask him?' suggested Anna.

Ed frowned, 'I'm not sure if he's even able to talk to us any more and we can't waste any time. Let's go upstairs and see if we can find anything in his work that might help.'

Anna swallowed hard. She felt safe in the kitchen holding Ed's hand. The thought of having to walk past the lounge again filled her with dread.

Ed saw her worried expression, 'we're safe Anna, they aren't strong enough to attack us. We have my Talisman and that is enough protection for both of us.' He smiled weakly, 'I promise you that we're safe.'

With that they made their way upstairs. Anna couldn't sense where the entities were at first, but as they passed Ed's bedroom where Albotain lay, a cold icy chill passed through her. It was as if she had walked through something, something waiting outside the door. She shivered and hurried to keep up with Ed.

Once in the attic room, Anna sat down in the old battered armchair whilst Ed began to inspect the contents of the table. He mulled over Albotain's birth chart. It still seemed unreal to Ed that his friend was born all that time ago, in an era that he had no real understanding of. Studying the birth chart, he could see his friend's strengths and weaknesses. He could connect with the essence that was Albotain, but it still couldn't provide him with the answers that he needed.

'That tells me about him, but what we need is a way of getting rid of those things forever.' He sighed heavily, 'and I have absolutely no idea how to do that.'

He turned to see that Anna was fast asleep curled up in the chair. It must be late he thought, looking at his watch, it was past midnight, no wonder they were exhausted. He lay his head on the table using his arms as a pillow, just to rest his eyes for a moment he told himself...

Chapter XXIV

He woke up, not in the attic room, but on an astral plane, the brilliant, blue sky almost blinding him. He blinked – he was in the middle of a desert, the sand was soft and golden though, not harsh or searing as it is on earth. The land stretched as far as he could see and the horizon was just a faint line. In the distance he could see a camp of some kind, what looked like Bedouin tents were swaying gently in the breeze.

Then, sensing someone beside him, he turned. It was Albotain. His heart almost burst with joy as he saw that his friend was glowing with health, his eyes were vibrant and clear and his skin was like porcelain. The astrologer was wearing a beautiful midnight cloak that shimmered with turquoise and aquamarine in the light. In his right hand he held a long golden staff, a beautiful snake was carved into the shaft. It was adorned with jewels that sparkled with a multitude of luminous colours, some of which Ed had never even seen before.

'You're here, you're well again,' he cried as he hugged his friend.

'Yes, Ed, thanks to your magic, the entities cannot reach me for the moment, which is what has allowed me to show myself to you now.' He added, 'the Talisman charm you performed was excellent!'

'Thank goodness, we thought that you were going to die!'

'What you see now is my real self, my spirit. My physical body however is in a very different state,' His expression became grave. 'Now, you must listen to me very carefully. Do you know who you are? '

'I've no idea,' came the reply, 'I guess I'm not the next Sapphire Soul, I think you would have mentioned that earlier somehow.' He smiled ruefully, 'I'm probably destined to be his dogsbody or something.'

'No Ed, you're correct, you are not the next Sapphire Soul. However, you are to be his earth father. You must teach your son what I have taught you and he will bring Light and Love to the world. He will banish hopelessness, greed and cruelty. It will be a gradual process affecting all of Mankind over the next few centuries. Through this third Sapphire Soul and his descendants and followers, the balance of the world will be restored. Your son will lead the way for many more highly developed souls to incarnate safely, to bring their gentleness and goodness to the earth plane. Man will finally be at peace and there will indeed be Heaven on earth, I can promise you that.'

Astonished, Ed looked at his friend, 'but how do I know I'll do it right? How do I know that I'm able to teach him properly?'

'You are ready Ed, you are much stronger than even I realised. The Talisman will serve you well, it will guide you. I am no longer needed on earth and I can leave you knowing that my work with you is complete.'

Ed frowned, 'that sounds like you're saying goodbye.'

Albotain just smiled gently and placed his hand on Ed, 'in a sense I am. But your heart is strong, you have a great future ahead of you. Be joyful my friend.'

'But I've saved you once and I can save you again,' Ed's voice was thick, his chest felt like it was being squeezed by a vice.

'No Ed, you cannot save me. I must go.'

'You're going to die, you're going to leave me?' Tears welled up in his eyes, 'NO, NO!' he shouted, his voice echoing in the vast landscape. 'I won't let you. You can't go.'

Albotain looked at Ed, his eyes soft and loving. He said gently, 'Ed I have to ask you to help me. There's something you must do for me.'

Ed, head down, refused to look at Albotain, 'not if you're going to leave.'

'This is not for me that I ask, but for the whole world, Ed. The entire future of the earth is in your hands. Please, will you help me?'

Ed shrugged still staring at the ground. Eventually he replied, 'what do you want?'

Albotain went quiet for a moment, then, 'I need you to take away the protection you've created. I need you to remove the Talismans.'

Ed couldn't believe what he had heard. Despite the fact that he wasn't actually in his physical body, he felt like he'd been punched. 'But that means that they'll attack you again and you'll die. I can't do that, no way.' He paused, confused, '*Why* would you want them to kill you?'

'I have to give myself to them. They are obviously not powerful enough to affect you at the moment. They will withdraw for now, but they will come back with reinforcements, with stronger, darker souls to claim us both Ed. Next time, they will win. I can't let that happen, not to you and not to the world.'

'How will your death help that?'

Albotain paused. Ed noticed that the light in his eyes dimmed just for a second, 'I will offer myself to them, agree to serve them and return with them to the Underworld.'

'*What* …I don't understand. How can you joining them help in any way?'

'I am powerful in my spirit state and they will want me. They will agree to my terms.'

'Then what, you'll be one of them?' Ed was incredulous.

'I am not one of them. They may overcome me and take my soul and use it. However, I think that perhaps when they begin to devour me, to absorb me into their mass, they will not like the taste of my soul. They will realise that I am not innately corrupt nor am I spiritually deformed and then they will reject me, spit me out.'

'What will happen to you then? '

Albotain looked away from Ed for a second and said quietly, 'that is in the hands of the Gods.' But he was very aware of what was going to happen to him. Once he returned with them to the Dark World, the entities would become incredibly potent. He knew that he would never be able to overcome them and he would be trapped there forever. The Hellish creatures that resided in the Darkness would enjoy enacting their revenge. They would take great delight in torturing his soul, tearing him apart over and over again – for eternity. Of course, he knew full well that this wouldn't stop them returning to claim Ed, but at least it would give the boy time to grow stronger, to become more powerful. Albotain knew he had no choice but to try.

Ed, however, was already in Hell. His friend was asking him to kill him and he just didn't think he could do that. However, if he didn't do what Albotain was asking from him then the future of the whole world was at stake. Albotain put his arm around Ed, 'I know this is so hard for you. I love you Ed, as if you were my own son. Please, do this for me.'

Ed sighed, crushed by the weight of Albotain's request.

'Will you let me know somehow if you are ok? I couldn't stand it if I never knew what had happened to you.'

'I promise that if I succeed I will send you a sign. You will know that I am well.'

Ed looked into Albotain's eyes for a long time, aware now that he was never going to see his friend again. He had never felt such pain, such sorrow.

'I might never see you again.' he said.

Albotain just smiled sadly, then his image began to fade slowly…leaving nothing but the desert in his place.

Ed woke up with a start. As he struggled to sit up, he rubbed his sore eyes. His heart was racing and he felt dizzy. The attic room was, however, unchanged and Anna was still sound asleep in the armchair. His mind began to piece together everything that his friend had told him. It couldn't be true, it just wasn't possible. Had Albotain really asked him to remove the Talismans so the dark entities could take him, could kill him? The reality of what was happening dawned upon him. He would have to do it. All he could think about was that he had promised his friend and he had to hold true to that promise. He sat for a while, head in hands, gathering his courage. He got up to go downstairs.

Then he realised that he couldn't leave Anna here alone and he certainly didn't want to wake her. She had had enough shocks for one day and what he was about to do would take a lot of explaining. He would need his Talisman with him, but he also had to provide some kind or protection for her whilst he was gone. He took the Talisman from his pocket and called for Catie. The room was suddenly filled with blue light and standing in the centre was the knight. His eyes were blazing and he was resplendent in full battle armour. He smiled warmly at Ed.

'Greetings friend. You require my help?'

Ed explained to him that he needed him to guard Anna whilst he helped Albotain. The knight nodded once, drew his sword and placed himself next to the sleeping girl, on guard. Ed knew she would be safe. As Catie was in spirit, Anna wouldn't be able to see him and so would be unafraid should she wake up. Just in case she did wake up however, Ed left her a note saying that all was well, that she was safe and to wait for him in the attic room.

Well, he thought sadly as he went slowly downstairs to his bedroom, at least the second part of the note was true.

Ed's feet felt like lead and his stomach was churning as he moved towards the bedroom door. He sensed the dark shadows near the entrance and shuddered, more for Albotain than for himself. He knew what they wanted and it took every ounce of his willpower not to attack them. He wanted to scream and shout at them to stop, to leave his friend alone. But he knew he had to stay calm. If he became angry, they would take his energy and use it against him. He clenched his fists as he passed through them into the bedroom. The dark forms stirred and then reformed into their previous shapes. He could hear them whispering malevolently and sighing with voracious desire, with lust for Albotain's soul. Ed had never hated anything so much in his life.

He closed the bedroom door and went towards Albotain. His heart was pounding in his chest and he felt like he was going to faint as he slowly began to pick up the metal discs. The whispering outside of the bedroom door became more audible and the sound of cruel laughter seeped into the bedroom. He couldn't bear it. He gritted his teeth and picked up the rest of the Talismans. Albotain stirred and half opened his eyes. He smiled at Ed just once and then closed them again. The eleven Talismans in his hand, Ed looked at his friend with tears in his eyes. He couldn't watch this, he had to leave, to go back to Anna. He silently apologised for his cowardice and left the room. As he exited, the dark shapes flew past him, their evil stench blackening the air. The maddening cacophony that signalled their victory deafened him. He half walked, half stumbled up the stairs back to Anna.

He almost fell into the room. He staggered over to the table and sat down heavily, hot tears streaming down his face. He was sad yes, but as well as that that he was angry. He was furious that he had had to do this terrible thing – that the Darkness had forced him to act this way. He thought about what was happening to Albotain downstairs and he began to sob. Anna woke up and stretched her arms above her head, yawning. On seeing his distress she stopped, rose quickly from the chair and put her arms around him, holding him tight to her.

'Are you ok?'

'No, I'm not. I'm really not,' replied Ed as he began to tell her what had happened.

Catie stood and watched them both sadly for a little while and then faded back into the night.

In the weeks that followed, they mourned Albotain together, walking and talking for hours on end, trying to absorb everything that had happened. As their friend had promised, the house was now clear of the shadows. However, their grief was further accentuated by the fact that there could be no funeral. Not only because Albotain was not supposed to have ever existed, but because there wasn't even a body to bury. They had returned to the bedroom early the next morning. Tentatively they had opened the door to the room. They did not know what they would find and were scared witless at the prospect of finding what was left of their friend. They found nothing though, nothing at all. The sun shone through the open window, a clean sea breeze kissed their faces and the birds sang their morning song to the blue, blue sky just like any other summer day. The bed was empty, just a few ruffled blankets lay across it. Anna gently lifted the bedclothes as if to confirm that Albotain had really gone. There, under the blanket, was a tiny blue stone, a sapphire.

They stood and stared for a while, not knowing what to say. Ed picked it up and held it, its blue light glinting in the sunlight that poured in through the window. There was nothing to say. They understood that there could be no real evidence of Albotain's short reincarnation, no sign that this man had revisited earth. Ed put the stone carefully in his pocket. He didn't know how, but he knew exactly what he had to do with it. Ed and Anna hugged one another for a long time, both saying a private farewell to the friend that they had loved, that they would always love. Ed just wished he knew what had happened to Albotain. He prayed with all his heart that his soul was safe.

They spent their days together finishing off packing up the remaining boxes. Ed wasn't sure what to do next though. The death of Albotain had brought him and Anna even closer. Bonded by their grief they were inseparable. Anna had moved into the house and had made it very clear to Ed that she wasn't prepared to let him go anywhere without her. 'Where you go, I go,' she said and refused to discuss it further. She had even invited her parents over to the house for dinner, so that they at least knew where she was living.

Not that they were really worried about her, she said laughing.

Her parents were, of course, very impressed by the house. Also, Anna's mother was totally enamoured with Ed, well actually with his extensive knowledge of astrology. Due to her recent experiences, Anna had decided that Ed was *just* about alternative enough for her family's approval. Of course, she realised that they would never know the full truth. That would be too much even for Anna's mother.

Anna's dad was small, bespectacled and dressed from head to toe in brown. He was very quiet and just coughed occasionally whilst surreptitiously handing, (the very grateful), Lionel pieces of steak under the table. Halfway through the meal Anna had had to put Gideon in the lounge. His language had become even more foul recently, thanks to Martin and Sparrow's visits and their 'extra special' language lessons. Consequently, her mother was becoming quite upset at the continuous tirade. It didn't help when the bird began to sing an extremely rude song very raucously – another fine contribution from the two boys.

Chapter XXV

A month or so after the death of Albotain, Ed and Anna sat in the lounge in front of the fire. The nights were drawing in and although during the day the autumn sun was valiantly struggling to keep the earth warm, it was becoming much cooler at nighttime. They sat on the floor drinking hot chocolate and eating hot buttered slices of Guernsey gauche that Mrs P had brought round earlier that day. Mrs P had become very fond of Anna and was happy that Ed had found himself such a lovely girlfriend. Lionel, having partaken of the feast, was fast asleep next to them snoring loudly.

Ed sat fiddling with the Talisman, which now hung around his neck on a fine gold chain. Anna had asked a jeweller friend of hers, Cathy, to mount it in a delicate circular holder so that it could be worn as a necklace without damaging it in any way. The symbols for the Moon and the zodiac sign of Pisces could be clearly seen. They reminded Ed not only of Albotain, but also of his own good qualities. To him the symbols represented the best in him. It reminded him of who he could be if he believed in himself. Incorporating the Talisman into a pendant was the most wonderful thing anyone had done for Ed. He'd always been afraid of mislaying this, his most precious belonging, somewhere. He still had the other eleven Talismans safe in his rucksack, each inscribed individually with the symbol of the Moon, one of the remaining zodiac signs and various other protective symbols. He knew that they were special, but wasn't sure what he was going to do with them yet.

As he sat there he pondered upon his life. Recently he'd been thinking, thinking a lot and he wanted to talk to Anna about the future. The boxes were finished and he couldn't stay in Guernsey. Much as he loved the island, he knew it was time to move on and he knew where he wanted to go – he wanted to find his dad. He'd saved up enough money now to last him and Anna about a month. He had an idea that once he'd found his dad, he could then look for work nearby so that he could get to know him.

'I know it's mad,' he told her, 'but I just feel it's the right thing to do. I've got an address I found in Lance's stuff, but I don't even know if he still lives in Wales,' he paused, 'and to be honest I don't even know if he wants to see me.' Anna stared at him for a moment and then kissed him on the cheek.

She just said simply, 'where you go I go.' Then she grinned, 'Wales here we come!' Ed smiled at her enthusiasm and kissed her back. The flames in the fire leapt and danced with glee and the only shadows in the room this time were of Ed and Anna embracing.

It was a bright sunny autumn morning and they stood outside looking at the house for the last time. The morning sun shone thinly on their faces, the trees were stark black lace against the blue sky. The furniture had been removed the day before and the 'for sale' sign was now posted in the lounge window. Their bags were packed and placed in the gateway ready to go. Lionel was next to Ed pawing at the ground trying to dig through the stone driveway. This was a futile mission but he seemed quite content to keep trying.

The auctioneer's truck had just left packed full of Lance's artefacts. Ed had spoken to the auctioneer who said he would probably buy some of the more precious objects himself and then donate them to the Guernsey Museum in St Peter Port.

Ed thought that Lance would have been pleased to know that his dream had, at least in part, come to fruition.

Ed and Anna had watched the lorry go trundling haphazardly up the narrow lane that led to the main road. Ed had felt very sad, it had been a poignant moment for him. It marked the end of a very special time in his life. It also reminded him of Albotain. He still felt the loss of his friend very acutely and watching the men load the boxes earlier, he almost felt as though he was losing him all over again. He was grateful though that his life had changed so much. He turned to Anna and she squeezed his hand. She knew what he was thinking and she felt much the same. She felt sad as well, but she had also found something special here, something that had changed her for the better. She was softer now, more trusting and forgiving. Most importantly, she knew that her future was with Ed. Her Ed, the loveliest, kindest most amazing soul she had ever met. Despite her sadness at losing Albotain, she felt a surge of gratitude for all that had happened over the past few months and silently thanked whoever was in charge of fate.

Mrs P strode over the driveway, her brilliant turquoise tracksuit almost glowing in the sunlight.

'Hello, you two. Are you about ready to go?' she smiled widely, although Ed noticed that he eyes were a little red and she was clutching a rather soggy handkerchief.

'Yep, the boat's in a couple of hours,' replied Ed feeling genuinely sorry that he had to go. He reassured Mrs P, 'we'll be back in a few months. Anna wants to be at her parent's 30th wedding anniversary bash, which is just after Christmas. We'll come and see you, I promise.'

Anna just smiled and rolled her eyes. It was hardly a strong desire of hers to attend the party; it was more like she'd be struck off the will if she didn't attend.

'Also,' continued Ed, 'we have to come back to see Martin and Sparrow. They're not too impressed that we're leaving them behind.'

'Good, I'm glad I'll see you two so soon.' Mrs P smiled again. Then she added, 'you know, Gideon's settling in to my house quite nicely. I'm quite surprised. He's not too bad. Of course, I'm keeping him away from the coffee which helps.'

They had decided only a few days ago to give Gideon to Mrs P. He may not have been her favourite addition to the animal kingdom, but he was the last remaining possession that had belonged to Lance. Ed smiled to himself as he remembered how when they had visited her to give her the bird, Mrs P had glared at Gideon and had told him to behave or he was out. It was strange, Ed noted, but at the same time she was admonishing the parrot, she was eyeing up the tin foil. As they left, Ed could have sworn that the bird had winked at him. Just the once – slowly, deliberately and not altogether innocently. He figured that Mrs P and he were a good match.

Mrs P bent down and patted Lionel. 'I'm so glad you're taking him with you.' She crouched close to the ground and hugged him round his furry neck. 'Now you be a good doggy woggy.' Lionel just stared at her, then lifted his leg as if to relieve himself. Mrs P got up quickly and brushed herself down and Lionel casually put his leg back down. Shortly afterwards he wandered off to try to dig up a different part of the driveway. A few minutes later the three of them made their way up the hill to the bus stop, intermittently waving goodbye to Mrs P. As they climbed the hill, Ed only had one real regret, he just wished he knew what had happened to his friend...

Albotain lay still, not daring to move, taut and stiff with apprehension. He kept his eyes closed tightly, very, very afraid of what he might see. After a few moments he dared to try to breathe properly. However, only jerky gasps escaped from his chest. Where was he? Well, it wasn't cold, neither was it unbearably hot as he would have imagined Hell to be. He tentatively reached out to his side, eyes still firmly shut. Nothing. He did the same with the other arm, same result. So, still no clues. He strained his ears, it was quiet, but he thought he could just make out whispers and faint footsteps. His heart lurched. Was that them? Were they coming to get him – to begin the terrible torture? He tried to move his legs, they obliged. He wasn't tied down then, perhaps he could run. He almost laughed to himself, *run*, run where exactly? He was in Hell – as far as he knew it was a pretty big place and he certainly didn't possess a map.

He lay there, not moving for a while. It felt like eternity. *Well it would do wouldn't it?* He was surprised that he seemed to have regained a little of his former sense of humour, something that had been sorely lacking for a good while before his demise. He put it down to hysteria. After all, it wasn't every day that you got to watch your insides being boiled and your head being peeled like an onion whilst you could still feel was it? Something touched him and he jolted like he'd been electrocuted. His eyes opened involuntarily in response to the brief contact. He tried to close them again quickly, but it was too late. He drew a breath and held it in, in disbelief. He sat up stunned. Actually, he was more than stunned, he was astounded. Standing in front of him, as large as life with his arms folded

275

was *Micah!* Albotain closed his eyes once again and covered his face with his hand.

'I do not know what you are, but I do know you are not the Archangel Micah.' He began to shake, his whole body trembling with fear. He felt a hand on his gently lifting it away from his face.

'Albotain, it *is* I, Micah,' said a beautiful, gentle voice, floating like flute music into the air. Albotain held out his hand cautiously and touched Micah's gown. It rippled and shimmered like a rainbow in water, colours spilling into one another.

'It is you!' he cried, looking around for the first time at his surroundings. He recognised the beautiful hall, the marble columns and the crystal clear light spilling in through the windows.

'But I don't understand, I'm supposed to be in Hell.'

'No, no you're not my friend. This is your home and you belong here.'

'But I gave myself to the Darkness.'

'You gave yourself to Ed, not the Darkness.'

Albotain frowned and repeated, 'I don't understand.'

You're a hero Albotain, you not only saved Ed and the fate of the next Sapphire Soul, but because of you the portal to Hell, the channel between the Underworld and the earth, is blocked. It's not permanent, but it will take the Dark Ones some time to clear it.'

'How? What did I do?' Albotain couldn't remember performing any even vaguely heroic acts. The last memory he could recall was seeing the Dark shapes fly towards him as he lay in Ed's bed. He'd been petrified with fear.

'You are a Soul of the Light. You have worked hard to right your wrongs and so you carry within you the purest energy. This energy was further strengthened by you sacrificing your soul for Ed, for love. As the Dark Ones attempted to carry you into the chasm, the place of the Eternal Shadows, they realised that they couldn't. As you descended into the Underworld, your radiance lit up the universe. You were too bright for them, you blinded them and they were forced to release you at the Gateway to Hell. As they did, you of course began to ascend to Heaven, your rightful home. But you left behind a residue, a surge of Light that came from your heart, one which obliterated the Darkness at the edge of Hell. The Dark Souls cannot pass through that Light and so are trapped on the other side, powerless to leave. For now, the world is safe from evil.'

'What about the Sapphire Soul? Does this mean that I am pure enough to care for him when he incarnates onto the earth plane?'

'Yes, of course, you are now a Divine Being. When the time comes, you will be his guide. However, you will no longer be earthbound and you will certainly never have to reincarnate in a physical sense again. You will still be able to connect through the Talisman, but you are a free soul. The future for you, my friend, is bright.'

Albotain looked at his friend. 'So Ed is safe and I am free?' He stopped and added, 'I can stay here this time.' He was close to tears. He felt like a small child asking to come home to his parents. Micah smiled and led him outside. They walked together though the magnificent halls and into the golden sunshine.

Ed and Anna sat next to one another on the ferry. As the swell carried them up and down the Channel, they sat sipping hot tea, trying not to scald themselves. Lionel lay under the table, chewing an old burger box and licking meat juices from the inside of the lid. Anna's engagement ring glinted, a multitude of blues sparkled vividly as she lifted the cup to her lips. Ed smiled with pride, he couldn't believe that she had said yes to becoming his wife. Albotain's sapphire had been the perfect choice for the ring.

Ed went outside to the deck and watched the island of Guernsey disappear slowly into the mist.

He knew that wherever he went his heart would always belong to this little speck of land in the middle of the Channel. It was so small, but oh so mighty. It had changed his life and he missed it already.

He knew that they would be back, but they had so much to do before they could return, so much to learn, so many places to go. But still, one day they would need to come home again for good. Ed knew that Guernsey was his home, not just physically, but spiritually too.

Battling his way back to the upper deck, he collapsed back into his seat. Lionel was asleep now. He'd given up on the burger box, which now lay partially chewed and screwed up between his feet. Anna was dozing, but smiled lazily up at Ed as he sat down.

Opposite them sat a young woman and propped up on her lap was a small baby. Ed reckoned it was a boy, but only because he was dressed in blue. They all look the same he thought. He was cute though. He had dark brown eyes and curly blonde hair. He gurgled and squealed happily as his mum tickled him gently and kissed his chubby little neck.

Anna was awake now and was also watching the baby. She looked pensive though and was biting into her lower lip with her teeth, her hand resting gently on her stomach. After a while she turned to Ed and whispered something in his ear. He didn't respond at first, he didn't move at all. He just looked shocked for a few moments, Anna watched him worriedly. Then he turned, he smiled and grabbed her. He pulled her up from her seat and he hugged her hard. Triumphantly, he swung her off her feet, swinging her around until she laughed and begged for mercy. Eventually he put her back down, his arm draped protectively around her. He grinned down at her and kissed her again.

They left the boat, arm in arm, Lionel trailing behind them on his leash. Ed went to throw the boat tickets away in the litterbin at the exit door. As he did so, he glanced at his ticket. He stopped and looked at it again, frowning as he saw the name printed on it. It was not made out to *Edward Blyte*, but instead to *Edward Bryte*. *N*o one had mentioned it when they checked the tickets and he had never thought to look. Realisation dawned slowly but surely. An image of the plump solicitor Mr Arvil formed in his mind. Of course, Albotain had been in on the whole thing from the very start.

A great wave of love and warmth encompassed him and it was at that moment that Ed knew his friend was safe. The future was indeed Bryte he thought, smiling to himself as he, Anna and Lionel headed up the jetty towards the bustling town.

The Story behind the Story

The idea for *'Albotain's Treasure'* was born after astrologer Sharon Ward initiated an astrological jewellery concept in 2005. The Moon sign jewellery idea was born when Sharon felt that it was time that the world was introduced to other aspects of astrology other than the Sun sign. Astrology is an ancient and fascinating subject, one that is overly simplified by today's media. Until recently, the mainstream has focused only on the Sun sign. There are twelve zodiac signs and as each of us have a Sun sign, so we all have a Moon sign. Our Moon sign is equally as important as our Sun sign. The Moon governs our emotions, our intuition and our inner selves. It is also very much connected to our core, soul energy.

Fortune guided Sharon and the first jeweller she approached agreed to work with her to create the jewellery. The amalgamation of Sharon's astrological knowledge and conceptual skills with Catherine Best's talent as an innovative jewellery designer has brought a long–forgotten aspect of astrology back into the public eye. The Moon sign jewellery has become not only a successful product, but has led the way to more understanding regarding astrology. The public has embraced the opportunity to learn more about this fascinating subject. People have also responded to the opportunity to connect more fully with their own inner strengths, to learn about the deeper aspects of their own personality. This success has further fuelled Sharon's passion – to teach people that they can be empowered by astrology and to show them that life can be lived in a loving and productive manner.

'*Albotain's Treasure*' is a fictional story. However, it's another medium through which astrology and the other forgotten arts can be reintroduced to a world that is ready to embrace life on a deeper and more fulfilling level.

If you would like to find out what your Moon sign is, go to

www.sharonward.co.uk, www.moon-signs.com, or www.catherinebest.com

£1 will be donated to the Born Free Foundation

for every sale of '*Albotain's Treasure*'

www.bornfree.org.uk

Order Form

You can order further copies of this book direct from Saturnus Ltd

www.sharonward.co.uk or *www.saturnus.co.uk* – you can order a printed copy or download in eBook format from either of these sites.

To order printed copies of 'Albotain's Treasure', please send a copy of the coupon below to:

Saturnus Limited
Grove Lodge, Les Vaurioufs
St Martins, Guernsey
Channel Islands, GY4 6TE

------------------------------------- ✂ --

Please send me _____ copies of the book 'Albotain's Treasure'.

☐ I enclose a UK bank cheque or postal order, payable to Saturnus Ltd for _____ @ £11.79 per copy (£8.99 plus £2.80 postage)

NAME:

ADDRESS

POSTCODE

Please allow 28 days for delivery. Do not send cash. Offer subject to availability. We do not sell or share our customer's details.
Please tick the box below if you do not wish to receive further information from Saturnus Limited. ☐